300 DAYS

Jacqueline Druga

Copyright © 2024 Jacqueline Druga

All rights reserved

The characters and events portrayed in this book are fictitious. Any similarity to real persons, living or dead, is coincidental and not intended by the author.

No part of this book may be reproduced, or stored in a retrieval system, or transmitted in any form or by any means, electronic, mechanical, photocopying, recording, or otherwise, without express written permission of the publisher.

ISBN: 9798336852684

Cover design by: Christian Bentulam

Speciall thanks to Paula

CHAPTER ONE – ALL THE LEAVES ARE BROWN

The screams.
Those God-awful screams.
They weren't a part of his life plan. Of course, back in the day, they didn't call it a life plan. There really wasn't a name for it.
It was exactly what John Gardner called it, just plain life.
Work hard, reap the benefits of hard work and thank the lord for all you had.
John worked hard. He didn't drink more than the occasional social beverage. He went home after work, spent the weekend doing things with his family and went to church on Sunday.
John was the epitome of a family man.
He worked his way up from stock boy to chief executive officer for Sears and Roebuck. He had the fanciest station wagon in the neighborhood, and a two-story colonial in a quiet, upper middle class suburb out side of Chicago.
John was the all-American success story.
A beautiful wife and three children, one of which was only six months old when the screams occurred.
John never saw it coming.
Was he blind to the signs or was he just blindsided?
A month after Stacy, his youngest was born, he bought that property up at Big Bear Camp ground. It wasn't exactly rough camping, a two bedroom cabin in the campgrounds, isolated, yet

near other cabins.

A small camping community an hour away from their home in the suburbs.

An every weekend getaway.

He thought Jeanette, his wife, loved it.

When summer came Jeanette wanted to spend a week up there. John didn't understand that, after all, no one was really there during the week and he couldn't be there until after work on Friday.

She would be alone with the kids, but maybe the solitude was what she wanted.

Jeanette started doing it more and more. Taking the kids up early in the week and John would drive up right after work on Friday.

He didn't like the idea of coming home to an empty house after work, making TV dinners and eating alone. But he bought that cabin, he introduced Jeanette to the lifestyle, he had only himself to blame for her loving it.

Usually, he packed what he needed on Thursday, left work on Friday, and popped by the grocer to get some extra stuff. Although he always planned to fish.

This weekend was a holiday and slightly different.

John left work early like most Americans for the Fourth of July weekend. Traffic was heavy, but even then, he would be at the site before evening. Early enough to enjoy a walk with the kids and sit down for a meal with his family. He was in a great mood. He stopped by to cash his check, which had that bonus he wanted to surprise his wife with.

But John had an unwarranted sinking feeling when he pulled into the camp site.

Nothing pointed to it, just a weird feeling.

Then he didn't see anyone.

As he turned a right onto the road that would lead to the cabins, he saw a bunch of people running that way.

Then he heard sirens,

What was happening?

Not a tenth of a mile down the road, Jim Herbst was waving his arms frantically to John.

John stopped, his window was already down. "Hey, Jim."

Jim opened his mouth to speak when Fred Price zipped by on his motorcycle.

"What?" John asked. "What did you say?"

Like some sort of bad movie, Jim's lips moved but the only thing John heard was the siren of the Sheriff's car as it zipped by.

"Screams," said Jim.

"What are you talking about?" John asked.

"Your family, John, we heard them screaming. All of them. Not good screaming."

John wanted to plow through the people on the road, but like the police car and Fred he'd have to get off the road to quickly go around them.

And that was what he did.

Jim said he heard his family screaming.

Was there a fire? Something else?

John had never driven so fast in the campground as he did at that moment, arriving to the cabin right behind the police car.

As soon as he stepped from the car, he heard Jeanette screaming.

"No, no! No! Help me! Help my babies!"

"Mom. Mommy!" cried his eldest daughter, Macy.

John charged forth. "Jan!"

"John. John, help us!"

The sheriff blocked John. "Sir, you have to stop. We have back up coming. It's a hostage situation."

"A hostage—"

"Reed Warner," Fred Price approached. "I'll go in with you, John. Let's do this, I have my side piece."

"Oh, now wait." The sheriff lifted his hand. "You can not storm in there. Reed is armed. Okay. You go in you could cause him to shoot."

"He already shot once," said Fred. "Why do you think you were called?"

Reed Warner? John knew him. Not well, but just as well as everyone else. He owned the camp grounds, a small guy, he acted totally out of place. A wanna be cowboy in the windy city of Chicago, he had a wife and if John wasn't mistaken, Reed was a new father.

How was he even a threat? And why?

"Reed!" John shouted angrily, stepping closer to the cabin. "What the hell are you doing?" He struggled against the sheriff who pulled him back.

"John! Help," cried Jeannette. "He ... he ... he killed Darren."

Darren his four year old son.

It was a twisted sickening feeling that slammed into John, it went from John's heart to his bowels.

"It was an accident, John!" Reed yelled back.

John looked at Fred. "Let's do this. What's the plan?"

"Daddy!" Macy screamed. "Daddy, help us." She screamed and screamed, she was just nine. She had to be scared.

"I'm coming baby," John called. "I'm ..."

Bang.

John's heart stopped for a moment.

Macy stopped screaming.

Then Jeanette released a horrid, agony filled scream.

John wasn't waiting. He didn't care if Reed Warner was armed or not.

He reached the steps ...

Bang.

John jumped for the door, blasting in.

Oh God. Oh God.

He couldn't look, but it was hard not to see, Macy lay on the floor a pool of blood widening around her head. Jeanette was on the floor near the kitchen, and Baby John was next to her. His tiny feet resting on Jeanette's belly.

"I'm sorry, John," Reed put the gun under his chin.

"No!" John raged and dove his way.

Reed fired before could reach him and dropped to the floor between Macy and Jeanette.

John was certain he screamed out the word, 'no' over and over deeply and heartbroken. He felt it come from his throat and heart, but his ears were blocked by his rushing blood and beating heart.

The agony.

The agony he felt was immeasurable.

He wasn't just surrounded by death, he was surrounded by his dead family.

Who to hold first, who to check first. He loved them all the same and loved them very much. Who would he touch and kiss, or say goodbye to first?

The Sheriff, Fred Price and others rushed in. Voice shouted, calls for help were being made, and John just stood there.

It wasn't real. It couldn't be real.

At any moment it would stop and John would wake up.

Unfortunately, it was real, and John didn't have any clue as to why it happened.

CHAPTER TWO – AND THE SKY IS GRAY

It was a tragedy hard to comprehend.

Darren had died. Macy and Jeanette were gone. Baby John was alive, barely, and John held him in the ambulance as they rushed as fast as they could to try to save him.

Unfortunately, his youngest was taken from him as well.

Why? The kids didn't deserve what happened. Macy spent her final moments scared and screaming.

The only one in the massacre still breathing was Reed.

He didn't die. The bullet sheared off the left part of his jaw and John prayed that Reed would live.

For two reasons.

He needed answers and he wanted to kill him.

John's entire life was over and he just didn't care.

No one wanted to tell John the reason for the murder and attempted suicide at the cabin, but John was a smart enough man to figure it out before the Sheriff confirmed suspicion.

Jeanette had been going up there without John.

Everyone knew and suspected it. Everyone but John.

Jeannette and Reed were having an affair and when Jeannette tried to end it, Reed exploded.

If John hadn't been swallowed by grief, he would have been angry. Angry that no one told him what was happening.

Perhaps if they did, perhaps he could have stopped it and the tragedy wouldn't have unfolded.

But it did.

It was all over the news and John had to relive it every time he turned on the television.

He also waited for Reed to heal, to pay for what he did.

A life of disfigurement and pain wasn't enough.

The death of his family was the end of John's golden life and beginning of his tragic one.

His parents were still alive back then, they treated him with kid glove care, almost an unspoken suicide watch.

Who wouldn't want to end their life.

His parents were the main reason he didn't. They were suffering as well over the loss of all their grandchildren. He loved his parents enormously and couldn't cause them any more pain.

How he got through the funeral he didn't know. It was there he told his father that he didn't want to live.

His father replied, "I know. But what a disservice to the memory of your family if you choose not to carry that memory on."

John found himself repeating those same words to his father six months later when his mother passed away suddenly. The doctors said it was from a broken heart, John believed him.

He kept working, but stopped being good at his job.

He took a severance from Sears, sold the house, packed what he believed were his best memories in boxes and moved in with his father.

He had enough money saved to not have to return to his prior work, and be able to focus on another career.

The two of them spent time waiting for the trial. There wouldn't have been one had Reed not wanted to face the death penalty.

They went to the trial, sat through every single day.

That wasn't the first time John met Reed's wife, Peggy. He knew her from camp. A super nice woman. The first couple days of the trial, she avoided eye contact, like she blamed John. But that wasn't the reason, she was wrought with guilt and went to the trial, not to support Reed, but to make sure he paid.

John felt sorry for her, she was devastated as well. A mother with a toddler now, pregnant when it all went down.

She told John she had to go away and she was sorry for what Reed had done. She'd find a way to make it up to him. John told her it wasn't on her, her life was just as destroyed as his.

He felt sorry for her and her daughter as well.

It took two years after John's family was murdered for the trial to start, and a week to find him guilty. Reed was sentenced to death.

Peggy moved away, John promised he'd keep her updated when everything was done. They kept in contact for a year, through letters and postcards, when she settled in Oklahoma.

They no longer hung people in the state of Illinois and John worried they were going to abolish the death penalty before Reed was given the justice he deserved.

That didn't happen while Reed waited on death row. His attorneys argued he was suffering from mental illness, that he was sick.

It didn't work.

Eleven years, three days and four hours after John lost his family, he and his father, holding photos of the kids and Jeanette, watched Reed die by lethal injection.

Reed had no one there.

Peggy and baby were long gone out of the state, in their new life, a better life. John sent her a letter, but he never heard back. He figured she moved on.

Reed was gone forever.

Still, it was meaningless to John. He was an empty man, and when his father died it was the last of anything left in John.

He believed he was condemned to live on the earth alone and bitter. Live with the pain of losing everyone because he should have been able to save them.

All he had to do was save his marriage, but he hadn't seen that sinking.

Their deaths were on him, he believed, as much as they were on Reed.

John sold his father's house and with minimal belongings

and more boxes of memories than he had stuff, he bought a little house far away from anyone who knew him in another state.

There he could start fresh. He could be what he wanted to be, no pity parties for him because people didn't know his story.

At the age of fifty-two, six months after his father's passing, twenty years after he lost his family, John moved to West Virginia.

The only person he told was Peggy, and that was in a postcard. He simply wrote, 'I don't know if you'll get this, but I'm finally taking your route. I'm starting fresh, where no one knows my name.

He used his new address, but again, like the letter he sent about Reed's execution, he never heard back.

Maybe John was a painful reminder.

He never remarried nor did he want to. He never really healed from the pain, and the hole in his soul didn't grow smaller. He wouldn't let it.

John could have tried to heal, but he never believed he deserved it.

Like the executioner who delivered the lethal injection to Reed Warren, John took his own injection.

One of anger and loneliness. Void of allowing himself to feel happy. It was easier to be miserable and angry than to enjoy life.

And if he ended up being that grumpy old man on the block who yelled, "Get you ball out of my yard." So be it.

John was fine with that.

CHAPTER THREE – GRUMPY OLD MAN

"Get your ball out of my yard."

John just wanted to step out of the house and get some fresh air.

That was all.

In his eighteen years at the house in Ripley West Virginia, he never once had to yell about a ball in his yard. Not that he didn't want to, he did. John was set up to be that quintessential grumpy old man.

Before the new people moved in, renters, John had lived a decently quiet life. Not that they were noisy. They had just moved in. He wasn't even sure how many, but that ball was indicative of kids.

In addition to being the town grump, he was also the most hated man in the America, but people didn't know it was John.

He just wanted to speak his mind, not be PC and worry about some cancel culture. He was learning about radios, broadcasting and editing when he left Illinois. Most of his time was spent on that Hamm Radio, ranting and raving. Then someone suggested he put his thoughts out there.

Ten years later he was an unknown man, speaking his mind across something called a Podcast.

He'd put an image to it and put it on social media video platforms. Before he knew it, he got a notice of monetization and John started collecting little checks. He could have made a lot more if he had sponsors, but he wasn't doing it to get rich or famous. He was doing it so people heard his thoughts.

He spoke about everything and didn't care if he offended people. It was his opinion. He didn't want to change the world.

The reason he chose not to have sponsors was because he didn't want anyone to know who he was. His real identity. The only ones that did was the platform who sent him checks. Other than that, the more people that listened and hated him, the more people believed his name was Reed Warren.

John took that name, he wanted no one to like Reed Warren. To hate him like he did.

So many years had passed since his family was murdered, no one picked up on that.

Was John a nice man? He wasn't mean to people, he just didn't care.

His own doing.

His own self punishment.

And now that green ball a few feet from his back porch was gnawing at him like a starter ingrown toenail.

He stepped down the two steps from his back porch and looked down at the ball, then turned his head to the right.

The renters.

A lot of the houses on Second Avenue were close to each other. John's happened to be close to the renter house. A piss stream away, John called it. So close that he could step outside and smell what his neighbor was cooking.

Before the renters a woman John's age lived there. She used to make chicken soup, the smell carried to him when he'd go on his back porch and have a smoke. He never bothered to get her name. He didn't care. The only time he said anything was when he saw them moving her stuff out.

"She die?" John asked a woman who probably was her daughter.

The woman gasped at John as if he didn't ask a warranted question. She never answered and a for rent sign went up.

It was for rent a long time. John wondered what was wrong with it. Was it dirty? Did it smell like old chicken soup?

Then again there weren't many renters in Ripley. There weren't many people at all. Seventy five percent of the population was adult.

John drove by the elementary school one day, there were barely any kids.

People just didn't inspire to move their family to Ripley.

More than likely the renters and the green ball came from across town.

They were probably evicted from their other place. The green ball in his yard was disrespectful. Shaking his head John looked over to the back porch five feet from his property line.

Sure enough, sitting on the back porch was a young person. A teenager, maybe.

He wasn't sure if it was a boy or a girl. Sitting on the old back glider, they wore jeans and a big hooded jacket. The hood was over their head and they were slumped forward, staring down to their phone.

"Hey!" John yelled. "Hey!"

The hood kid looked over at John.

"Yeah?" the young person answered.

Higher voice, strands of brown hair pushed down in the face from the hood. It was either a girl or one of those 'Emo' wanna be boys who hadn't hit puberty yet.

Nah, it was a girl.

"Get your ball out of my yard," John told her.

She looked left and right. "Me?"

"Yeah, you. Get your ball out of my yard."

She snickered. "Do I look like I'm playing ball?"

"No, you look like you're up to no good. Probably making a mean video, posting it on Tak a tick or snap something while doing the marijuana pens they pass out in school."

"Seriously?" she asked.

"Yes. Get this ball out of my yard." He lifted it.

"It's not mine. I don't even have a ball." She looked back down to her phone.

After a short huff, John threw the ball at her. It landed at her feet. "Now you do. Keep it out of my yard."

Feeling better about that ball being out of his yard, John went back into his house and to his work.

CHAPTER FOUR – INCOMING

"And that is kids today," John said into the microphone which he had connected to a discount tablet. His eyes lifted to the photograph of his family he had on his desk. "Kids today. And that's it for me, meanest man in America, signing off." He hit 'end broadcast' and published it to the site.

Leaning back in his chair, he rubbed his eyes, thinking about what he'd make for dinner.

Then he heard the most unfamiliar sound.

A knock at his door.

A bit surprised, John stood up, He paused on his way out of the office and grabbed his bottle of gin. He poured a half of shots worth into a glass and downed it. Usually he did the Queen Drink, double gin and tonic before bed. Rarely did he drink it straight, but he guessed if he had to deal with people a shot would help.

After that quick drink he walked to the door.

Parting the curtains, he looked out. A woman stood on his porch. A younger woman in her thirties. She wore what John would describe as nightclub style clothes, her face was all made up as if she had some huge event to attend, and her hair was big. Too big. Even John knew it was too big for the times.

Figuring she was harmless enough, he opened the door. "If you're selling. I'm not buying."

As he went to close the door, he noticed she held the green

ball and she was just staring at him.

Staring as if in shock to see him.

"What?" John snapped.

She snapped out of her staring daze with a shake of her head. "Did you throw this at my daughter today?" she asked, looking down at the ball.

He couldn't place her dialect. It certainly wasn't southern. Maybe Cleveland, Midwest?

"Depends," John answered. "Who's your daughter?"

"Yely."

"Really."

"Yes."

"You named your daughter really?"

"Her name is not really it's Yely."

"Good Lord, you're confusing me," John said. "It sounds like really, but it's Yely."

"Yes."

"Never heard of her," John said. "And who the hell would name their kid Yely? What about Mary, that's a nice name?"

"Yely is a nickname."

"It's not a very good one."

She huffed. "I'm not here to discuss my daughter's name. She said you threw this ball at her today."

"If you're talking about the emo kid posting obscene videos and smoking marijuana on the back porch, then yes. I threw it at her."

The woman gasped.

"Gasp all you want. That ball is a dollar bouncing cheap thing from the discount store. Even if I whipped it at her full force, she felt worse at dodge ball if she, you know, goes to school. And I wouldn't have had to throw it at her if she didn't put it in my yard."

"She doesn't have a ball."

John shook his head. "Well, shame on you for not providing toys. Maybe she wouldn't have to puff those marijuana pens they give out to all the kids."

"Listen," she said firm.

"Did you just move in next door?" John asked.

"I did."

"This is not the way to make a good impression. What is your name?"

"Ruby."

"Ruby." John nodded. "Well, Ruby. Get off my porch." He closed the door.

Not a few steps away from his door, he heard the thump. He figured that was Ruby throwing the ball at his door.

He thought about going back, opening the door and throwing the ball at her, when he heard his fax machine.

While most people used email or messaging, John stuck with the fax machine. It was, to him, more secure, especially if people wanted to give him political or conspiracy theory scoop and information he could talk about on his show.

Everyone's secrets were safe.

When John walked into his office, he saw the pages in the fax machine and knew right away from the header it was from his friend Jarvis.

He grabbed the papers, they were filled with information and charts. Reading the first and last line of his accompanying note, made John reach for his chair and sit down.

He rubbed his eyes, exhaling heavily as he picked up the phone.

He didn't know if Jarvis would answer. It was after midnight where he was, however, Jarvis had just sent the fax so chances were he was awake.

"Jarvis."

"Evening John," Jarvis replied. "I take it you got it?"

"I got it. I haven't read everything yet, but I read the important stuff. Is this confirmed?"

"It is."

"Jarvis, you've been speculating for a while."

"I have and it's been confirmed."

"Anyone else know?" John asked.

"Nope. Read page four. Under wraps as long as possible. It's for the best if you think about it."

"Maybe," John said. "When?"

"Two weeks. Are you going to announce it?"

"Yeah, I will, but you know," John said. "I'm thought of as a crackpot so it won't be taken seriously."

"Me, too."

"What are you going to do?" John asked. "If your prediction is right—"

"Book a flight."

"Where?" John asked.

"Well, John looks like Ripley West Virginia might be one of the safest places on the planet. Location and such."

"I'm not letting that tidbit out," John said. "Book that flight. You're welcome here. Get some rest my friend, and thank you for this."

He said good night to Jarvis, then stared down to the multipage fax.

Even though they had discussed everything on those pages, seeing the finality, the confirmation was a hard pill to swallow.

If indeed it was true.

Jarvis was someone who had been listening to John for years. He gave John lots of information to share. But for all John knew, Jarvis wasn't a scientist like he claimed.

If there was a remote possibility the information in the fax was true, John had to believe it, he couldn't take a chance not to.

Before he let his small pocket of public know about the contents of the fax, John wanted to know it, inside and out.

CHAPTER FIVE – PREPPING

The Kroger's opened at seven and John was out front waiting for the doors to open. He had been out in the parking lot since six, when the store was still dark. He watched the lights come on and patiently waited. A simple crack of his window allowed for the smell of fresh baking bread to flow into his car. He wasn't there for the bread. He was there for the items that would last a long time.

John had a list and Kroger's wasn't the only stop he had to make that morning. It was why he started early. He also had to stop at the lumber yard to make sure all that wood was delivered to his house.

But Kroger's first.

He sat outside the store in his pick up, waiting for that manager woman to open the doors. He needed water, cases of it. There wasn't any time to get a pallet, but John had been buying cases of water since Jarvis told him what was coming. Now, there was a time frame and not much of one at that.

He had to plan that everyone would find out, hit the stores and the shelves would be empty.

John knew the recommended amount of water was a gallon a day, but he wouldn't drink that much. Still, he planned on it. There was washing, and dishes, and cooking to take into account.

Over the previous four months, John had purchased twenty-eight cases, they lined up his entire basement, and he knew another twenty cases was going to have to go into the garage.

He'd put four in the pit, a hole he hired someone to dig and cover with plywood, a hidden storage area.

That wasn't all he needed, John had an entire list.

Did he think the event would happen? No.

Did he plan on it? He did, but now with the evidence, he had six days to kick it into high gear. He figured three days before people found out.

He was grateful he lived in a small town, but his rounds after Kroger would take him farther out, to Sam's Club and Costco.

John wanted the shopping trip to be the only one and if he had to go out, it would be for things he forgot.

There was enough things stocked in his basement. If the event happened in an hour, John would be good. Would he be good for three hundred days? It would be pushing it.

John wanted to be good for two years.

So he set out to do just that.

Later in the day he would record a broadcast, but not mention the event yet.

He was still learning all the facts. Of course, Jarvis told him there were a lot of places on the internet that could help him. John's response was, "Is the internet going to be there after June tenth?"

Along with an answer of, "Probably not." Jarvis started faxing John all sorts of information. Probably stuff he got off the internet, but John had a paper copy and would keep it handy. He used the three hole punch on them and put them in a binder.

Jarvis also booked his flight.

He was serious about coming to Ripley.

The store finally opened and John was the first inside, other than aluminum foil and water, he was buying things most people weren't shopping for on a Saturday.

It was Memorial Day Weekend. They'd be buying hot dogs, burgers, wings, and ribs. Buns, too, they'd be hard to get. Of course, being Memorial Day Weekend, John would pick up a pack of hot dogs, they were on sale.

Nothing like a good hot dog. He was out of Kroger's in an hour and that included the twenty minutes it took to load his truck, then he'd hit the rest of his stops.

John was doing well. He was able to get everything on his list and was on his way home when he heard the 'ding' from his phone.

He knew what that meant.

"Ah, hell." He lifted the phone and glanced down quickly. John hated getting text messages, absolutely hated it and Jarvis knew that.

Clearly it was from Jarvis, even though John couldn't read it. Through his blurry vision, it looked like it said Jarvis. John knew if he was sending a text, it was important. So John pulled over, and grabbed for his reader glasses. He had just placed them on when he heard the 'bloop-bloop' of the siren.

He glanced at the rearview mirror and saw the police car pull over behind him.

"Son of a gun," John cussed. He couldn't figure out what he did.

He waited. That awful long time from the police officer in his car until he got out.

Of course, he knew the officer.

Giles Matthews.

He used to be a punk teenager with long hair delivering newspapers when John first moved to Ripley, now he was this buff acting cop wearing a high and tight haircut. One of the few that worked in Ripley. Everyone knew him and everything about him. Actually, his divorce was the big talk at Kroger's.

John stared ahead until Giles tapped on his window and then John wound it down.

"Morning, Mr. Hopper," said Giles.

"Giles."

"Do you know why I pulled you over?"

"I wasn't speeding," John said.

"No, you—"

"I wasn't weaving."

"No."

"Have something against senior drivers?"

"No," Giles replied with a chuckle.

"Well, Giles, I can't figure out why. Unless you're so damn bored you decided to pick on me."

"Distracted driving," Giles said.

"What? I wasn't distracted."

"You lifted your phone."

"And you saw that from behind?" John asked. "Nonsense, you're just pissed at me and trying to find a reason to pull me over because I turned you into your superior last week for distracted driving."

"That was you?" Giles asked.

"Oh, stop., You know it was me. You were sipping a Starbucks and eating a hamburger."

"I wasn't driving." Giles said. "And there's not a Starbucks within thirty miles."

"You were distracted I whizzed by you six good miles over the speed limit. You didn't pull me over then, so I can only figure this is payback. And I wasn't, I pulled up my phone as I pulled over."

"And you didn't signal."

"What?" John asked.

"You failed to signal."

"So did you."

"Excuse me?"

John nodded. "I watched you. You hit the siren, turned on the lights and pulled over."

"Yeah."

"Without signaling. I watched."

"You know what?"

"What?"

"Have a good day." Giles walked away.

John smiled, waiting until he saw Giles get into his car and then he lifted his phone to read the text. "Damn it," the smile dropped from his face.

'Three Days," Jarvis wrote. 'There will be no hiding it."

Three days? It didn't surprise John, he figured it wouldn't take long. He was just glad he was in Ripley and not Chicago.

After seeing Giles drive by in his police car, John, using his turn signal, pulled back on to the road and headed home.

※ ※ ※

The tripping up the first couple steps was a common sound Yely heard at two in the morning from her mother. One too many drinks at the bar, staggering in the house. But never did she stay out all night. It was five in the morning when Yely heard her mother.

She was waiting for her and had slept on the couch. The thumping on the porch caused her to sit up and wait for the door to open, and for her mother to come in and start yelling about something.

The door didn't open and Yely grew concerned. She peeked out the living room window, she didn't see her mother.

Fearful, she opened the door to find her mother sitting against the side of the house, her head slumped over.

"Mom." Yely crouched down, her mother reeked of alcohol. "Mom." She shook her. "Come on in the house."

"Leave me alone," her mother mumbled.

"Mom, come in."

"Yely!" Her mother swatted out her arm. "Leave me alone. I'm trying to sleep."

"Fine." Yely went back into the house. She couldn't leave her mother out there, even though it wasn't winter, it was still chilly. So Yely grabbed a blanket from the couch, took it outside and covered her mother. She was sure she'd hear about it the next day.

"Yely, why did you leave me on the porch all night?" her mother would probably say.

And there was no winning that one.

It didn't matter what Yely said, her mother would believe it was intentional.

She wasn't the nicest drunk, nor was she nice when she was hung over. Yely was used to it.

Her mother was all Yely had.

Yely didn't know her father. His name was never mentioned.

There was a time when her mother was actually a really good mother. Packing her lunch, making her breakfast, brushing her hair and never going out.

But that was when they lived with their grandmother. Of course, that was when Yely was little, and her grandmother passed away five years earlier when Yely was ten.

That's when they moved to Ripley and her mother spiraled.

The move to Ripley wasn't random, like throw a dart at the map.

Yely's grandmother always talked about moving to Ripley, like a dream retirement destination, but she never was able to afford giving up her job.

In Yely's mind, Ripley had to be some sort of amazing place, especially if her grandmother talked about it so much.

Her mother decided to fulfill her mother's dream.

To her surprise, it was just a tiny town and Yely couldn't figure out what it was about it. She went from being one of thirty kinds in a fifth grade class, to one of eight students in sixth grade.

When they first got there, everything was great. The apartment was nice, close to the school and a block from the diner where her mother got a job.

Then after a year there, her mother lost the job and then the apartment. They were kicked out.

Evicted.

They stayed in Ripley.

Yely couldn't figure out how her mother kept losing jobs in such a small town, but she wasn't thinking it was her mother's fault.

For three years Yely believed no one liked her mother despite how hard she worked and that was why they kept firing her. The pet store, the Kroger's. Losing her jobs and struggling for money was Yely's excuse for her mother's drinking.

Then came the eighth-grade prom, Yely was outside waiting on her mother. All the other kids were being picked up and Yely was still there waiting.

Alone, the last one.

Mrs. Connor the principal drove her home, even walked Yely into the house.

Her mother wasn't home and Yely was genuinely scared that something happened to her mother.

Mrs. Connor called the police.

Sergeant Matthews was about to end his shift but took the call instead of it going to the State Police. He promised to look for her.

That was the night that it all came clear to Yely.

It wasn't the other people. It wasn't Kroger, it was her mother.

The police found her passed out drunk in her car, she promised she would get help, she swore she would.

Three months sober and her mother was back at it.

The way Yely looked at it was her mother had a sickness and she had taken care of Yely for years and Yely had to take care of her now. Even if it included lying to child authorities.

And they came by a lot. Yely suspect the school called them.

Yely dealt with it, all the bullying, the lack of food, being called names like 'trash'.

She dealt with her mother's manipulation of people and Yely would do so until either her mother changed or she couldn't take it anymore.

Again, her mother was all she had. She didn't have friends despite the fact she had lived in the same school district and town for years.

Yely was hopeful on the latest move to Second Avenue next to the grumpy old guy. It was a nice house, the nicest place they rented. They were lucky because they had been evicted so much, renting a new place was hard. Her mother had managed to keep her bartending job at Crazy Carl's for six months.

When they were evicted from their fourth place in town, her mother did her manipulation thing with some really nice woman pastor at a local church. The church helped them to rent the house.

It was a fresh start … again. Only this time Yely was old enough to work, to pitch in with the rent. There was something about manipulating and using someone on God's team that scared Yely.

She didn't want to move again, unpack boxes, hear her mother repeat 'this time will be different'.

Yes, it would be different, Yely would make sure of it.

Taking care of her mother was something she was used to doing.

Tucking her into bed when she stumbled in after work, changing her bedding when she drunkenly wet her bed, cooked dinners, covered with the child services when her mother went on some excursions out of town for days, leaving Yely alone.

She loved her mother.

She hoped and prayed her mother would eventually get through and conquer her demons.

No matter how angry Yely got at her mother, guilt always set it. Just like it did when she left her mother out on the porch.

Yely had no intention of leaving her out there for hours, but she fell back to sleep and when she woke up it was nearly eleven.

When she woke back up, she grew nervous, fearful and praying her mother didn't die of alcohol poisoning or inhale her own vomit.

It was a horrible burden and fear for a fifteen-year-old to carry, but Yely didn't realize it.

It was her life and she left her mother on the porch.

Maybe when her mother woke, sobered up, and felt better, Yely could talk about cooking out. They had a house now, they could barbecue and it was Memorial Day Weekend.

First, she had to make sure her mother wasn't dead.

Scared and holding her breath, she walked onto the porch. Her mother was in the same position. Sitting with her back against the house.

Yely exhaled her anxiety when she heard her mother breathe.

"Mom." She walked over to her, grabbing her arm. "Mom, come on. Let's go inside."

Her mother groaned.

"Mom, come on." Yely yanked her arm.

It took three tries and finally her mother began to stand.

Just as her mother stood, she stumbled again and the grumpy guy from next door pulled into his driveway.

He stopped midway.

Yely cringed, then continued to try to get her mother to stand.

The old guy stepped from his truck and looked over, calling out. "She sick or something?"

"Something," Yely answered.

"You need some help?" he asked.

"No."

"Okay. Good luck with that." He got back into his truck and drove the rest of the way in his driveway to the back of his house.

Good luck with that. Yely repeated his words in her head.

She didn't need luck, she just needed her mother to stand up and walk into the house so she could sleep it off.

CHAPTER SIX – THE BACK AND FORTH

'John pick up,' Jarvis said on the answering machine. 'Pick up. I know you can hear me. You're the only person in the world who still has an answering machine. John. John."

That was followed by four text messages.

'Call me.'

'What are you doing? I'm freaking out.'

"Oh, Good … Lord." John shook his head looking at his phone and finally, he called Jarvis.

"Thank God," Jarvis answered the phone.

"Jarvis, what is wrong with you?" John asked. "To respond to your messages, I am calling you. And I couldn't pick up the phone because I am a seventy-two year old man who had to dig up his supply ditch while some drug addict teenager emo girl watched from the window. What is so important?"

"My flight leaves tomorrow morning."

"Okay."

"John, after you Americans celebrate your Memorial Day, this thing will be known," said Jarvis. "I just want to make sure this address you gave me is correct."

"It is. Why would I lie?"

"You lie about your name," said Jarvis.

"Oh, this is different. So, you are coming here?"

"Yes," replied Jarvis. "From my calculations that area, your area, is the safest place on earth. I leave here tomorrow morning. I have several flights and should arrive in Charleston on

Memorial Day."

"Charleston? And you're renting a car?"

"I am."

"Then I'll see you when you get here and we can get things ready. Good thing for you that you won't have to return it."

"We'll store the battery and starter in your supply hatch. That way if there is an EMP it should be protected."

John was looking for a reason to end the call, but didn't need one when the doorbell rang. "Sounds good. Someone's at the door. Looking forward to meeting you."

After ending the call and making his way to the door, John thought briefly about letting a stranger in his home. After all, Jarvis could be a killer. John wasn't worried, being murdered really was the last thing on his mind.

He peeked out the door and grunted when he saw the officer there.

"This is harassment," John said "Officer Matthews."

"You know," he nervously said. "It's actually been Sergeant Matthews for a while now."

John nodded. "I see. But I get a pass because I was the only one who called you by your real first name when everyone thought your name was Matt Giles. Now what do you want?"

"I got a complaint," Giles said.

"About?"

"Are you burying a body in your yard?'

"Yep. Wanna see?"

"You ... you are?"

"Oh, don't be silly." John waved his hand. "It's my supply hatch. For burying some supplies, in case of looters and as Jarvis says protect the car battery from the rental car he plans on stealing."

"I'm sorry, what?"

"I'm not repeating. You can go look."

Giles shook his head and put his little notepad away. "No, that's fine. Thanks Mr. Hopper."

"It was that drug addict next door huh? She turned me in.

Nosey son of a gun. Probably high on the marijuana."

"Mr. Hopper, Ruby has problems, it's not drugs. At least not that I know of."

"Ruby, the mother?"

"Yes."

"Oh, I'm not talking about her. I'm talking about the kid. The kid was peeking out the window. The mother was in no condition to call the police. Hell, she was passed out on the porch still in her hooker clothes when I left for Kroger's. The emo kid with the weird name was trying to drag her in the house when I came back."

"Ruby was passed out on the porch all night?" Giles asked.

"She your girlfriend?"

"What? No."

"Because that is the type of woman that a divorced man goes after when he dumps a nice girl."

"I'm leaving. Thank you." Giles turned and stepped off the porch.

"Giles," John called him.

Giles stopped. "Yeah."

"Hey, you didn't hear that from me about the mother on the porch. For all we know she had a stomach bug and didn't want to give it to her kid. We don't need you doing that mandated reporter thing and having the welfare service giving them a hard time."

"That's oddly nice of you," Giles replied.

"It's selfish because they'll knock on my door."

"And don't worry, I'm just going to have Pastor Judy check on them."

"Pastor Judy?" John asked. "Why?"

"She was helping them. Actually, helped them get the house."

"Thank you for the tip. Looks like my donation will be cut in half this week on the offering plate. Have a good one." John started to close the door.

"Mr. Hopper, wait, what do you need a supply hatch for?"

Giles asked.

"End of the world." John closed the door.

He waited a second to see what Giles was going to do. The officer stood there, looking a little dumfounded, then he got into his squad car and didn't go next door to the new neighbors.

He watched as the police car pulled away, then John went to his kitchen for some hot dogs.

* * *

John opted for a short nap in his reclining chair. That peanut butter sandwich he had after getting home kept him from getting hungry, but when he woke up from his short nap he was pretty famished.

It was pushing dinner time, the sun was still pretty bright. After getting his wits about him following his late afternoon nap, John knew it was time to cook.

He was ready for his Saturday, Memorial Weekend solo barbecue.

He grabbed his hot dogs, buns, butter and a platter and headed outside to his yard.

He had a decent grill and kept it a good distance from his house, about ten feet from his back porch.

When he started his propane grill, he heard arguing coming from the renters.

His peaceful neighborhood had been uprooted. Maybe they were just having adjustment issues. John only hoped the arguing wasn't a regular occurrence.

Then again in a few days, what would it matter.

They were the type that weren't ready for things. They'd either flee to somewhere not safe or get desperate and try to steal from John.

He was ready for that.

In a desperate situation such as an extinction level event, John was prepared and he had no qualms shooting looters, neighbors or not.

The grill was hot and ready and he placed his all-beef hot dogs on the grill. He then buttered his buns. He loved a grill toasted bun. As he gently rolled his dogs on the grill for perfect cooking and grill markings, he saw through the smoke of his culinary works, the teenager next door, standing in her yard.

He looked at her once, then again.

"If you're wondering about that body buried in my yard," he shouted over to her. "Cooking him up right now. Figured, it's better to get rid of him with the law lurking around."

He laughed.

She didn't.

John looked down at the eight hot dogs on the grill and the buns he had just buttered. "You hungry? You want a hot dog? They smell pretty good."

The moment those words escaped his mouth, he thought, 'wow, that was too nice of me', and he meant to correct it by telling her he was kidding, but before he could, the teenager said.

"Are you sure?"

John couldn't say 'no', instead he just waved his hand over to her and before he knew it, she was standing next to him at the grill.

"What are you doing with those buns?" she asked. "Why do you have them cooking?"

"Heating, toasting, glazing them with the good stuff, my secret," John said. "You have to admit, everything tastes better with butter."

"I never had butter."

"What do you mean you never had butter?"

"Well, not the real stuff," she said. "Not butter. I had the yellow stuff."

"Margarine?" John asked.

"I guess."

"That's not butter."

"My mom said butter is expensive."

"It is. Here." John removed one of his buttered grilled buns from the heat. "Give this a try. Break off a piece, tell me what you think."

She looked down at the grilled bun, broke off the end and gave it a try. She chewed slowly at first then smiled. "This is really good. Can I eat it?"

"You go ahead," John said. "We already have an uneven amount, but what the heck right, what's one more?"

She just stared at him.

"Ten hot dogs? Eight buns?" he questioned.

She didn't say anything, she just kept eating the bun. "Thank you," she said. "Mister …?"

"Hopper," he replied. "But you can call me, John. And what is your given name? The legal one. Not the Really Yely one your mom calls you."

"Beverly."

"Beverly." John placed the hot dogs and buns on the plate. "That's better. Let's go inside Beverly. Get some condiments and some of that Kroger macaroni salad I grabbed today."

She was quiet, John thought. Maybe she was scared of him.

They entered through his kitchen door. "What do you like on your hot dog? Ketchup, mustard, onion, relish?"

"Yes," she replied.

"That a girl." He set the platter of hot dogs on the table and walked to the fridge. "Get yours on the bun. "Take two if you want. Paper plates are on the table.""

"Thank you."

He began pulling things from the fridge, setting them on the counter next to him when he notice she was looking around. "Everything okay?"

"It's really nice in here."

"Thanks." John knew she was referring to his modern kitchen with updated cabinets, appliances and so forth. "It wasn't always like this. Probably wouldn't have changed it had it not been for the fire." He placed the condiments on the table. "I'll get that macaroni salad."

"Fire?"

"Oh, yeah, a year ago. I blame it on Pastor Judy. She talked me into getting one of them air fryers. I was sitting in the living room, eating chicken wings and watching old reruns of Masked Singer when boom, the darn thing just lit up and caught fire. No one told me to unplug it." John shrugged. "As you can see, I don't have one now."

"I'm sorry about the fire."

John handed her a plate. "I guess fate was saying it was time to modern up. Right? I mean now I don't have to vacuum, got rid of all the carpet. Not that the fire spread, but that fire smell got into the carpet."

"I bet." Yely fixed the condiments on the hot dogs.

"Take some of the salad. I think it's good. Did you want to eat on the porch?"

Yel nodded and then paused.

"What?" John asked.

"That picture." She pointed to the large, framed picture that hung on the dining room wall. It was one of many, but he knew which one she pointed at. John had it taken at a portrait studio just a mere two months before the tragedy.

"What about it?" John asked.

"Is that your family?"

"It is."

Before John could say more, there wasn't just a knock at the back door, but more of a pounding.

He raised his eyebrows a few times. "Wanna bet that's your mother?"

"How do you know?"

"Because no one ever knocks on my door."

"I have to go," Yely said. "Can I take this with me?"

"You go on." John walked to the back door and opened it for her.

Roby, Yely's mother stood there. "Where's my daughter?"

Yely looked up to John as he opened the door wider.

"Let's go." She said with a snap to her voice. "Now. Why didn't you wake me?"

John cleared his throat as he peeked out. "Sometimes it's best to sleep it off."

It was a mixture of a growl and huff the sound mother made. She shook her head and took Yely by the arm, nearly yanking her out. "What do you have? Give it back."

"Mom, he was …"

"I don't care. Don't eat his food. Give it back."

Yely turned and extended the plate to John.

"Nope," John said, then looked at Ruby and spoke with a gentle stern voice. "I invited her. She took the food, she gets the food, she eats the food. Hear me. She eats the food." He paused. "Would you like one?"

After another huff, her mother stormed off with Yely trailing behind her.

The young girl looked embarrassed, and John felt bad for her. He rarely felt bad for people, but he did for that young girl.

He only hoped she did get to eat those hot dogs.

CHAPTER SEVEN – NOT MY BUSINESS

'Tomorrow morning' Jarvis time, meant John was still sleeping. His flight left London at 9:30 am and when John woke up in West Virginia at nine am, Jarvis was four hours from landing in Charlotte. According to the text, after the layover, he'd be in Charleston by four and John planned a late supper for him when he drove down.

Together, with Jarvis as an expert guest, John would announce the impending doom.

John didn't want to sleep so late, rarely did he sleep past seven. But he had some audio issues recording his little show and it wasn't technical. Most came from noise … next door.

They bickered, screamed and fought all night.

Actually, into the early hours of the morning. John finally fell asleep. What could a mother and daughter fight so long and hard about?

He didn't hear the daughter as much as he heard the mother. She was loud. And by how obnoxious she sounded, she was probably drunk.

But he didn't want to make assumptions.

His quiet neighborhood was being shattered by a dysfunctional family.

That was the least of his worries, their worries too, they just didn't know it.

He still was up in plenty of time to go to church, something he never stopped doing. Although he changed denominations many times, he still attended church services.

Before doing so, he sat on his front porch, enjoying his coffee and weekly Sunday cigarette.

Truth be known he would sneak one here and there. At his age, it wasn't smoking that would kill him, and in light of the upcoming event, it was probably the last thing that would take his life.

Jarvis.

The man he never met was supposed to be on a flight and John expected him to send a text when he landed and waited for his layover, but John would probably be listening to one of those long winded, 'where is this going' Pastor Judy sermons.

Still a part of John was anxious about Jarvis, a man who knew pretty much what was going on.

As the time inched close to Jarvis arriving, John wondered a lot. Did Jarvis really have the information or was he making it up?

Maybe Jarvis put on a good British accent and was actually some weirdo from Pittsburgh scamming him.

John would find out soon enough.

If the end of the world approached, Jarvis was legit, if not, John would handle it.

His coffee was good. He always liked it when Kroger's had that fancy brand on sale. John didn't need to add that creamer powder to his brew to make it better.

He enjoyed the warm, quiet morning.

At first, he thought they must have finally fallen asleep next door. Battled it out and hit the hay. Then he saw their car wasn't in the driveway.

Clearly, the mother had left.

He hoped if she was drunk, she had sobered up before she drove off.

Of course, it had been several hours since the screaming matches started. A part of John felt guilty, maybe he shouldn't have had the girl over for hot dogs.

Rarely if ever was John neighborly. Actually, he couldn't

remember being neighborly.

Even though he felt bad for the girl, he felt a sense of relief for her. The mother Ruby wasn't home. Which meant, Yely or rather Beverly could get some rest.

When did the mother leave? Clearly it was after two in the morning, because John was still tossing and turning as their voices carried into his bedroom.

At least it was quiet now.

John finished off his coffee and weekly official smoke, then went back into his house.

He'd make some eggs, eat and then get cleaned up.

John would absorb normalcy. Go to church, smile and greet people. Then he'd hit up the coffee store, grab an expensive coffee and figure out what he was making for supper. Especially if Jarvis was coming. If everything went as planned, he'd be there by seven.

Jarvis was English, though he didn't have an English accent. He'd figure out something to make him. Then again, it was Memorial Day Weekend, maybe he'd make some hot dogs again. Even though, John had all that trivial stuff swirling around his brain, he couldn't help but wonder about the emo teen and if she were alright.

He'd mention it to Pastor Judy.

CHAPTER EIGHT – COOKIES AND CREAM

"And your reason for visiting the United States?" the customs agency asked when Jarvis approached and showed his passport.

"I was born here. So I'm visiting family."

Which was a lie.

Jarvis couldn't tell him the truth. It sounded ludicrous. That he was on his way to meet a stranger whose voice he knew from the internet, to find a safe haven in West Virginia for an extinction level event.

He knew this for a fact because his ex-wife was a scientist and she told him about the event. Of course he could have moved to the US six years earlier with her when she got the big NASA job, but he didn't. He wanted to stay as far away from her as possible, and he loved London

Now the same woman who he hated was saving his life.

Was she headed to the safest place on earth, too?

She had her own government safe haven. In which she had been invited to long before she told Jarvis anything.

Then again, she didn't have an exact date until recently.

Jarvis checked through customs and paused when there was an alert on his phone.

Delayed.

His connecting flight was pushed back an hour. He already had a three plus hour lay over. Now it was even longer.

Jarvis would find a place to charge his phone and rest. And if his flight was delayed any longer, he would just rent a car. No reason to sit for five hours when he could be driving.

❋ ❋ ❋

The cookies looked fresh. Not that the church had stale cookies for pre service coffee hour, but they certainly served ones they kept in the freezer. They always lacked luster and were cold to the touch.

John picked a cookie where the raspberry filling kind of glistened.

"Morning, John."

John didn't have to guess who said that. He knew right away it was Megan, the forty-year-old divorcee, a vet tech. She was the only person at church under 50 that called him John.

Then again, most people just nodded.

Megan talked to him. For a while he thought she was getting her flirt on with him and he'd have to break her heart by saying she was too young. But that wasn't the case, she was just being nice. Megan was always nice.

John didn't know her story or when she divorced or even why. It wasn't his business, and he never asked anyone, he didn't want anyone to ask about his life in return.

"Morning," John replied.

"The cookies don't look frozen," Megan commented. "People must have dropped off fresh ones."

"Looks that way."

"Oh!" Pastor Judy approached the table. "Fresh cookies. How are you Mr. Hopper?"

"I would be better if I had more sleep," John answered.

"Something bothering you? Are you sick? Worried?" Pastor Judy asked.

"No I have loud neighbors fighting at all hours."

Pastor Judy cringed. "I'm sorry. But I'm sure they'll work things out."

"Weren't there any other properties in Ripley you could help them get?"

"Yes. But God told me to put them next to you."

"God told you, huh?" John said. "Did he give any particular reason or was he vague?"

Pastor Judy smiled with a slight laugh. "You're funny. We'll catch up later, John."

When she walked away Megan asked. "So you finally got neighbors in that house?"

"Yep. Odd duo. Loud mouth drunken mother and an emo teenage girl sitting on her porch doing the marijuana."

"Maybe the emo teen does marijuana because her mother is a drunk or is all this you guessing?"

"The marijuana thing is a guess."

John popped the cookie in his mouth and started to walk away.

"John? Do you have plans for supper tonight?" Megan asked.

"Are you hitting on me or asking me on a date?"

Megan giggled. "No. Kroger had corned beef on sale and I was gonna pop one in the slow cooker. Thought I'd see if you wanted to have a nice corned beef dinner."

"You know they're left over from Saint Patrick's day."

"Oh they are not."

"I would love a corned beef dinner, but I'm expecting a friend from out of town around seven."

"A friend?" Megan asked. "Oh, now I'm curious. There's plenty. I can bring it over."

"You know what? That's a great idea. He may like that. He's from England so it sort of counts as Irish."

"Then it's a plan. I'll be over about six to get things ready."

"Good. I'll see you …" John's eyes strayed when he saw Yely walking into church alone. It just struck him as odd. What teenager in their right mind would willingly go to church alone?

Immediately Pastor Judy walked up to her.

"John?" Megan called his attention.

"Will you excuse me? That's my new neighbor who walked in."

John was pretty sure Megan said 'certainly' as John made his way to Yely and Pastor Judy.

"Beverly," he said to Yely. "You okay this morning?"

"Yes. Thank you."

"Good. Just checking." John started to walk away.

"Mr. Hopper," Pastor Judy called him. "Why don't you have Yely sit with you."

"Sure."

Pastor Judy faced Yely. "Can you give me and Mr. Hopper a second?"

"Go get some cookies," John said. "They're fresh."

"Okay. Thank you," Yely said and walked away.

"She's a good kid," Pastor Judy told John "Things aren't easy for her."

"Alright. So why are you telling me?" John asked.

"Because all that fighting you heard. I assume it was because her mother left."

"Left where?" John asked.

"Ripley," Pastor Judy replied "I got a text from Ruby this morning stating she had a business opportunity out of town."

"She one of the 'I go where you pay prostitutes?'"

Pastor Judy gasped. "John. She's not a prostitute."

"Well she ain't a business executive either. And she up and left her kid? Isn't that illegal?"

"We can all keep an eye out on Yely for a few days."

"How long is the mother going to be gone?" John asked

"One week."

"Hmm. Well guess we'll be keeping an eye out for a long time."

"Why do you mean?"

"Worlds gonna end before she gets back. Now if you'll excuse me I need to tell Megan we have one more for corned beef."

CHAPTER NINE - ALERT

"Flight 5102 to Yeager Airport is now boarding. We'll now board those who need assistance" the gate agent announced.

"Oh thank God." Jarvis gasped out and took the final sip of his soda. He tossed it in the garbage can even though he had a while to board.

He should have been landing in Ripley at that moment instead of only boarding his flight. He was irritated when the guy at the bar told him he could have driven there before the flight left. Jarvis knew that. He tried to rent a car to drive, but there weren't any available. And judging by how empty the gate was, he guessed a lot of passengers had the same idea.

What irritated him most was that home cooked, corned beef dinner he was missing out on. John said he'd save him some.

He waited his turn by staring at a women working on a tuna fish sandwich. He watched her wrap it up when they called his section of the plane.

He really hoped she wasn't sitting next to him. Especially with that tuna sandwich she was rationing.

It was only an hour though. He supposed he could deal with the smell.

They boarded the plane and Jarvis watched all those with carry on luggage fight for overhead space. He shot one more message to John before shutting off his phone. He'd be there soon enough.

He'd get his luggage, his car, and after setting his GPS, he would be there soon enough.

By his calculations and his ex-wife's, the event would occur on the fourth of June. Surely that was correct or else his wife wouldn't have already disappeared into that survival government bunker.

Five days.

What worried Jarvis more than the event was when the world found out about it.

Once the news undeniably broke, he didn't want to think about the chaos that would ensue. But if all went well, Jarvis would be safe and sound in Ripley, West Virginia when all that happened. Once he landed it was a forty-minute drive to Johns.

He didn't know John more than their over the phone conversations. He caught his podcast once and after becoming an avid listener, gave John inside government scopes no one yet knew. John never claimed them as fact, he only used them for speculative commentary.

Jarvis couldn't wait to meet John. A hard ass, opinionated man who made Jarvis laugh with how politically correct he wasn't.

Soon enough he'd meet John, begin their safety preparations and unlike others, get ready for the end of the world.

But the hopes of seeing John soon were dashed when the pilot announced that the plane was being rerouted to Washington DC.

It was unavoidable, the pilot explained and everyone would be at their destination soon enough.

Jarvis never heard of such a thing happening before they were even in the air and that worried him. There was no reason for a disruption of air travel except for … the event. And if that was the case that meant the news would break sooner than later.

If Jarvis wasn't in a rental car and on his way to John's when the news broke, then Jarvis stood a chance of never getting there.

❈ ❈ ❈

"That," John said as he set his napkin on the table and stood. "That has to be the best corned beef I have ever had."

"Thank you," Megan replied.

"How'd you get it so perfectly sliced?" John asked.

"Electric knife." Megan then looked at Yely. "Did you like it?"

"It was really good. I never had it before. My mom doesn't usually make strange foods."

"Strange?" John chuckled. "Corned beef isn't strange. Then again maybe it is. Where did you say your mom went? Pastor Judy said it was business."

Yely shook her head with an embarrassed smile. "She went with her boyfriend. I guess she was waiting to tell me."

"I'm sorry."

Megan reached over and grabbed Yely's hand. "Do you know where they went?"

"Bahamas."

John whistled. "Hate to be the bearer of truth news, but that isn't a spur of the moment trip."

"Yeah I know," Yely said. "She's done it before. She doesn't tell me because I get mad that she leaves me alone."

"Well, you're not alone now," Megan told her. "John is right next door."

John was about to say something sarcastic, try to lighten the mood when both Yely and Megan's phone made a strange buzzing sound at the same time.

John's phone didn't. Then again, it was in the other room and he didn't have one of those fancy smart phones.

"This is weird." Megan looked down at her phone. "Usually, it's a storm alert or Amber alert."

"What's it say?" John asked.

Yely replied. "To watch the president for an important announcement at seven."

"That's fifteen minutes from now," said Megan. "Wonder what is so important they have to send a national alert."

John shrugged. But he had a gut feeling he knew what it was.

Admittedly, Yely was leery about following John down to the basement. It was creepy, they cleared the table after dinner, and then the alert came and John changed.

"I need you to come with me," John told them.

Yely didn't think too much about it until they headed down the basement stairs.

"John," Megan said. "Why are we going to the basement?"

"I need you to see something before the president comes on. I think I know why," John replied. "That amber alert sounding thing wasn't anything good. And again, I think I know what it is."

They walked down the flight of stairs and ended up immediately in an office. There was a small laptop, microphone, fax machine, and old radio on a desk. The area was small, but then John unlocked a door.

Yely grew nervous, was he going to trap them in the basement?

"I think you're scaring Yely," said Megan.

John paused in opening the door. "She should be scared."

Yely screamed.

"What in God's name is wrong with you?" John snapped. "Scared of what's going to happen, what the president is going to say." He pushed open the door and turned on the lights.

With an 'Oh my', Megan stepped in first. "John, what is all this?"

"This is enough food and water to survive for, well, three hundred days. Longer by myself."

Upon realizing that John wasn't leading them to slaughter and seeing the shelves of supplies like it was some mini warehouse, Yely stepped farther in. "Why do you need this many supplies?"

"To live," John replied. "Something is going to happen, something big. Something that is gonna make me need these supplies."

"John," Megan said his name. "If you knew something, why didn't you say something."

"Well, I was given bits of information. Nothing concrete until a day or so ago. But based on the outlandish predictions of a scientist named Jarvis, I started prepping. And who is gonna listen to a crazy old man. Other than the people who listen to my radio podcast, I would have been dismissed like half the other nut jobs who have predicted the apocalypse."

Yely gasped. "The apocalypse."

Megan reached to calm her, laying a hand on her back. "No, I'm sure he doesn't mean the end of the world. Do you John?"

John just stared and didn't give an answer.

CHAPTER TEN – HERE IT COMES

Jarvis wasn't exactly sure how long they sat on the tarmac, no air conditioning, no news, no means to use the bathroom or get a drink of water.

Thankfully, Jarvis had his own water bottle.

He was told they were going to Washington DC, they rolled a bit more toward the runway and stopped. There they sat.

No one really giving updates, no one really saying anything.

Then the plane started moving, People expressed their relief outwardly, but the plane wasn't moving toward a runway, it moved back to the terminal.

This was turning into the flight from hell. Jarvis was approaching nearly a day of traveling.

What was going on? They pulled up to the terminal and Jarvis watched through the window as they attached the walkway.

The tones for an announcement rang out.

"At this time, we'll deplane. FAA has grounded flights at this time. Thank you for flying with us."

Wait. What? Jarvis thought. That was it? He was in the first row after first class and stood. People questioned and guessed, talking to each other, but he just wanted to get off of the plane. He didn't have a carry on, just a small backpack with his laptop. He easily slipped from the aisle and noticed the flight attendants weren't making eye contact.

"Excuse me, what about our checked bags?" he asked a flight

attendant. "We'll be able to get them, correct?"

"Sir, I don't know," she replied. "You can ask inside."

Even though internally Jarvis screamed in frustration, it wasn't her fault. She didn't delay the flight and ground all planes.

Quickly he made his way off the plane, across the fly bridge and to the terminal.

He turned on his phone and immediately thought about renting a car. He stood at Gate B25 with dozens of other people on their phones. He thought surely they were doing what he was doing, looking for a car. Then he got out of his own head for a moment and heard it.

Everyone's phone was making a buzzing sound, like an alarm.

Why wasn't he getting one? Was it because he was from the UK?

He stepped farther from the gate and looked around. He saw the sign 'Car rental' and headed that direction. While he did so, he called John.

"Jarvis, where are you?" John answered the phone.

"Still in North Carolina. The FAA grounded all flights."

"That's news to me."

"So you don't know what's going on?" Jarvis asked.

"Just that the president is making some announcement. You may wanna find a place to catch it. You have eight minutes," John said. "And Jarvis. I think this is it and it's early."

Jarvis ran and the entire time he did he ran down every cuss word he could think of. If it was the event, he still had days before he thought the news would break.

All flights were grounded, he was in North Carolina and needed to get to West Virginia. While it wasn't that far, it wasn't walkable before the event. He might as well have been back in England if he couldn't get a car. With flights grounded, he didn't see that happening.

Jarvis knew once the news broke, people would react in one of two ways. They'd be in denial and calm or out of control.

Maybe it wasn't news of the event.

The next day was the American Memorial Day holiday, maybe they grounded flights because of a terror threat.

He needed to find a television in the airport that wasn't showing advertisements only.

Finally, he came across a lounge and raced inside.

"Paying customers only," someone told him.

"I'll pay." He injected his way to the bar, wedging between a thicker built man and a woman that smelled like body odor and perfume.

The bartender was busy, and Jarvis waited for his moment.

He pulled out a hundred-dollar bill, waving it as the bartender passed. "You can keep the change, get me a double bourbon straight."

The bartender walked by, stopped, backtracked and grabbed the hundred.

Without asking what kind of bourbon, he grabbed a bottle and glass, poured more than a double and slid the glass to Jarvis as he went back to work.

The liquid splashed some on his fingers as he lifted the glass. "Thanks," Jarvis said. The bartender didn't say anything.

Sipping his beverage he turned to face the television on the wall. His fears of not being able to hear vanished when everyone around him were encouraging others to be quiet.

Then the president came on.

CHAPTER ELEVEN – NOTHING NEW HERE

It was nearly everything John expected to hear. Only one thing was new to him. He knew eventually the president would address the nations as would other leaders of the world. Well timed so that not one place broke the news before the other.

A message of concern and ending as one of hope.

"We will not stop, we will keep trying to stop this, globally. Not as one nation in the world, but one world coming together. God willing, we will succeed."

That wasn't going to happen.

As the president gave his speech, he assumed Megan and Laney understood John's basement bunker a little better.

John always wondered how the president would start his speech about it. Like the man he was, the president minced no words.

"Look, I'm going to come right out with it," the president said. "We're in trouble, not as a nation, but as a planet. Sort of the same kind of trouble the dinosaurs faced sixty-five million years ago."

Megan gasped and so did Yely. John kind of chuckled, not that it was funny, but the blunt way he delivered it was.

He told about how it wasn't as big as the rock that nailed the dinosaurs, it was half the size and it was a comet, not an asteroid or meteor.

The Comet was named Silverstien after the astronomer that discovered it.

Who happened to be Jarvis' ex-wife. That wasn't mentioned by the president.

There was hope because NASA called comets 'dirty snowballs', they had a chance that most of it was ice and would break up upon entry.

It was due to arrive on or around June fourth and while they were watching for a while, confirmation of its imminent collision with earth was just learned. Not enough time to launch a big space 'destroy it' project.

There was limited time, so the government was doing all they could to move supplies to expediated shelters in big cities.

The president urged people to be calm, humane, do not loot or hoard.

Another thing that wasn't going to happen.

They estimated the impact point to be Northwest Africa. Around Morrocco, but the scientists couldn't say if it would be a land or sea hit.

Either way, Spain and Portugal were screwed, and the Canary Islands gone.

Not to mention the huge mega tsunami that would hit if it slammed into the ocean.

He encouraged people to use the next few days to move from coastal areas, and possibly to areas that have mountainous protection. He listed some areas, about thirty of them, thankfully, Ripley didn't make that list. The president did mention Clarksburg, which wasn't too far from Ripley.

In other words, it was going to be a mad race exodus.

The information John didn't know, that Jarvis and his ex-wife failed to say was the comet wasn't coming alone. It was accompanied by thirty-two other rocks, some as small as cars, others as big as buses.

Thirty-two. Maybe it wasn't something they could see until it was five days out. Plus, it could rain small meteors as it broke through the atmosphere.

The president wasn't sure if they would come before, during or after. But to get ready.

John was ready. He was ready for a single celestial object colliding with earth, he didn't expect it to come with offspring. But really what were the odds one of them would hit Ripley?

The president mentioned the smaller impacts, then mentioned earthquakes, possibly tsunami on the coasts.

What he didn't mention was all the other little things, like ejecta, or wind blast, the exceptional heat then cold.

He left that out, but John needed that information. He had it and even more if Jarvis ever showed up.

* * *

For a half hour after the president made his announcement it was absolute mayhem at the airport. It was bad enough all flights were grounded and Jarvis didn't know why that was. He tried to text his ex-wife, but she wasn't getting back.

He drank his double while watching the president. The moment it was over, everything erupted. People panicked, rushing out of the lounge, some not paying their tabs.

Jarvis had been standing, but a stool opened up almost immediately and he sat down.

He had a great vantage point seat. On the other side of the bar, watching not only what happened in the lounge, but outside the lounge doors in the terminal.

Jarvis wasn't moving. Why would he? He had no where to go except get his checked bag and he didn't want to be in the terminal at that moment. Not yet. Even if his checked bag wasn't there, everything important was in his briefcase bag.

His eyes went from his phone to try to get a rental car, back to the commotion. More so the commotion. Watching it all, one would have thought a bomb was going off the way they all ran, bumping into each other, hitting each other with carryon luggage.

Insanity.

He was the only one in the bar. He and one bartender, who

like Jarvis, just watched.

Jarvis pulled out another hundred dollar bill and the bartender instead of pouring him a drink, gave him the bottle.

"Thanks," Jarvis said. "I appreciate it."

"Waiting for the madness to stop?" the bartender asked.

"Yep, then I'll hopefully collect my luggage."

"Then what?"

Jarvis took a sip and shrugged. "I haven't a clue."

The bartender handed him a bag of pretzels. "Obviously you aren't from around here."

"Nowhere even close. I was originally from Oregon, now I'm across the pond."

The bartender cringed. "Yikes. You are far. Where were you headed."

"This was my layover to Charleston."

"South Carolina?"

"West Virginia."

"Eh." The bartender waved out his hand. "It could be farther. It could be Oregon. Hold on." He pulled out his phone.

"If you're looking for car rental. I can't find one."

"No, but I found a bus, it leaves in like four hours."

"Seriously?" Jarvis grew excited. "That's fantastic. It's not cancelled?"

"Not that I can see." His fingers moved. "Nope. Still running. But you better hurry. It looks like there are only six seats left."

"Shit. Didn't realize it was that popular of a place."

"I don't think it's the place," said the Bartender. "I think it's the last bus out until tomorrow morning, or rather the last bus getting away from the east coast."

"We aren't that close to the coast, are we?" Jarvis asked as he sought the bus reservation on his phone.

"A hundred and fifty miles," he replied, then again lifted his phone. "And, if the armchair experts that are coming on line are right, if that tsunami comes, right here will be like Atlantis."

Jarvis got it, a seat, and in between reserving his lone bus ticket, he listened to the bartender. "What are you going to do?"

"Like everyone else. I'm going west. What choice do I have, right? But I'll take the long way which is every single back road. I've seen movies."

Jarvis smiled. The bartender was right. He was glad he spoke to him and got that seat on the bus. Hopefully, he would be on the road before others rushed to leave, cramming the highways and making a safe escape impossible.

CHAPTER TWELVE – WHAT ARE THE PLANS?

John said, "Bus."

To which Yely replied. "There's a bus?"

"Yep. He booked his ticket." John peered down at his phone. "He just needs to get from Charleston to here."

"I'll get him," said Megan. "When does he arrive?"

"No," John told her. "Driving those roads now that the news broke, that's not good. Maybe here it will be fine, but out there, no."

"It's forty miles, John," said Megan.

Yely muttered, "They said Clarksburg."

John snapped his finger. "Exactly. It was one of the places mentioned. Everyone is going to head toward those places that were called out."

Megan shook her head. "No, John this is your friend. This is the man that told you about the event."

"In my defense …"

"Don't." Megan wagged her finger. "You have been talking to him. He came all the way overseas to get here. Now he's stuck. I understand you not getting him, but there's no reason I can't. I won't take any of the main roads. I'll take Charleston."

John sighed out. "What if I make him walk out of city limits?"

"I can work those details out with him," said Megan. "I need his number so I can stay in touch with him."

"I'll call him," John said and lifted his phone. Before he dialed he noticed Yely walking back toward the living room. "Are you leaving?"

"I was going to watch the news," Yely replied. "See if there's a reaction, see what they're saying."

"You can't watch the news at your own house?"

"John!" Megan snapped.

"Just saying."

Yely shook her head. "No. We don't have cable and we didn't get the antennae thing yet like you."

"Okay then watch away," John told her and dialed his phone. After a ring, Jarvis answered. "Jarvis, hey, I'm gonna put you on speaker phone."

Megan asked. "Does your flip phone have speaker phone?"

"Yes it has speaker phone," John quipped and placed on the speaker. "Jarvis?"

"I'm here."

"Jarvis, I would like you to say hello to Megan. She's going to meet up with you in Charleston and give you a ride here."

"Oh, that's fantastic, thank you so much."

"It's nice to meet you," said Megan. "Sadly, under these circumstances."

"Well, there's still a half percent chance it won't hit," said Jarvis.

"Jarvis," John said. "I'm going to give her your number, you can work things out with her and come up with a plan B, too, just in case."

"Just in case what?" Jarvis asked.

"You get stuck somewhere."

"On it and thank you, John, thank you Megan."

"Be safe." John ended the call, then noticed the look on Megan's face, she seemed offended. "What?"

"You just hung up."

"It's fine. Now where's she going?" John asked.

Megan turned. "She's probably leaving because you were

mean."

"Oh, I was not." John walked to the living room, the television played and news anchors were on. He paused to look, they were repeating what the president said, announcing experts would be on shortly.

He thought maybe Yely left, but he saw her on the porch and he stepped out to join her.

"Thought you were watching the news," John said.

"They showed a picture of the ocean." Yely gripped the porch railing.

"Okay."

"My mom is in that area."

"Okay."

Yely looked at him. "I'm never seeing her again, am I?"

"More than likely not." John saw her head lower. "But you don't know. She may not have gotten on a plane. They cancelled all flights. Do you have her details?"

"You mean what flight she took?"

"Yes."

Yely shook her head. "No, she said she'd call when she got there."

"Have you tried calling her?"

"Goes right to voice mail," Yely replied.

"Maybe she's not on vacation. Seems like an awfully fancy vacation to take for a single mother relying on the church, for a place to live."

"Where else would she be?" Yely asked.

"Tulsa."

"Why Tulsa?"

John shrugged. "Just throwing it out there. Look, I'm just saying, the chances of her finding a man that's all of the sudden taking her to the Bahamas is slim. She's not far, I don't believe that. Not now that the news broke, once she turns her phone back on, bet she'll come back home."

"You think?"

"Yeah, that's what I'm thinking."

"Thank you." Yely, without warning, hugged John.

"No, no. No hugs." John moved her back. "I'm not emotional like that."

Yely nodded.

"Why don't you go grab your left overs and head on home and get some rest. You had a hard night last night, I don't suppose you got much rest."

"Okay. Thanks." Yely walked by John and opened the porch door. When she walked in, Megan stepped out.

"I don't know what your story is John," Megan said. "But the compassionate side really is fighting to come out."

"No, it's not," John stated. "It won't. I don't really care about anyone Megan."

"That's not true."

"It is," John said.

"You don't or won't."

"Both." John stared out. "I can't."

"She's a teen ..."

"I won't. I can't," John repeated adamantly, then after a beat said, "Don't be thinking I have some criminal record with kids involved."

"I don't."

"Good. I don't. I've always tried to live my best life."

"And you think not being nice in your final chapter in doing so?" Megan asked.

"I think God is fine with me. Let's change the subject."

Silently, Megan stared out for a second. "You said Plan B with Jarvis."

"I did."

"Do you think it's going to be that bad already?" she asked.

"Not that I have experience with an end of the world panic, but," John said. "I do. And it won't be long before we find out how bad it will be."

CHAPTER THIRTEEN - WAITING

Bartholomew Stevens was a very interesting person. A character perhaps that Jarvis would have seen on some BBC television show. Despite Bartholomew bragging he was a self-made millionaire, inventing a new dental device, Jarvis just smiled and knew that was probably not true. After all, if he was a millionaire and invented something dental why was he missing his two front teeth.

He wasn't an old man, probably late thirties or early forties. His hair disheveled as if he hadn't combed it in days. He didn't smell, that was a good thing and he didn't look dirty, just in disarray.

Of course, Jarvis enjoyed his company at the bus station. After being the last one to collect his check-in luggage, and getting a ride from the bartender Stan, Jarvis got to the bus station early and Bartholomew was sleeping on a bench. The station was crowded and it seemed everyone was trying to avoid asking him to move over.

Not Jarvis. He tapped him politely on the shoulder asking if the seat was taken and that was when Bartholomew sat up, making room for Jarvis conveniently by an outlet so he could charge his phone.

Bartholomew patted down his hair, apologized and introduced himself. He told Jarvis he had been at the station waiting for the next bus going west.

Seemed everyone was.

Bartholomew told him that the trains were sold out and that happened instantly. He himself was on a flight to Los Angeles, first class of course, when his flight was diverted back to Charlotte, then cancelled.

Jarvis didn't question him. He supposed the man needed someone to finally talk to him.

He offered Jarvis half of his sandwich. Jarvis declined even though he was hungry.

Stan the bartender gave him a few bags of pretzels and Jarvis was saving those.

"Are you sure?" Bartholomew asked. "It's fresh from the vending machine." He pointed for Jarvis' behalf.

Jarvis glanced in the direction he pointed. Sure enough there was a vending machine and no one was really using it.

"Wow. You enjoy your sandwich. I'll see wat they have," Jarvis said.

After glancing at his watch and seeing he still had two hours until the bus, Jarvis asked Bartholomew if he would watch his seat and if he wanted anything.

Bartholomew said he was fine and laid back down when Jarvis got up, to secure his seat and watch his Phone.

A part of Jarvis wondered if he should be so trusting especially in desperate times, but it wasn't in his nature to mistrust. Hence, partly why he was divorced.

There were three vending machines. Food, snack, drink.

"It only takes cash," a woman told him as he approached the sandwich vending machine. "The card reader isn't working on any of them."

"Thanks," Jarvis replied and pulled out his wallet. He had cash. After giving up his hundred dollar bills he only had small bills remaining but enough to stuff his briefcase.

The choices were limited. Turkey, bologna, and tuna. Jarvis opted for bologna. He bought five bologna sandwiches, four bags of M n Ms and three bottles of water.

After allowing himself to eat half a bologna sandwich, he would save the rest for later with those pretzels if he needed it.

Jarvis thought positively.

He believed he'd get on that bus, get to Charleston, and meet up with that nice woman Megan woman whom he'd been texting all night.

He returned to Bartholomew and his spot.

"Got all of your stuff?" he asked

"I do, thank you." Jarvis took a bite of his sandwich.

"Where are you headed?"

"Charleston now," Jarvis answered. "But Ripley, West Virginia is my final destination'

"Never heard of it. You have family there?"

"Friends"

It was then it hit Jarvis. Bartholomew didn't mention the comet. Surely, he knew about it. Then Jarvis started to listen. Listen to those around him. Eavesdropping as he ate his sandwich.

People talked about where they'd go, what they would do. Most sounded calm. No one was panicking. Maybe because they had a bus ticket and they would be out of the city soon.

It was still early. On his way to the bus station Jarvis didn't see chaos or fighting. He had a good feeling.

His phone bleeped taking him out of his observation mode. It was Megan asking how he was.

He replied that he was fine, met a nice man named Bartholomew, was eating bologna and would see her soon and as planned.

Jarvis was confident in that.

At this stage in the game, he was still ahead of things and what could go wrong

* * *

It was after midnight, Yely wasn't tired. She had another piece of corned beef and kept her phone on the charger. She would be lying if she said she didn't check it every few minutes.

Mr. Hopper offered for her to stay and watch a movie or sit in while he did his radio show. Megan offered to stay with her as well. Both of them claiming that in light of the recent announcement, she shouldn't be alone.

Yely didn't want to be alone, but she didn't want to show how upset she was with her mother. She wanted to appear strong, unaffected.

But she wasn't.

Her mother left. She just left. Up and went on vacation without warning, and it wasn't the first time. The only difference was, every other time she did, the world wasn't going to end in five days.

Yely tried calling, but there was no answer.

She sent text after text ... nothing.

It was possible she never left the United States and was held up somewhere like that man Jarvis.

Staring out the window, she saw all the wood John had in his yard and it made sense now to her. All those supplies. His lights were still on, he was probably working on his radio show. Yely wanted to reach out to her mother, even using an app, but data charges applied and she had to prepay.

Finally John's lights went out, she had to figure out what to do. She went into the kitchen and did a count of what she had as far as supplies. A lot of canned goods from the food bank, some peanut butter. Fortunately, most of it was nonperishable.

A little after two in the morning, her phone rang.

It was on the charger and Yely raced to it. She saw it was her mother and she answered with a rushed, "Hello."

"Are you okay, are you hurt, in trouble?" her mother asked.

"No."

"Then why the hell do I have eight missed calls and too many texts to count."

"Mom, I ..."

"I told you, I would call you. It costs money for these calls."

"But you didn't text or call," Yely said.

"No, I didn't. I took a nap. I didn't sleep last night and we just woke up."

"So you haven't watched the news?"

"Oh my God, I just said …" her mother then started talking to someone in the room. "No, put them over there. There. We'll trip on them. Just leave the small one on the bed."

The male voice in the back said, "Don't you wanna get to your clothes?"

"Mom," Yely tried to interject, feeling frustrated.

"I'll unpack later. I just want to pull something out to wear now. Hopefully, we can find some place open."

"Mom!"

"It's two in the morning," he replied. "We can try. But every minute you're the phone, is another minute wasted."

"I'm talking to my kid, you asshole."

"Just saying."

"Mom …"

"What, Yely?"

"Are you really in the Bahamas. I need to know."

"Are you serious?" her mother snapped. "I told you this is where I was coming."

"But I just thought—"

"Goodbye, Yely, go to bed."

"Mom, you need to watch …"

"Goodbye."

Done. Call ended.

She didn't get to tell her mother she loved her. She didn't get to tell her anything. She figured soon enough, her mother would know.

Maybe it was time for Yely to try to sleep.

CHAPTER FOURTEEN – WAKING

Flying across multitudes of time zones, delays in travel, too much booze, Jarvis was wiped out. After saying goodbye to Bartholomew, he boarded the bus. It took a while, which Jarvis didn't understand.

People fought over seats even thought they were assigned. They carried items on that were stacked upon their laps.

Obviously they were running for their lives, but did they know where they were going?

He tried to listen in on conversations, most people seemed like it was a random bus they booked a ticked on just to get west.

He was exhausted, but held no expectations of going to sleep.

How could he?

With all that was happening in the world, the crowded bus, people talking and that baby.

Jarvis sat in an aisle seat and the young mother sat in the seat next to him across the aisle. She was alone and had a baby that was six months old, and the child kept crying.

He thought once the bus started moving, the baby would calm down.

That didn't happen.

She shuffled the baby, bounced him, tried to get him to eat, but the baby wasn't having it.

Before getting annoyed, Jarvis remembered an opinion piece he had read at one time about how people, instead of getting angry with single parents traveling with fussy children, one should ask if they needed help.

"How old is your baby?" Jarvis asked.

"Six months."

"Are you traveling by yourself?"

"Yeah. I have to get out of town, right? Away from the coast. Better now than later."

"True. But we're going north, not really making headway from the coast."

"I have a connecting bus to Cincinnati," she said.

"Not quite sure where that is."

"It's farther west." She then shushed the baby, trying again to comfort him.

"Do you ... do you need help?" Jarvis asked. "I'm not a dad, but I'm happy to help."

"That's nice. I'll let you know, okay?"

Jarvis smiled and nodded. "Absolutely. If you need a break, just let me know."

He heard his phone beep and he lifted it.

It was Megan.

'How's it going?' her text read.

'Good. Finally the bus is moving," Jarvis replied. 'I'll have a full charge on my phone and power bank as a backup."

'So you should arrive in Charleston on time.'

'I hope. The bus is crowded.'

'Is it full of people trying to get out of town?' she asked via text.

'Yes. It was the last bus tonight leaving Charlotte. We're headed north, not west.'

'Into the mountains,' Megan texted. 'Higher ground.'

'True.'

Beep. Another text came through.

'Keep in touch. I'm going to try to sleep for a couple hours, then I will head out to get you. You'll need to get out of Charleston and do some walking. I am going to take the back roads.'

He didn't think about how she was waiting up to text him and come for him. It was two in the morning, he was overwhelmed by her kindness.

'Sounds good. Thank you again. You are very kind.' He messaged.

There was a delay in her response, then finally she sent her last text of, 'Try to sleep.'

Jarvis found that funny. It was going to be an impossibility. They had a six-hour bus trip, which he figured included a short break.

His stomach rumbled a little in hunger, but even though Jarvis had food, he didn't want to eat, not yet, just in case.

He did offer the young mother a bite to eat.

After placing his phone on battery saver, Jarvis put his rest back. He thought about how unbelievably hard the trip ended up being. It wasn't supposed to be like this. The news wasn't supposed to break until after he arrived in Ripley. That made him curious about what may have happened that his ex-wife didn't tell him about.

He sent her several messages and she didn't reply. She would. He knew she would when she had a chance.

Surprisingly the trip moved smoothly. No delays and just as he felt himself nodding off, they stopped for a twenty-minute rest stop two hours after they had left Charlotte.

The baby still fussed, not as much as earlier and after the bathroom break, Jarvis thought he could get some rest. If he didn't, he would when he met up with John.

He fell fast and hard into a deep sleep, and it wasn't a crying baby that woke him, it was the sound of his phone messaging going off.

It sounded loud and he realized the bus was quiet and wasn't moving.

Figuring it was another scheduled stop, he didn't think much about it and Jarvis looked at his phone.

It wasn't Megan, it was from his ex-wife. A phone call, not a text reply to his question, 'Why was the news released early? Is something else happening.'

"Lil?" Jarvis answered the phone.

"Were you sleeping?" she asked.

"Yeah, briefly. I was worried about you."

"I'm fine. I'm safe. Sorry I didn't get in touch sooner, security just gave me my phone back."

"That's fine," Jarvis said. "You're calling."

"I came up for fresh air," she replied. "Jarvis, the news had to break early. S is still coming in four days, but what precedes it can happen any time."

"I'm sorry. What precedes it is happening at any time?"

"Yes. The massive family of smaller meteors. They picked up speed and are passing 'S'. Most of them are coming before it. It's going to be bad."

"Jesus," Jarvis said aloud then wrote. "Okay. When?"

"We don't know."

"Is Ripley still safe?"

"Are you in Ripley."

"Not yet," Jarvis replied. "But close. I'm on my way. Is it still safe to be there?"

"From S yes. Jarvis, unless you are two hundred feet underground, nowhere is safe and we don't know where they'll land. It will be like throwing a fist full of pebbles into a lake, they will scatter and land anywhere. I have to go. Call me or text me when you get to Ripley."

"I will. I promise."

"Be safe and Jarvis, I will always love you."

Jarvis paused. "I'll always love you, too, Lil."

She hung up first and Jarvis slid the phone from his ear. He was in his own world on that bus and it took the slam of what sounded like the hatch to the under carriage to snap him out of it.

No one was on the bus.

He stood, figuring he'd take this rest stop moment to get something to drink and stretch his legs. He threw the strap to his briefcase crossbody over his shoulder and walked up the aisle.

When he arrived at the front of the bus, he realized they weren't at a rest stop.

They were somewhere, a highway, and from the windshield of the bus for as far as the eye could see where cars, trucks, traffic and people.

Everything was at a standstill.

He looked out of the driver's window to the other side of the highway, the middle median strip was filled with cars and the other side of the highway was traffic going in the same direction.

It was then he stepped from the bus.

"Excuse me, sorry," a man bumped into him carrying a suitcase.

"Good luck," said the woman's voice, then Jarvis looked. It was the young mother from the bus. She carried the baby on her back as she moved down the side of the highway, pulling her suitcase as she pulled her luggage.

Jarvis looked to his right, the bus driver stood by the closed hatch and the remainder of the luggage was on the side of the road, including from what Jarvis could see, his bag.

He walked all the way to the end of the bus, just like a head of the bus, traffic went as far as he could see.

A glance at his watch and Jarvis was stunned. It was eight in in the morning. Three hours after that bathroom break and a half hour from their scheduled arrival time in Charleston.

The bus driver, a stocky man in his late fifties just stared to the sky.

"Excuse me, what's going on?" Jarvis asked.

"The sleeper."

"I'm sorry, what?"

"You were sleeping on the bus," he said. "You were so out people thought you were dead."

"I'm not."

"Obviously."

"What's going on?" Jarvis asked. "Why is my bag over there?"

"This is it. We aren't going anywhere, not anytime soon," the bus driver replied. "Traffic is at a standstill past Charleston.

Apparently, an accident and no one can get through to clear it. Southbound lanes, median strip, they are all jammed. I suppose people are leaving their cars, making it worse. We slowed down and stopped about ninety minutes ago."

"And everyone just got their luggage and left?"

"They weren't going to until another bus radioed and told about the standstill."

"What do I do?" Jarvis asked.

The bus driver shrugged. "Walk maybe?"

"Walk." Jarvis nodded. "How far are we from Charleson?"

"We just passed a placed called Burnwell, so thirty some miles."

"Okay, thank you."

"Good luck," said the bus driver.

"You, too, mate."

Thirty some miles. That was roughly fifty kilometers. When Jarvis was in the British Army, he used to walk fifteen kilometers with heavy packs and armory in a day for a fitness. He was confident. At the age of forty he was fit, and could easily handle the walk.

He grabbed his suitcase, pulled out his phone to send a message to Megan and began his walk up the side of the highway, following everyone else that made their way north.

CHAPTER FIFTEEN – WALKING

John had been up for a while, how could he not. It was a matter of days before the event happened and he just wanted to make sure he had everything he needed. Going to the store was no longer an option.

According to Megan, Kroger's closed their store until the president gave instructions on what limits would be placed.

No panic shopping was allowed.

John had enough, he didn't need to panic shop.

He just needed to organize. Prepare for the heat, then the cold and before that, the EMP that could happen when the comet drew closer. Not since the dinosaurs had anything this big hit and despite what the scientists claimed, it was still a guessing game.

He had just hung up the phone with Megan for the third time.

She was taking responsibility for getting Jarvis far too serious.

"He'll be fine," John told her. "You gave him the best route to take."

"I did, but it looks like he has to walk the highway for a good twenty miles. Seems like they stopped between Burnwell and Standard."

"Never heard of them."

"It's a lot of uphill on I-64."

"He'll be fine. You wait before you get him, you hear?" John said. "We don't need you out there and stuck."

"What about your friend?"

"He'll be fine."

John believed his words. Jarvis wasn't overseas or even that far. He was in the same state. He'd arrive eventually.

What John did worry about was Yely. And that bothered John because he hadn't worried about anyone in a long time.

He was about to go check on her, even if she was asleep, when he heard the knock on his door.

It had to be her. Who else would be knocking on his door at nine in the morning?

John was wrong.

He opened the door to see the police officer, Giles Mathews standing there.

After a slight huff, John shook his head. "Well, if it isn't the poster child for authority harassment."

"Morning Mr. Hopper."

"Mr. Hopper?" John laughed. "I don't recall you calling me that since you were a teenager."

"Actually, I call you that all the time."

"Then maybe you should call me John since you're always stopping by. If you're here for trouble, no I am not burying bodies and I didn't even pick a fight with the teen emo girl. Fed her corned beef."

"That's nice. That's not why I'm here," Giles said.

"If this has to do with the mother leaving town. I don't want to hear it. She asked me to watch the girl."

"Ruby didn't ask you," Giles stated. "But I'm not here for that either."

"Well, what the heck are you knocking on my door for?" John asked.

"When I was here last …"

"Which time?" John interrupted.

"About burying the body."

"Ah, yeah." John nodded. "That time."

"You mentioned supply hatch and looters."

"I did probably."

"And rumor has it you pretty much cleaned out every firewood place in this county."

"And some," John said,

"Why?"

"The firewood? For my wood burning stove. Gotta stay warm."

"Mr. Hopper …"

"John."

"John, were you prepping for this event?" Giles questioned.

"Is this business or personal?"

"Business."

John shook his head. "Then nope."

"Why?"

"You ask me if I was prepping for the event, right? Well I tell you, then all of the sudden you're here invoking section 801 of Executive Order for National Defense Resources Preparedness."

Giles stuttered. "I … uh, what?"

"Section of a law, executive order that gives the law, you, the authority to take all my stuff. Well, I have nothing so have a good day."

"Okay fine." Giles stopped him from shutting the door. "I'm not here for your stuff or to invoke some law, I'm here to ask for your help, for your town. You obviously know what's happening and have for a while. The mayor wants to set up three shelters. He wants you to come in for a meeting to help plan."

"You can't plan to shelter a thousand people for nearly a year in just a few days."

"We have to try, John," Giles said. "Will you help?"

In a strange twist of emotions, John felt a sense of obligation. He looked down at his watch as if to project to Giles that he had better plans, then exhaled.

"I'll give you three hours."

❊ ❊ ❊

"What the heck?" Yely thought as she looked out the window. She got a little sleep, was getting a cola when she looked out the window and saw John being put in a squad car.

Why was John arrested? Yely wondered and she had to find out. She raced from the house, but it was too late, they were pulling away. Immediately her mind went to the fact that he was preparing for the event.

Was that illegal?

Lifting her phone she immediately did an internet search for, 'Is it illegal to stockpile supplies?'

It was amazing what came back. Almost as if, with all that was going on, everyone was searching for the same thing. Yely didn't click on anything, like most people, she read the headline and the preview text and went into a panic.

Other than her mother, she had three people she knew in town and had phone numbers for two of them. Pastor Judy and Megan.

She didn't want to call Pastor Judy, she had feeling there would be no sympathy for John, but Mega was different. She brought John corned beef and was going to pick up some total stranger.

In Yely's young mind, there was no time to waste.

From what she was reading they were gonna come and take his stuff. That had to be why they arrested him.

Poor John. He worked so hard to plan and to have it all taken away. She didn't know what to do so she called Megan.

"Yely?" Megan answered. "Is everything okay?"

"No. No it's not. I'm sorry to call you but they took John. Mr. Hopper is arrested."

"What do you mean they took him, who took him?" Megan asked.

"The police."

"He was arrested?"

"Yes, just now."

"Are you sure?"

"Positive," Yely replied, pacing as she spoke.

"It's a holiday, he'll never get before a judge until tomorrow."

"If ever," said Yely. "It's more than a holiday, they may not let him out at all."

Megan's sigh carried over the phone. "Let me finish getting my things packed in my car for when I have to go get Jarvis and I'll head to the station. Sound good?"

"Yes."

"In the meantime, if I hear anything, I'll let you know. I'll try to call."

"Thank you." Yely hung up. While she was grateful Megan was going to call and eventually go down there, Yely couldn't wait. After she got dressed, there was something she had to do first for John, then she'd walk to town to find out herself.

※ ※ ※

.   Jarvis thought about the Season two premiere of The Walking Dead. He loved that show, but it came to mind as he walked that highway. The scene in the show were all the undead walking in a giant hoard, picking up more zombies every mile, because they of course, just followed along.

When he exited the bus, he was about ten feet or so behind the woman carrying the baby on her back, along with shouldering a heavy bag. He was the last of the bus. It took him nearly a mile to realize people were following him. Well, maybe not him in particular, but like the zombies they were following along.

He felt bad for the young mother, even though she kept her pace, nobody was walking fast, how could they. It wasn't a straight, flat road.

When he noticed too many people separated him and the young mother, he picked up his pace. He didn't want to be a creeper, but he kept thinking about who travelled a week prior to Northwest China with her two children, alone. Her husband was there already, he left to secure them a place to stay in a village near his parents.

But what if it was his niece stranded and walking. The bus woman couldn't have been more than twenty-five.

Finally, he made his way to her. "Hello, I'm not some creepy old man," Jarvis said, as he walked. "I want you to know that. I just … I have a niece about your age. She travelled alone with her children, and I … can I help you? I know on the bus you—"

"Yes, please, thank you." She exhaled. "Please, if you can carry my bag."

"Absolutely," Jarvis took it. The purple bag was heavier than it looked and rather clunky. "Wow, how did you carry this so far."

"It's not so far, only three miles."

"Three miles!" Jarvis snapped. "I swore it's been more. What the heck's in here?"

"Baby formula. Food. Diapers."

"Water?" Jarvis asked.

"Do you need water?"

"No. No. You didn't mention it. I have water."

"I have a little. I'll be fine. What is your name?" she asked.

"Jarvis. And you?"

"Holly, and this little guy on my back is Denver."

"Denver? After the city?"

She smiled and nodded. "Yep. Home. I wish I was there. I would be safe."

"You'll be safe," Jarvis assured her. "They're saying it isn't coming for a couple days, right? We'll be good."

"Thank you for helping me."

"It's not a problem. I'm happy to and happy to have the company on this walk."

"My only worry is where to go when we get to Charleston," Holly said. "Obviously I'm going to miss my bus."

"Hold on." Jarvis pulled out his phone.

"You're phone's not dead."

"I have two fully charged power banks. I'm on my last one but … let me send a message to a friend, see if she can find out anything about shelters in Charleston."

"Do you think it will be safe there?" Holly asked.

"I do. It was listed, right? I heard it on the news. If it's listed, they have to have shelters. I would think." He watched her nod her understanding, then he shifted his eyes to Denver. He was asleep in the back carrier, his little face poking out of the top. She had him secured in there well. Admittedly, Jaris was concerned about that. Not that he knew about kids and baby carriers.

He continued walking, sending not only a message to Megan but to John as well. To see if they knew of a shelter in Charleston.

Even though she was a stranger, he hated the thought of her having no direction.

He couldn't ask John to take her in, he knew how John was. And this was a survival situation. Yet, if she asked if she could go, could he tell her no?

He didn't know why he was so worried about this stranger, yet he was. It had to be the niece connection.

Jarvis didn't know when he was going to tell Holly he wasn't going all the way to Charleston. Maybe she wouldn't care. Maybe by that point, she would be fine on her own, not that she wasn't already. But he should tell her. He would. According to Megan he had to leave the highway at a town called Marmet and after she took all little back roads, Megan planned to be there the next morning at a Kroger's to meet him.

He wasn't quite sure meeting at a grocery store was wise. All stores were closed until the president of the United States made his proclamation of laws. He could only imagine the panic that had set into people over having enough supplies.

Jarvis had to focus on walking. It was taking a lot out of him. The uphill climbs were rough on his legs and lungs. If Holly was right and they only walked three miles, he still had close to twenty until he got to Marmet. They were walking less than three miles an hour, with a break that would be due soon, he didn't see them getting to Marmet before night fall or even collapsing.

His phone beeped with a response. It was from Megan.

'I'll search for shelters. They posted a list once. I'm leaving shortly to allow enough time to get there and wait for you. I'll be in the lot across the street.'

Jarvis replied. 'I appreciate it. I'll shut down power until I need it.'

Beep.

'Turn your power on every hour on the hour.' Megan instructed. 'And Jarvis, there may be a lot of people there. What do you look like?'

'Hold.' After sending the message Jarvis lifted his phone.

Holly laughed. "Are you taking a selfie?"

"I am." Jarvis sent it. "My ride has never met me."

"You have a ride?"

"She's meeting me, yes."

"Maybe she'll give us a ride."

A twitch of nervousness hit Jarvis. He didn't know what to say. "Maybe."

Beep.

Jarvis looked down. "Shit."

"What?" Holly asked.

"Nothing. She's just trying to find another friend." Jarvis shook his head. But it wasn't nothing. The message from Megan simply said, 'BTW John's been arrested. I am on that. Check back in one hour.'

What a cliffhanger to end on. He really debated on shutting down his phone to conserve power. John was arrested? What did he do? What happened?

Before powering down his phone, Jarvis decided he was going to get in touch with his niece or at least try to make sure she was alright. Then it would be like pins and needles waiting on news about John.

Arrested?

Knowing John as he did and how crass his online friend could be, a part of Jarvis wasn't surprised. He just hoped John was out of jail before everything went down.

CHAPTER SIXTEEN – TELL IT LIKE IT IS

"Thank you," the mayor extended his hand to John when he welcomed him into the office. "I appreciate you coming."

"I don't know how good or how much help I can be," replied John. "But the coffee is good, Mr. Mayor."

"Call me Jim."

"Jim, Thanks."

The mayor pointed to a long table in his office. Seated there were two women and another man. "John do you know our town council?"

"Not personally."

"Well, this is …"

John waved out his hand. "I won't remember names. I'll just refer to the. as council woman one and two and council man."

"That's fine. Please, have a seat."

John nodded and sat at the table, away from the others.

The mayor sat down. "Sergeant Matthews informed us you knew of the comet ahead of time."

"Giles has a big mouth. What else did he tell you?"

"That you knew and were preparing."

"Sort of preparing," John replied. "Not much. Just what I would need to survive the three hundred days."

"He mentioned that, too."

"You said he only mentioned that I knew and was preparing."

"For three hundred days."

"He has a big mouth. What else?"

"What else what?" Jim asked.

"What else did he tell you?"

Council woman one huffed. "Mr. Hopper we're not here to play games."

"I certainly hope not, because I hate playing games. I am too competitive."

"John," Jim looked at him. "I don't care how you knew it was happening, or what you have done. I want to know why three hundred days and what can we as a town do to help as many of our citizens survive."

"I can tell you that we're in a good place," John said. "They didn't mention it on the news and that's a good thing because we don't want a bunch of strangers coming into town. We also have to make due with what is already in town. Kroger's is closed?"

"Yes," the mayor replied. "Until we figure out what to do. We have people watching it."

John nodded again. "You're gonna have folks that won't want to be in a community shelter. Limit the supplies they can get. I suggest pre boxing and bagging. I would come up with a percentage."

Council Woman Two asked, "What do you mean?"

"How many are staying in town, how many are leaving. Before you open the doors to Kroger or any other shop in town that people can get stuff, including the Stop and Gas, find out who is leaving and who is staying. I think by tomorrow you'll have a good idea."

"Why do you say that?" asked the Council man.

"It's another day closer to the event, they're gonna wanna leave soon. There are eleven hundred people in this town. Estimate maybe ten percent will want to leave, another ten percent hunker down. I would put eighty percent of all supplies into community context. Eight percent of everything. Every canned good, candy bar, box of cereal. Everything."

"What if eighty percent aren't in the shelter," Jim

questioned.

"Still lock it up. Even if say only four hundred go to your shelter, you're gonna have people coming to you for food and water. You wanna be able to give them something. You can't do that if you let people take what they want."

Council Woman One asked, "What about water? They say a person needs a gallon a day to survive."

"That's healthy, everyday environment. That's not gonna be the case," John said. "I was told about a liter if they're just hanging about. More if people are working, less for smaller people. But I will guarantee in Jesus time they didn't drink a gallon of water a day."

"That's because," Council Woman Two said. "Back then the water was deadly. They drank wine."

"There you have it. Close the liquor store and Katie's Winery." John smiled. "But you have to remember that after the three hundred days, we have to keep going, so maybe look into a little hydroponics. Set up and plot places that people may or may not hit, like warehouses and so forth. It doesn't end when it clears up."

Jim waved a pencil. "That's the number. The three hundred days. Some experts are saying two years."

John nodded. "And it will be in some places, but here, three hundred days. From the time it hits until it's livable and tolerable to think long term."

"We are safe here?" the council man asked.

"From the comet. Just because we are not ground zero doesn't mean we won't be hit. There are other factors to take into consideration."

"Like?" the mayor asked.

"Well those meteorites that are tagging along," John explained. "They said like thirty some?" he made a raspberry sound with his lips. "Yeah, try hundreds and they can hit before, during and after. Like God throwing stones, they can land anywhere if they don't break up."

"Then after the comet and we make it through, we're safe?"

the Mayor asked.

"Not quite. They comet is gonna hit something solid, even if it lands in the ocean, it'll hit bed rock. All that rock goes up and it comes down. That's called ejecta. Fore balls raining from the sky. We may or may not get it ... "

"Then the nuclear winter."

John chuckled. "Not yet. We will feel the earthquake first, about twelve minutes after impact. Then a cigarette's length of time later come that ejecta. A couple hours after the blast winds, that we could lose some windows maybe. Thankfully no tidal wave."

"Then the nuclear winter, right?" the mayor asked.

John whistled. "Nope. A heatwave like no other. Imagine the worst summer ever. Add about twenty degrees. We're gonna luck out here, we have a lot of trees, shade, mountains, but we aren't spared. For about three or four days it will be so hot, every tree will die. Things will burn. People will want that water, but use it sparingly. On that last day of hot, have people go out because about that point the sun is going to be blocked."

"Then the nuclear winter," the mayor said.

John snapped his finger. "Absolutely. So while we're all sweltering, you need to start gathering every bit of wood to burn or figure out right quick how you're gonna keep people warm in that shelter. There will be a time frame for about two months, I was told it starts three weeks after impact that it could get sixty, seventy below."

It was at that point, everyone just sat back in their chairs.

"John," Jim said. "How long have you known about this?"

"Year and a half, maybe a little longer."

"Why didn't you say anything?" asked Jim.

"I did. On my radio show. If you listened, you'd know. But," John replied. "If I came in here screaming the sky is falling, the sky is falling, would you have listened or sent me to Homeford Living for crazy seniors?"

"I don't know." Jim shook his head. "I don't know if I would. It seems ..." He paused and looked up when the door opened.

"Sergeant Matthews, can I help you?"

"I'm sorry, your Honor for interrupting, but," Giles said. "Can Mr. Hopper come out and calm a situation?"

"Can't you handle it?" the mayor asked.

"Nope." Giles shook his head. "Only Mr. Hopper. She won't believe he's not arrested until he walks out and tells her himself. She's causing quite a scene out there."

"Megan?" John asked.

"No, sir. Yely," Giles replied. "She came to rescue you."

John smiled then quickly drew a serious look. "Damn weed addict, emo girl." He stood. "I'll handle it. Do you need me anymore?"

"We could use you to help formulate a plan with the stores," Jim said.

"Alright. Let me get the kid." John walked to the door. "She latched on to me for some reason." He walked by Giles. "Must be the corned beef."

He knew his last words in that room confused them, but it didn't matter. For some reason, Yely coming to 'rescue him' really made John feel good, but he wasn't going to show it.

"Now, get up off that floor," John ordered Yely when he saw her sitting against the booking desk. "This isn't a 1975 hippy protest."

Yely jumped up, but when she did, she couldn't race to John, she had to untie herself first.

John shook his head.

"They let you out. I knew it would work." After untangling herself, she raced over to John.

"Yes. It worked. Thank you. Now, go home and try to reach your mother. In fact …" He reached into his pocket and handed her a set of keys. "I'd appreciate it if you would go to my house, in case Jarvis calls on the landline."

"What's a landline."

"It's a phone on the wall."

"Oh. Can't I walk with you?"

"No." John shook his head. "Still have some paperwork to take care of after the arrest, but I'll be there. I need someone at my house."

"Okay, I'll go." She quickly embraced John.

John, slightly taken aback and a tad uncomfortable, patted her on the head. "Good. Good. Go. And thanks for getting me out of the cell. That Bruno guy was scaring me."

"Who is Bruno?"

"The cell mate they gave me. I'll tell you all about him at home."

"Alright, see you soon. And I'll call Megan to let her know I got them to let you out."

"Good. You do that."

Yely started to leave but stopped. "Why did they arrest you?"

John looked at Giles then to Yely. "An unpaid ticket."

"I would think they have other things to worry about."

"You would think. Go."

"I'm going."

"And have some of that corned beef in my fridge," John hollered as she ran out.

"Why didn't you tell her the truth?" Giles asked.

"She tied herself with clothesline to the desk. I didn't have the heart."

"See, you can be nice, Mr. Hopper."

"I feel bad for her. If her mother really is in the Bahamas, by the way, what's the boyfriend's name, do you know?"

"Yeah, I think it's Jeremy Bernstein."

"Like the bears?" John asked.

"I think that's Berenstain Bears."

"Whatever, does he have the means to up and go to Bahamas.":

"Damn it. Okay. If she did go, more than likely never seeing her again, and worse …"

"Worse?" Giles questioned.

"Worse. It's the apocalypse. No power for that phone she's always buried in and there goes that marijuana habit she has."

"You joke, but I see it," Giles said. "For the record it's nice that you're taking the kid under your wing."

John's head went down, he took a moment and looked up. "I'm doing no such thing. No kid under my wing. I just met her a few days ago. I don't know her, and I really don't want to get close to her. I can't. Her well being is in your hands and this survival committee you guys are building. I'm sure you guys will take care of her, just fine."

"That's harsh, Mr. Hopper."

"Yes it is. Life is harsh. And it's about to get a lot harsher." On that he turned, walked away and headed back to the meeting.

CHAPTER SEVENTEEN – PRELUDE TO HORROR

When Jarvis began his journey, it was over thirty miles to Charleston, less to the two of Marmet. It was slow, but after he made friends with Holly, the walk seemed to move faster.

Or at least time didn't drag.

They stopped a lot, taking breaks here and there to rest, feed the baby, change him.

Jarvis honestly believed he had it in him to make it the last five miles to Marmet and probably would have kept going even though the sun was setting. But authorities forced everyone off the road. Helicopters flew over head making announcements that weren't easy to hear through the chopper noise.

From what he could make out, water and provisions would be provided and they were directed to an old, abandoned strip mall a third of the mile from the highway.

A lot of people veered that way, Jarvis wasn't sure if there was trouble ahead, an unforeseen emergency or just a way to clear the roads.

Either way, a few hours rest would work out for the best. When they arrived, they waited in line for a half hour to get one of those military meal packs, a blanket along with water, and then he and Holly found a spot to settle.

"Do you think Marshall law went into effect?" Holly asked.

"I don't know. That is entirely possible."

"Seems like they were rushing us."

"It's an unprecedented situation, they're all flying by the seat of their pants," Jarvis told her. "Although it is safer to be off the roads at night. Safety in numbers, right?" Jarvis peered around.

Holly nodded. She had some trouble opening her MRE and Jarvis helped her. She looked tired. The baby was already sound asleep on the blanket next to her. Jarvis imagined it wouldn't be long before she fell asleep as well.

While he boasted the safety in numbers line, the truth was, Jarvis was worried with all the people. He worried about not only losing their stuff, but something happening to Denver.

His body was tired, his mind was not. It would be quite some time before he fell asleep, if that even happened.

※ ※ ※

It was a bit smaller than the Kroger's in her hometown, at least the parking lot was. That was oddly the first thing Megan noticed when she pulled into the lot across the street from the grocery store chain.

Maybe it looked smaller because people were camping out there, waiting for it to open the next day.

Two policemen were positioned out front, there was no mayhem or chaos, just people waiting.

Like Megan. Only she was waiting on Jarvis.

She was so close to where he was. He sent her a message about being made to leave the road, that was when she saw how close they were to each other, she decided to go to him. But after two miles, like Jarvis, they told her roads were closed for safety.

She turned around and went back to the original plan.

She had a cooler in her car. Jarvis would need food as well, and she pulled out one of the corned beef sandwiches she had in there.

While enjoying that, she texted a few times with Yely. Assuring her John was fine even thought he wasn't home. She made contact with Jarvis, too. It wasn't until she was scrolling through news stories that she noticed she forgot her charging cable at home.

Just in case, she sent a message to Jarvis telling him, she was going nowhere and that her phone was going to die. If he had any 'juice' in his phone left, to let her know when he was up and moving.

If Jarvis left at first light, he would be there bright and early.

Megan thought about her life as she sat alone watching the people meander in the Kroger's lot as if they were waiting on Concert tickets. Thinking about her life was something she rarely did, because there was a time when it absolutely sucked. Not so much anymore. Once in a while something would cause her to reflect back.

Like the current extinction level event.

Her story was a sad one, not as sad as John's. Although he tried to hide his story, anyone on the internet could find out about him, plus, there was an episode on 'Jilted Killers' that featured what happened to John's family. Megan saw it, John never made an appearance.

What happened to John was bigger news than John wanted to admit.

What happened to Megan barely got noticed by the media.

She married her high school sweetheart at eighteen, then after ten years of marriage he met someone else and just left. She didn't know who this person was or even how they met, he was gone.

A note. A simple note left on the kitchen counter of an emptied house.

'Starting over with someone new.'

It was horrible. She was at a Tupperware party and came home to a mattress, a can of corn, a spoon, fork and knife.

If that wasn't bad enough, it was worse, he took their son, Peter.

The police were helpful but turned up blank. No one knew where her husband went and it was about a year before cell phones were everywhere. No way to trace or find him.

Megan never stopped looking. Her ex husband had family and she spoke to all of them. They had nothing. At least they said they didn't know. She posted fliers, followed every clue and tip. Offered a reward ... nothing.

She thought it would be easy then she realized how big of a country it was.

She never heard from her son again. One thing she was certain of was that her child was safe. Her ex would never hurt Peter.

Megan never found out why he left and why he took their son, but he did.

She was a good mother, a God-fearing Christian.

As if she were an abuser, he vanished without a trace.

Megan was never the same.

Peter was taken when he was seven.

People rallied around Megan and then slowly, they went on with their lives.

Then one day, three years earlier and eighteen years after her ex and Peter vanished, she received an email from a retired Ripley Police Officer. The subject heading was, 'Is this Him?' and in the body of the email was a link to an obituary.

The Officer, Todd Matthews, father of Giles, never stopped looking either. He came across it when he did his weekly search.

The obituary was for Grant Evans, her ex. It was several weeks old, but it confirmed he died. And worse, it confirmed something else.

'Preceded in Death by his son, David Peter Evans'

Grant had switched Peter's middle and first name.

Preceded in death.

Her heart was crushed, her soul wiped clean of any hope. She missed him every day of her life and would never get to see him again.

Never hug him or tell him how much she loved and terribly missed him.

Seeing how his sister was listed in the obituary, Megan

reached out to her.

Eileen, the sister and Grant had been estranged for years, in fact she wasn't speaking to him when he passed and she got Megan in touch with Grant's widow.

The widow never knew Megan existed, she believed, like Peter that Megan had died.

Peter passed six years before his father, when he was nineteen of a drug overdose.

The widow told her all she needed to know, but shared a lot about her son.

She even gave Megan pictures and videos. It didn't make up for the time lost with her child but it gave her something.

Now, as she sat in the car waiting on Jarvis, watching the people in the Kroger's lot, a part of her was relieved her child didn't have to face the horrors of what was to come.

John asked, Pastor Judy asked, why she focused on Jarvis and wanted to help a stranger so badly.

Megan didn't have an answer that was suitable, but she knew why.

Helping and waiting on Jarvis, gave her a focus, something to think about, something positive.

Yes, Megan was at church every Sunday. She did church events, volunteered, made dinners for folks, worked her job at the clinic, but Megan never stopped thinking about her son. Never stopped missing and mourning him.

Despite the smile she placed on her face, Megan wasn't happy. It was all a front.

Helping Jarvis was a goal. One of many she had tasked herself with to get through each day.

Any focus on a positive was better than a focus on a negative.

Megan would get Jarvis to safety, she would keep smiling, she would put on the front that she was trying and willing to survive. The truth was, she was done.

It was only three years since found out her son, Peter had died.

The comet, the apocalypse, couldn't come soon enough.

But even the impact wasn't going to dull the pain she felt deep in her soul, it would just put her focus elsewhere.

CHAPTER EIGHTEEN – RAIN DOWN

'Baby, I am so sorry,' read the message Yely got from her mother. 'Please answer'.

It wasn't that Yely wasn't deliberately ignoring her calls, she was getting things ready. She received a call from Pastor Judy that Sergeant Matthews was going to be picking her up to bring her to the community shelter at the church. So, she needed to pack things.

When Yely saw the 'please answer' message, she immediately called her mother via video message.

Her mother answered. She looked frazzled and was outside.

"Yely, oh my God, I am so sorry," her mother said,

"Mommy, tell me you never got to the Bahamas."

Her mother lowered her head, then looked at the camera. "I'm sorry."

Every ounce of her being sank. Yely really hoped and believed that somehow her mother wasn't far away, that she was not telling the truth. But as soon as Yely saw her mother's reaction she knew, her mother was not only in the Bahamas but somewhere that wasn't safe.

"I'm trying, Yely," her mother said. "There are so many boats leaving here, trying to get to safety before the comet comes. We're at the dock, we maybe be getting on a boat going to Savannah. A red cross ship. What?" Someone spoke in the background, and Yely couldn't understand them, they were breaking up. "Four."

"What?" Yely asked.

"Red Cros ... Hamas four."

"Mom, please get on that boat, if it hits and you're there ...."

"I know," her mother said, "Listen. Listen to me." Like a bad TV reception, her mother glitched. Her words broke up with intermittent static. "Drawer. Know. Wait, but can't."

"What? What did you say. Mommy, you're breaking up."

"In my top ... there's a ... I was gonna wait ... now."

"Mom? Please say that again."

"My top drawer. There's ... brown ... lope. Under ... Get it. I was going to wait ... Tell. But ... now. Show it to ... Tell you more."

"Mommy. You're really breaking up."

"I know." She looked over her shoulder.

Yely could see that her mother was somewhere waiting in line.

"Yely, just live okay. Live."

"Try Mom."

"I will. Yely ..." her words broke up again. "Love you. I ... You much."

"I love you too, Mommy."

Static.

Gone.

Yely started to cry, she cradled her phone and sobbed.

Even with the mistakes she had made, it was her mother. Yely felt so alone.

What was her mother trying to tell her? Something in her drawer. She started to head to her mother's bedroom when there was a knock at the door. She walked over to the door and opened it, Giles Matthews stood there.

"You ready, Yely?" he asked. "We have to get going. The shelter is filling up."

Yely nodded, then grabbed the two big bags she had waiting by the door. She had food, clothes, a blanket, she honestly didn't know what all she had to pack. Then she thought about what her mother said, about something in her drawer.

"Yely?" Giles called her name. "Did you forget something?"

"Um." She looked over her shoulder then down to her phone which was still in her hand. "No. Let's go."

Giles grabbed one of her bags, she grabbed the other and as they walked out the door, her phone and Giles' made that alert noise.

On the front porch they both stopped.

The message warning was simple, it told how the object was now visible in the sky, along with an alert of potential small meteorites coming through the atmosphere.

It wasn't until she stepped off her porch and looked to the sky that she knew what the message meant.

There it was, huge and bright in the sky, positioned like a massive star. It looked threatening, how could it now?

"Is that it?" Yely asked, Giles.

"I believe so."

"How does it look so big and still be a couple days away?"

"I don't know." Giles walked her to the squad car and opened the door. He placed her bags in the back.

"It has to be big," Yely said.

"It is."

A shudder of fear went through her looking up at it. It was bigger than any star and almost as big as the moon sitting there in the sky waiting to drop.

As she got into the car she heard the squeak of a screen door, she looked back to see John stepping from his house.

He glanced at her with shock and confusion, then he waved as she got in the police car.

Yely waved to him, looked to the sky and got in the squad car.

She told herself that was the last time she would look to the sky. She didn't want to see it. It was a symbolization of the end of everything she knew.

Where the heck was she going? John thought. Obviously,

they weren't arresting her or were they. He had been with the mayor all day into the evening. In fact, he stayed until they started to stock the basement at the church and community center.

He was actually on his way to thank Yely and see if she was okay. Pulling his phone from his front shirt pocket, John dialed Megan.

She answered quickly. "Hey, John, I can't talk long. I left my charger and want to make sure Jarvis can get a hold of me."

"I won't keep you long. Have you spoke to Yely? I just saw her getting in the squad car with Giles."

"She's not under arrest. I got a text from Pastor Judy. They're bringing her to the shelter."

"Which one?"

"Does it matter. She's safe. I have to go. I'll see you soon."

Click.

"What the heck?" John stared down at this phone, but not for long. He caught it from the corner of his eye. The neighbor two doors down, high tailing it like a mad man out of his driveway. The silence of the neighborhood was suddenly broken by the sounds of slamming car doors, horns and screeching tires. *All of this because the comet was suddenly spotted in the sky?* Where were they going?

Then John looked up.

The objects started to appear, like distant explosions bright and orange. Hundreds of meteorites burst through the atmosphere, raining down in fiery streaks from the sky. Some small and far away, some big and John knew they were landing close.

Figuring if something was going to happen close by, John wanted to see it coming, he sat in the chair on the porch and watched.

CHAPTER NINETEEN – QUIET SCREAMS

It went from people quietly waiting and also getting too tired to scream.

Megan had closed her eyes, wanting to nap after her brief talk with John to getting out of the car.

She leaned back, closed her eyes and heard the commotion.

What was happening?

She couldn't see anything and at first she believed maybe a fight broke out, but as soon as she stepped from her car, she saw the sky.

There were so many of them falling, the world was big, what were the chances. Like watching a falling star, really, why were people panicking?

The odds of it hitting close were slim.

That's what she thought.

She was wrong.

While others far away watched a brilliant light show, the falling meteorites painting the sky, she witnessed a horror show both in sight and sound.

They not only made a roaring sound as they drew near, they caused booms and crashes that sounded like thunder and lightning.

The sky lit up and the wind whipped as if the worst storm were coming.

Crackling, booming. Flashing white lights.

It all happened so fast, but yet it seemed like it was in slow motion.

It was coming, it was close, but where would it hit?

How big was it?

Megan had looked up meteor hits and remembered the one that hit in Russia, and that it was the size of a school bus, and had exploded with the force of seven atomic bombs.

She was out in the open, with nowhere to run or hide, all she could do was stand there watching, and hoping that whatever was coming missed her.

* * *

Flash.

Before the screams, before the running, the shaking, the fire, the flash … it was quiet.

The campfire had burned down and was reduced to glowing embers like when it started.

Jarvis was awake, as were others. But not many. The quiet sound of chattering conversation carried to him. He was near Holly, who had fallen asleep with Denver curled up at her side. She was using a big purple bag as a pillow.

Sleep was not on his agenda. Jarvis was too afraid someone would steal their stuff. There were too many strangers around. A lot of desperate people. Obviously, so was Holly, the strap to her bag was around her arm, as if someone would take it, she'd feel it.

He had turned off his phone, many people did, because he only heard a couple phones ring out that emergency alert sound.

He didn't know what the alert was, and before he could turn on his phone to find out, he saw others standing and looking up.

When he raised his head, he saw it.

At first, the only thing that was different in the sky was the comet. It was visible. It was close.

Within seconds … they appeared. The meteors they had warned about. The rocks accompanying the comet were faster, smaller and making their way to earth as a prelude.

A destructive prelude.

Jarvis didn't worry or think too much about it, after all, there were a lot of them, while there was a chance they would land nearby, what were the odds, really?

Unlike his ex-wife, Jarvis wasn't an expert. But he was able to gauge by his knowledge that they would impact earth during several minutes.

He watched them, then as two of them appeared bigger, Jarvis worried.

"Holly," he called to her. "Holly, wake up."

He felt the hair on his arms raise as the sky flashed, like when a storm was brewing.

Louder, he called out, "Holly! Get up now! We have to run for cover."

Cover, he thought, *where would they go?*

Holly sat up fast. "What's going on?"

"Grab the baby. It's not safe out here."

Her eyes widened as she saw what was happening. "Oh my God." She stood. That purple bag was still attached to her arm and the heaviness teetered her some. Jarvis tried to help, but she got her footing and she grabbed Denver, blanket and all, cradling him close to her chest.

It was total chaos.

People ran, screaming, tripping over things, all running for coverage of the strip mall.

Jarvis heard the crash of breaking glass, someone had cleared a window, then another was broken. Would the strip mall provide protection? Maybe there was a basement there, something.

Anything was better than outside. They would have to run for it, they weren't as close as others.

No, this isn't happening, Jarvis thought. *One is not going to fall on us, it's not, I know the statistical odds.*

Jarvis extended his hand to Holly, but when he looked, he realized why she didn't take it. She wasn't there.

With a deep feeling of desperation, he looked for her, then finally spotted her near the mall. She wasn't waiting, she ran fast.

He didn't blame her. She had Denver to think about.

Jarvis picked up the pace to catch her, but didn't make it far.

No one, not even his ex-wife told him what to expect.

There was no sound, just a sudden bright, blinding light, he stopped running, raising his arm to shield his eyes. When nothing happened, he lowered it.

The blast sound was at a distance, they were not ground zero, but whatever hit was huge.

A massive fireball was on the horizon beyond the strip mall and within seconds, a wave of heat, moving fast and furiously, barreled through, it shattered half the strip mall into splinters and hit Jarvis so hard it threw him in the air.

That was the last thing he remembered.

❈ ❈ ❈

It was close.

Close enough that everyone was thrown into a state of shock and panic. The Kroger's parking lot wasn't packed anymore, people had run. Megan wondered if they ran away or ran for cover inside the store.

Megan was glad she stepped out of her car when she did because the windows in her vehicle burst into thousands of pieces of flying glass. She had stepped out when the flash occurred and then seconds later her windows were gone.

Another thing she was happy about was she had shut off her car.

Unlike a few others, she was able to start it. Some sort of electromagnetic pulse John had rambled on about.

She didn't leave it running for long. Long enough to try to find a radio to listen to, something, a newscast, but the airwaves were dead.

This was it. The prelude to the end. The rocks that fell from the sky weren't anywhere the size of the one that was coming.

It was just the beginning of much more to come.

There was a sense of relief for Megan, she didn't have much time left in this world, soon she would finally be reunited with her son.

No way, no how, humanity was going to survive what was coming. They'd live, but a savage world would slowly become where only the strong survived.

Megan was not strong.

She was fine with that.

She stepped out of her car again, making sure it showed no signs of being a working vehicle, the last thing she needed was someone to steal her car. She had a mission and a promise to keep.

She was going to help Jarvis. A stranger from across the ocean. She didn't know him, had no responsibility to him, but for some reason, without really thinking about it, he became a purpose to her.

John looked at her as if she were nuts, more than likely because it was a dangerous world, but Megan didn't care.

She didn't fear death.

Standing outside her car, she looked toward the glowing orange sky in the distance. It reminded her of the time she was in California and there was a wild fire.

She was close to where it had fallen.

Something was burning.

Knowing the area, it had to be trees.

But where.

Walking around to the back of her car, she opened the trunk and searched for her emergency kit. Since she started to drive her father always told her to keep an emergency kit in case she was ever stranded on the highway. In her kit were flares, a flashlight, first aid kit, Atlas Map and compass. She regularly rotated the water and protein bars.

She pulled out the map and compass. Megan knew the small

town wouldn't have an enlarged map, she was only trying to figure out where the meteor hit.

Holding the compass, she determined the fires were coming from the south.

Her heart sank, that was the direction Jarvis was traveling from.

But she wasn't giving up nor was she leaving.

Just because the meteor landed in his direction didn't mean he was close to it.

Megan would wait. If Jarvis didn't arrive an hour after first light, then she would go looking for him.

They were only a few miles apart.

* * *

The ringing in his ears was intense, almost as intense as the pain in his head.

Jarvis didn't know where he was or how he ended up by an overturned minivan, but he was alive. At least he thought he was.

He couldn't hear anything but that ringing.

The pain in his head was so sharp, he felt as if he had been impaled. He moved his hands around his head for a foreign object that may have hit him. But nothing.

He did hit his head, it ached internally and when he touched the top of his head, it felt damp, like blood.

When he finally made it to his knees, he lifted his head to try to see what was going on.

For the first few moments, everything was blurry and Jarvis felt dizzy. Those first few moments he wasn't thinking about anything but his own predicament.

Then he rolled from his back and got on to his knees.

Enough to look around.

The ringing was loud and strong in his ears. He couldn't hear anything else. He caught his bearings and looked around.

It was still night, and the orange glow of fires was all around. He saw people running, their mouths open wide with a look of anguish on their faces.

He couldn't hear their screams, but he could imagine them and how they sounded.

They were obviously screaming.

Mouths open, crying out, probably for help. Many looked injured. Jarvis didn't know if it was his ears or just the adrenaline and fear he had stopping him from hearing.

Were they screaming out in pain, for someone to aid them, or were they crying out for someone they were with.

The moment Jarvis thought that, he thought of Holly.

Suddenly, his senses came back, he snapped into some sort of survival mode. He was bombarded with the horrible cries of pain and the smell of burning flesh.

With each beat of his heart, his head pounded.

'Michael!'

'Dixie'

'Mommy, where are you, mommy? Where are you?'

So many people called out and Jarvis moved closer to the burning destruction. Closer to where he last saw Holly.

Not far from him was the strip mall. Half of it had been obliterated and the other half burned.

Burning wood debris scattered about and the closer Jarvis got, the more bodies he saw.

He didn't know if they were men or women, some were so badly burnt, they were black stone objects.

Walking carefully, Jarvis looked for Holly and her baby. A sick feeling filled his gut, because the nearer he got to the strip mall, the more bodies and body parts he saw. He wanted to call out, but he would just be one of many voices. He wasn't going to quit, even though his head pounded. She had to be out there. They had to be out there somewhere.

The last he saw her she was running with the baby, that purple bag swinging.

The purple bag.

Thump!

Jarvis swore he not only felt his heart sink to his stomach, but heard it as well, when he saw the purple bag. Not the bag in its entirety, most of it was charred beyond recognition, but a third of it was untouched. Crouching down to examine it, knowing instantly it was Holly's also gave him the vantage point to see her.

Holly.

Had he not gotten down and close to the ground, she would have been missed. Blending into everything like any other piece of debris.

Almost completely face down, she lay not far from the bag, maybe ten feet.

Was it her? It was hard to tell. Her hair had been singed off, her head, back, arms and legs blackened and bleeding.

Her size, and the fact that the purple bag was near her was Javis' reason for believing it was her.

He scooted around to see her face.

Her eyes were open and half her face was burned, not charred, but burned. Enough was unscathed for his confirmation.

That was it for Jarvis. His heart ached for his new friend. How protective she was of her child. Never letting him out of her sight and now her child was nowhere to be found.

Jarvis didn't have it in him to look for Denver's body. He didn't want to see him. He could only imagine how horrible it was. Holly was dead, burnt, killed. Denver was so tiny and little, so frail that he could only imagine that what was left of him wasn't much and nothing Jarvis wanted to see.

He lowered his head, said a soft prayer and started to stand when he heard it.

A cry.

A baby's cry.

He supposed it was there all along, but Jarvis was so focused on Holly he didn't hear it.

Where was it coming from? Was it his imagination? He

started to stand to follow it when he realized it was close.

He listened. Despite all the noise around him, Jarvis listened.

Stepping away from Holly's body, the sound grew distant, but when he was close to her, it was louder.

He moved as close to Holly as he could and the cries were the loudest he heard.

How was Denver near her?

He didn't see the child.

Then it dawned on him.

Holly was cradling the baby in a blanket as she ran.

He reached for Holly, lifting her gently. When he moved her, he heard the crackling of her skin and then he heard the baby's cry even louder.

That blanket he was wrapped in was under Holly.

No wonder she wasn't completely face down to the ground. How could she be? She was cradling the child to her chest, wrapped protectively in a blanket under her body.

Holly was hit by the fireball, but by some miracle, the baby wrapped in the blanket was spared and the reason she wasn't completely face down to the ground was because the child was under her.

Jarvis gently took hold of the baby wrapped in that blanket. He wanted to look for injuries, see if he was hurt, but it was too dark. He couldn't tell if the baby was crying from being scared, hungry, or hurt. He didn't know how to distinguish a child's cry. He did know one thing, he had to get help. He had to make sure the baby was okay. Before he left, he said a prayer for Holly and he whispered, "I'll get him some help. I'll take care of him for you."

Could he?

Jarvis wasn't a hundred percent. His head ached and it felt as if his entire body tingled in a weird pain, but he didn't feel weak.

He wasn't worried about himself as much now as he was worried about Denver.

Holding the baby he glanced around to the chaos.

People running, crying and hurt.

He and the child were one of so many.

Not long before there were military people all around. But Karvis couldn't see them. He couldn't see anyone giving aid or offering it. That was when he knew. Finding help was going to be impossible.

But he would try.

CHAPTER TWENTY – IT IS COMING

John had ways to find things out that others couldn't and he needed to use his resources now because something didn't feel right.

The amount of asteroids or meteorites, whatever they would be called, the amount that fell from the sky was mind boggling.

It was like something out of a sci-fi movie. They came down, and they just kept coming. After one would drop, another would appear. Relentless destruction. How they didn't hit every corner of the earth John didn't know. They could have. But they didn't hit Ripley.

He sat on his front porch watching it all unfold. Watching as his mild mannered neighbors fled their homes in a panic.

Watching the rocks fall, there were times during the terror shower of rocks that one would look so bright and big John believed that was it. The end

But they were spared

A part of him thought with so many rocks falling from the sky, maybe the three and a half mile comet had broken up. That was a possibility.

After it was over. After the rocks stopped falling and flames blazed the horizon in the distance. In the midst of the noises, sirens and shouting that carried in the night air, John went in to his house.

He had to get information first and foremost before he

ventured to do the other important things.

Immediately he called Jarvis. Jarvis talked a lot, not as much as his ex-wife. But Jarvis phone never even rang, it went directly to voicemail.

Then he tried Megan.

Maybe they connected and were together.

Megan answered after one ring. She sounded sad and desperate.

"Please tell me you're alright," she said.

"I'm fine."

"Yely?" Megan asked

"She's fine, too."

"Is she with you?"

"Not at this moment. Giles came for her. I'll handle it. None hit here, but they looked close. You?" John asked. "Did any hit around you guys?"

"Not here. But John it was close. All the windows broke, the ground shook."

"Jarvis?"

"I haven't heard from him in a while. I think … one hit near him."

"Megan come home," John told her

"I can't leave him behind."

"Yes, you can. Come home."

"At sun up. Okay. I'll give it until sun up," Megan replied.

"Okay, then come home."

"I will. And you?"

"I am trying to find something out."

"What?" Megan asked.

"It's off Megan. This is all bigger than predicted. Too much is happening right now for a comet that's not supposed to come for four days."

"So what are you trying to find out?" Megan asked

"I need to find out if the time line changed. If we really have four days before the big one drops."

"Do you think it changed?"

"I do," John replied. "And I think I can find out, but sadly, even if I can, nothing can be done to change it."

"If nothing can be done then why even worry?"

"Because a change in impact time means a change in ground zero. If it's gonna be close to us," John said. "I need to know."

"Can it land closer to us?"

"Yes. And if it lands early," John said. "'More than likely it will."

❅ ❅ ❅

In her mind, Megan knew John was wrong. She absolutely couldn't go home. And John was wrong about Jarvis. He was showing up. Last she spoke to him he was close.

But Megan needed to make a decision.

She was sitting there with a useful car, across the street from where panicked people raided Kroger's. Screaming and shouting. Fighting as they ran out with arms full of food. Those who pushed carts were easy targets. Their carts were snatched easily from them.

She couldn't feel too sorry for them as they were stealing just like everyone else only they did the work for another looter.

How was this happening in such a small town?

From calm to chaos in 2 seconds flat. Megan had much more faith in humanity than she was witnessing.

She had a working vehicle and needed to get back to Ripley, she started to fear that if someone knew, they would just take it from her.

Megan couldn't chance that.

So she choose to camouflage it.

With the key in the ignition, she turned it gently enough so as not to start it, just to put it in an unlocked ignition position. She put the car in neutral and in the midst of all the pandemonium, allowed for her car to drift.

It didn't move fast or catch a roll on a big hill. It just moved slowly forward. As it did she turned the unpowered steering column to a hard right. And the vehicle drifted into another, then it just stopped. The hood resting against the door of a gray SUV.

With the windows busted and the car appearing as part of a pile up, Megan was hopeful no one would take it.

She needed it and needed it close by so she could leave in the morning.

After leaving the car she walked back to the lot across from Kroger's.

Even though she was ready and wanted to go home, Megan couldn't do so without Jarvis. Not yet, she wasn't giving up.

She was tired and scared alone out there in the middle of the riots.

She tried not to think of the comet coming early or landing closer. She had to just think of making it through the night, getting back to Ripley, but doing so only after Jarvis showed up.

* * *

"Someone, anyone," Jarvis called out trying his hardest not to yell too loudly, the baby wasn't crying as much and he didn't know if that was a good sign or bad. "Is there anyone out there who can help me? Please."

He moved slowly, his body ached, but he figured that was from being thrown. He started to cough some from all the smoke.

He moved away from the strip mall because there was no help there.

Remembering where he and Holly came in from, he headed toward that direction.

At the very least he was five miles from Megan.

Five miles.

He could do that even with the baby. However, Jarvis knew he had to get the baby checked out.

That was most important.

CHAPTER TWENTY-ONE – THE BACK CART

Jarvis didn't have to walk far. He followed people and soon made it to the highway. Not far after arriving on the road, he noticed a line of maybe ten people. It was obvious, they were waiting for something. Ahead by a vehicle, a small fire burned on the side of the road for warmth and light.

Jarvis asked what they were waiting for and a woman with a bleeding eye told him, they were injured and a woman ahead was helping people.

As soon as Jarvis heard that he felt blessed and took his place in line.

Her back was to Jarvis when it was finally his turn, working out of an SUV. She moved nervously, probably frightened.

"I don't have a lot of supplies. Only minor stuff," she said, then turned around. "How can …" She paused. "How can I help you?"

"This baby," Jarvis stated. "He's the son of a woman I was traveling with. She died. I just need to know if he's alright. He's been crying."

She looked at him compassionately, then took the baby.

The frazzled woman examined little Denver in the open hatch on the floor of her SUV.

"He looks fine, I don't see any injuries," she replied. "His head doesn't have any bumps or abrasions. I think he's fine." She wrapped the blanket. "He's crying because he's scared, maybe hungry. I do suggest you both go to the medical center to get checked out."

Easier said than done, Jarvis thought. He was polite and gave her a nod. Jarvis didn't know her story. He didn't see anyone with her. He saw only a couple of suitcases in the back of her SUV and a medical kit.

Why was she helping?

"I think he's fine," she repeated and handed the baby to Jarvis. "What about you?"

"I'm fine."

"Are you sure?"

"Yes." Jarvis nodded. "I need to make it five miles, maybe less. I have someone waiting for me in Marmet."

She tilted her head curiously. "That's very specific."

"A friend. We're going somewhere else. Ripley."

"What's in Ripley?"

"Survival. A good chance. What about you?" Jarvis asked her.

"I don't know. Maybe Ripley."

"Good call. How did you end up taking patients? Out of your SUV of all places?"

"It's not mine, it was abandoned, so I am using it as a work station." She smiled tiredly. "I'm a nurse. My husband and I live about a quarter of a mile from here. We saw it hit and we came to see if we could help."

"That was nice of you."

"Thanks. I helped a man with a cut and then it just started, a line forming. Are you walking to …"

"Marmet? Yeah." Jarvis nodded, adjusting Denver in his arms. "It's right off the highway, I mean a few hours of walking."

"Go to the medical center," she said. "It's right on the outskirts of Marmet."

"You said that before but, I think once I get to Marmet my friend will be there. It's the same walk either way, right?"

She paused, looked at him curiously, then shook her head. "Oh, I am so sorry. I didn't mean for you to walk to the medical center. My husband and another neighbor are taking people there. My husband is already on his first trip. Dan, our neighbor, is leaving soon. A little up the road you'll see people, a campfire and a man with a horse and cart. Tell him June said you and the baby need to go. He'll take you. It may be a bumpy, off the road ride, but you'll get there."

"To Marmet?"

"The medical center, and please you may feel fine, but have them check you out."

"Okay, I will." His words were more pacifying. He didn't need to get checked out, but it wouldn't hurt to have Denver looked at again.

Jarvis felt better. No more walking. He was going to get a ride even if it was only by a horse drawn cart. It would give him a chance to rest and to try and feed the baby. He had his own bag still, and knew he had food in there. Hopefully he had something the baby could eat.

It wasn't long after leaving the medical woman that Jarvis found the place she mentioned.

Some of the survivors were around the campfire. Many of them looked really bad. Some burned, some bleeding. It reminded Jarvis of the nuclear war survivors in movies he had seen.

Jarvis made his way there and found a spot. He was about to sit down when he saw the horse and cart. A man then approached the cart, helping someone inside. Before sitting he walked over to him.

"Hi," Jarvis said to the man. "June said to tell you that me and the baby need to get to the medical center."

An older gentleman with a worn jean jacket, he wore a 'Wild Cats' baseball cap and his eyes cased Jarvis. "I see that. Hop on in. We leave in a few."

"Thank you. Thank you so much." Jarvis stared at the back end of the cart. It was about the height of a pick up truck. Typically, it wouldn't be a problem, but Jarvis held the baby, the blanket and his big bag.

The man must have noticed how awkward it was for Jarvis climbing in there, in that he lent him a hand, holding the baby while Jarvis climbed in and got situated.

But the man stared at the baby.

"Sir?"

"He's one lucky fella," said the man. "You must have been holding him tight and out of the way."

"Actually, his mother was holding him."

"And she is?"

"Gone. He was in her arms, under her and alive."

The man whistled. "Then he is lucky." He handed Denver back to Jarvis. "Don't let go of that one, he'll keep you safe."

Jarvis already knew that, after all if it wasn't for Denver, they wouldn't have a ride in a cart.

"Thank you again." Jarvis said. "You and June are really kind."

"We help each other out, right?"

"Right."

The man walked away to get someone else.

Jarvis looked at the man already in the cart, he was in bad shape. Missing a leg and he had a tourniquet on it. He quietly sobbed in pain, not looking at anyone, arms tight to his chest as he trembled. Jarvis supposed others would be just as bad and he realized how fortunate he and Denver was. If it wasn't for the baby, he wouldn't dare get in the cart.

Let people who really needed help, get help.

June spoke about a medical center, so she had to be positive one was operational or else why take people there.

Denver wasn't crying as bad, more of a whimper. "Hey, little guy." He uncovered Denver and allowed him to sit more on his lap. "We're going to be okay. We're going to be fine. I promise. Now let's get you something to eat."

Jarvis opened his bag. He wasn't sure what he had in there that a six month old baby could eat, he'd get him something. At the very least, he could take the cheese from his vending machine bologna sandwich.

For the time being he was able to sit, feel safe and confident that he was eventually going to get where he needed to be.

With John and Megan in Ripley.

CHAPTER TWENTY-TWO - DAY ONE

John sat back and exhaled. Getting the information he needed was harder than he thought it would be. It certainly took longer than he wanted.

Hours.

It wasn't as if he could pick up the phone and call. He did try though, but with no luck, he had to resort to the old-fashioned radio. That took some time to get a response. The rain of meteors was everywhere.

It reminded him of when the fireworks on forth of July would fall from the sky only the meteors didn't disappear, they landed.

He got the answers and information he needed, and it wasn't good. Now he had to share it.

First person he tried was Megan again.

Fortunately, she answered.

"Are you on your way home?" John asked.

"No, I'm ... I'm walking."

"Home?"

"No, down sixty-four."

"Why in God's name would you do that?" John asked.

"Because this is the way I told Jarvis to go and I'm only gonna go about a mile John."

"Megan, you're a lovely woman, but you don't know Jarvis."

"You do," she replied. "Wouldn't you try to find him?"

"Probably."

"I'm not looking, I'm just going about a mile," she said. "Out of town. I don't see anyone walking the highway at all. No movement."

"Well, don't dally. I need you back in Ripley," John told her. "It's gonna get really bad out there."

"It's bad out here now," said Megan. "Everyone is panicking."

"It'll get worse. Megan, you have five hours."

"Five hours until—"

She started saying something, but the line died.

John shook his head. "Unbelievable. I left her on a cliffhanger." He glanced down, it wasn't his phone, it had to be Megan's. Noticing the time, John wondered if it was too late, but he couldn't delay any more.

He grabbed his jacket and truck keys, then he paused. It was only a few blocks into town. He didn't want to take his truck. It was already hidden in the car port.

The jacket would suffice, and John began the journey. He was old, but he wasn't so old that he couldn't walk a few blocks.

John didn't know what he was expecting. Ripley was a pretty mild mannered town that took care of its own. Yes, John worried a little that all hell would break out, but it sure didn't.

He had faith in the town and people and it looked like they pulled through.

Faith.

Where was that damn church. He was used to driving.

It was quiet and dark, no body was on the streets. Occasionally, a car would zip on by. Was it a Riplian? Or a passerby.

Even though it was late, John knew what he had to do. He just hoped he wasn't too late.

"Hey, John," he heard the male voice call out through the quiet night.

John knew the voice and turned to see, Giles Matthews

leaning against the wall outside the post office. "That high on a looter list?" John asked.

"No, I'm having a smoke and hiding from my wife," he replied.

"Got news for you, she'll smell it."

"I know, but it makes me feel better, besides." He lifted a cigarette and lit it. "We're at end times."

John cringed. "Don't say that. I always think of God when people say it's end times. Speaking of God. Is Yely at the church?"

"Why would she be there?"

"You took her."

"Not to the church. That's secondary shelter for overflow. She's a kid, so she's in the main shelter at the community center. Probably the gym. Not sure."

"Thank you."

"John, it's nice of you to stop by to see if she's okay."

"Oh, I'm not stopping by," John said. "I'm taking her."

"What do you mean you're taking her."

"Taking her with me. I would have stopped you earlier, but I couldn't."

Giles chuckled. "John you can't just take her."

"Why not."

"Her mother called Pastor Judy."

"Her mother is away," John stated. "And Yely can make her own mind up if she wants to come with me or not. Right?"

"I suppose. But John, really, she's fine in the shelter. She'll be safe."

"I know. But I want to ask her. Besides, I got corned beef in a can for the real down and deep survival days. Thanks, Giles." John changed direction, started walking and stopped. "Hey, uh, Giles?"

"Yeah?"

"It's coming days early."

"What is?"

"The big one."

"How?"

John shrugged. "I don't know, that's what took me so long to get down here. I was reaching out to my contacts to get information and confirm my suspicions. It's gonna land somewhere near Puerto Rico. Not Morrocco and while we will be safe, we may get some damage." John continued speaking as if he were rattling off a grocery store list. "Like shaking and windows breaking, some fire from the sky. That stuff comes after, we'll have about twenty minutes to prepare for it."

"When does it come John?"

John looked down at his watch. "About four and a half hours. Which means I gotta get moving."

"Four and a half hours? We need to tell people. Half the town left in a panic"

"Makes it reasonable for survival now. Besides some of them will come back," John said. "Tell the mayor and folks on the survival committee, they know where to find me to get information. Right now, I have an emo teen to get."

When John arrived at the community center, there was a nice young woman he didn't know, working the table. The place was pretty packed. People weren't sleeping in the halls, they were sitting there chatting in whispering voices.

He asked the young woman which way the gym was and she pointed him in the direction.

He walked by the people talking, some he knew from church or just seeing in town. He acknowledged with a nod. Passing rooms, he could see people sleeping.

John always wondered how people were able to sleep under stressful situations.

When his family was killed, he didn't sleep for days. Before the trial and waiting for any legal decision about Reed, John couldn't sleep. Yet, there they were with most people passed out.

He found the gym and it was dark in there. The sounds of slight snoring and people sleeping carried to him.

Had it not been for the single lone glow of a LED flashlight in the center of the gym, he wouldn't have been able to spot Yely in the dark.

She gave her own light. Sitting on a cot, reading a book or something.

John walked through the maze of cots. They weren't packed in, but given it was dark, John bumped into a few.

He muttered out apologies and that was when Yely looked up. Almost shocked, she jumped from the cot.

"John, Mr. Hopper I mean."

"John is fine," he replied. "Get your stuff."

"Why?"

"I want you with me and Megan. When she gets back. I have corned beef in a can. I think it will be better for you. Not the corned beef in a can, but you coming with me. Unless you don't want to."

Yely smiled, at least in the dark John thought it was a smile. Without saying any words, she grabbed her backpack and duffel bag and started to pack them.

"I'll take that as a yes." John nodded. "Good girl."

It didn't take her long, the bed wasn't hers. The pillow was and that was all she took, the rest was in bags and Yely walked out with John.

Just as they stepped onto the street. Someone called out.

"John Hopper you stop right there!" the woman yelled.

"I know that fire and brimstone sound." John stopped and turned around.

Pastor Judy was running his way.

John waited. He figured if she wanted him to stop so bad, she could come to him.

Slightly out of breath and looking frazzled, Pastor Judy walked up to him. "Where are you taking this child?"

"Isn't it obvious?" John asked. "With me."

"No, she is safe here and I promised her mother …"

"Look," John cut her off. "No offense to your promise, but there has to be at least a hundred people in that gym and who knows how many others. How many people are you responsible for taking care of?"

"It doesn't matter, I am responsible for her well being."

"Well seeing that this town wouldn't have a plan if it wasn't for me, and I would still be locked up if it wasn't for her, I can be responsible for her well being a heck of a lot better."

Pastor Judy huffed. "John, this is not up for discussion. Yely, take your things back into the gym."

Yely looked up at John with a sad look.

"All due respect, Pastor," John said. "She's not. She's coming with me. You can stand here and argue with me on the street or you can go do your pastoring thing. I'm four blocks away. She'll be fine. She'll be safe."

"This is false concern John."

"Says who?" John asked.

"Says me."

"You're wrong."

"You have not cared about a single soul since you moved to this town," Pastor Judy said. "This is a huge event. Life changing. The child needs someone who is going to care. Someone who is there for her."

"Well, I'll be there. We bonded. We had hot dogs and corned beef. Unless she says she wants to stay here she comes with me, and like you said, it won't be up for discussion."

"You're just going to send her back to her house, aren't you?" Pastor Judy asked.

"What? No. Go back to your church," John waved his hand. "Yely, if you wanna stay, no hurt feelings. But if you want to come with me, we need to move. We have prepping to do."

Yely looked at John then Judy. "I want to go with him."

"Then that's that." John took hold of Yely's arm and they started walking.

"They'll come for her, John," Pastor Judy hollered. "I'll tell Giles."

John stopped walking and spun around. "I know it's your job to help the flock. And if she's one of your flock, help her by letting her be in the best place she can be. That's with me. Now, we have work. You wanna send the law, send the law. Let's go Yely."

As they walked farther from Pastor Judy, Yely looked up to him. "John, thank you. Thank you for doing this for me. I feel safe with you."

John wanted to muster up something sarcastic, but her words were genuine, and all John could do was say, 'thank you' and keep walking.

※ ※ ※

Megan would say it was a hunch, but it was more of a given and a decision that made sense. She had made it to the highway and planned on just waiting there, watching people make their way north, like Jarvis was supposed to do.

She saw the sign in the distance, a small medical center off the highway. That was where Megan waited.

Not that she knew if Jarvis was injured, she didn't. But going there was worth a shot. She knew one of the meteors landed nearby and maybe those injured would head there.

Also, she was in a good position. She could see anyone walking up the highway, and if Jarvis kept walking and didn't stop, then he possibly could be arriving.

She would spot him.

When she first got there, there wasn't anyone. No one was walking the highway.

That filled her belly with fear because according to Jarvis, everyone was walking that way, heading north.

What happened to stop the influx of people?

Only one thing.

The meteor.

Not long after she was there was when Megan noticed that people were walking in the area off to the side of the road. She noticed it after spotting a man riding a horse, pulling a cart, appearing as if he were leaving the roadway from the hospital.

Hating to leave her highway position, she mentally flagged

that man as if he was someone that may have answers. But when she drew closer, he kept going. A man on a mission. That was when she spotted others walking her way.

They walked close to the highway, yet not on it. Covered in blankets, huddled in groups, they looked helpless.

Then came another cart drawn by a horse. The cart moved by them, passing some of them.

"Where are you coming from?" Megan asked the travelers.

They were in shock, they looked at her and kept walking.

She noticed that the horse cart was full of people. Were they injured? Surely, they had to be or else they'd be walking as well.

Standing nearly in its path, she waved her arms, but he wasn't stopping.

A baby's cry caught her attention as it moved by her and it was a glimpse, just a glimpse, but she swore she saw Jarvis.

Megan couldn't be positive because after all, she had only seen him in a selfie.

"Jarvis?" she called out. "Jarvis!" she cried again as the cart passed her.

The man sat up with attention. In his arms, he had a baby, he looked back. "Megan?"

"Yes!" It was him.

Soon the cart had pulled farther away and onto the roadway for the medical center.

Megan exhaled heavily, bending over and grabbing her knees as she caught her breath.

She found him. Her instincts had paid off. He was on his way with others to the medical center and Megan with renewed energy, followed.

She had kept a steady pace on the highway, but as soon as she knew she found Jarvis, she picked up her pace.

It was a goal, one she became obsessed with. Find this stranger and get him back to John's. For a brief moment, she didn't think that was going to be possible.

Now it was.

They were maybe a mile from where she placed her car. She

could drive if Jarvis was injured.

Was he injured?

At the end of the road, Megan saw the small medical center. There weren't lines of people waiting, but it was busy. The lighting was dim, almost as if it was emergency lighting.

The cart was parked out front and Megan slowed down, she was almost there.

She watched the man walk around to the back to help those in the cart get out.

That was when it happened.

A boom, or rather crack as if someone hit a baseball bat against something right near her ear.

It was loud and vibrated through her being. But it was nothing compared to the shaking she felt beneath her feet. It wasn't an earthquake, just a deep vibration that carried in the air.

Megan looked up.

❈ ❈ ❈

There were times when Yely felt like a grown up, adult enough to do things. Independent would be more of a word, but walking back from town with John with all that was going on, Yely felt like a child.

Younger than her fifteen years.

She felt like that six-year-old girl, looking for the hand of that fire fighter when she was lost at the fair.

He was assuring, strong, and Yely wasn't scared when he took her hand.

There were very few male influences in Yely's life. A teacher here and there, no grandfather, no father presence.

Her mother had lots of boyfriends, but they didn't come around, her grandmother shielded Yely from them.

Giles Matthews was sort of one, but John ... there was something about the cranky, miserable old man who yelled at her the first day she moved next door to him.

She knew it wasn't her, it was him. Something about her worried him. Perhaps it had to do with that picture of his family that he hadn't told her about.

It was an old picture and he had kids in the photo, and a wife.

What happened to them? There was a sense of sadness. She couldn't see his family just leaving him. He wasn't some sort of vile criminal or else Giles would step in.

Then again, Pastor Judy didn't want her to go with John.

Yely wanted to.

Even though it was only a couple hours, being in that community shelter was scary and she felt alone. No hand to grab, at least with John she felt that lifeline.

This was it.

She felt it.

A sense of sadness and doom swept over her every time she thought about her mother.

They fought, her mother had her faults, but she was still her mother.

John didn't say much on the walk back. He asked her if she was okay. He seemed focused on getting back.

Things were quiet on the streets as they mended their homes. A few cars whizzing by. Nothing like when the meteors fell, People ran to the roof of the community center to watch.

Not Yely. She didn't want to see.

At that second, she didn't have a choice.

Four houses from John's it started.

"When we get back," John said. "If there's stuff, you immediately need from your house, go get it. If not, we should ..."

It was a bang.

The loudest noise Yely had ever heard. It sent a jolt through her as if someone slammed a door waking her from a deadened sleep.

Nearly jumping from her skin, Yely didn't have time to ask what that was. A rumble, not shaking started under her feet, and it moved like a soundwave through the air. Within seconds, the pre-dawn sky lit up bright as day as a roaring began.

John stopped walking, his head raised up.

"John?" Yely called his name with fear.

"Take a look, look up. This is it."

Yely looked at John's face, it was more than what he expected. Yely didn't know what to expect, what occurred above them certainly wasn't it.

It was massive, a huge white fireball soared over them with a trail of blazing smoke that covered the sky.

The loud roar blocked out any other sounds, causing almost a gravitational pull as it slowly moved.

It was massive, so much so that Yely thought it was bigger than anyone expected, closer, or both. With the comet still moving above her, Yely filled with panic and fear and she just ran.

She ran as fast as she could.

CHAPTER TWENTY-THREE – NEAR MISS

John saw her run, but there was no way he was catching up to her. He kept an eye on her all while counting.

'Ten one thousand, eleven one thousand …'

Please, John thought, *get to thirty seconds at least.*

At the rate that the comet was coming, he was told sixty kilometers per second. He was told to count once it flew overhead.

Thirty seconds was nearly a thousand miles. Fifteen seconds took it to the coast, thirty dropped it in the Atlantic, the farther the better.

John held his breath with each number he uttered.

The tail was gone at six seconds, and the comet was out of sight within twenty.

That was safe enough, a few more seconds, he wouldn't feel the impact.

It was a big rock, before its early arrival, they stood a chance of very little physical impact until the weather changed.

But now, John estimated they had about an hour before ejecta arrived and only twelve minutes before the pressure winds.

He had things to do in his little house, things he should have done sooner, like opening the windows and closing the shutters. He didn't because he was trying to get information, and then finding Yely.

Before he did the final prep work, he needed to find Yely once more.

John watched her run into her house and John followed.

"Yely," he called out as he stepped in. "Yely!"

It wasn't a big house, like John's, all was on the first floor, nothing above them but the crawl space. Two bedrooms, a small kitchen, dining room and living room. She wasn't in the living room and as he walked into the dining area, she wasn't there either.

"Yely, come on now. We need to get prepping," John said, calmly.

She wasn't in the kitchen either.

Like his house, Yely's had a basement and John walked to the small hallway where that was located across from the bathroom.

Just to be sure, he checked the bathroom as well.

As he reached for the door handle, John knew at that moment, Yely was hiding.

If she wasn't in the basement, maybe the crawlspace.

Then the word really struck him ... hiding.

Hiding.

John closed his eyes. Yely was a child, even though she was in a teenage body, she still was a scared child and John changed direction and went into the smaller bedroom.

His eyes zoomed in on the closed closet door. When he did, his mind flashed back forty years to that tragic day.

"Macy tried to hide in the closet," the sheriff said that tragic day. "We believe that. But she came out."

Earthquakes, tornados, fires ... kids hide in the closet as if it were some magical protection place.

John opened that closet door and Yely sat on the floor. Her arms wrapped around her bent up knees, head down.

"Let's go." John held out his hand. "We have work to do."

Yely didn't move, in fact, John could hear her crying.

"Yely ..."

"I don't want to die. I'm so scared, I don't want to die, John," Yely wept.

John felt it when she said those words. In fact, he felt them in more ways than one. His eyes welled up listening to her fear. He thought of his daughter, probably thinking the same thing. In his mind he could see his little daughter, probably hiding and sitting the same way as Yely.

John couldn't save his child.

"I don't wanna die."

"Well, then let's make sure that doesn't happen." John touched her arm.

Yely grabbed his hand, raised her hand and then stood. She wiped the tears from her face. "Promise."

"I promise I will do everything I can to keep you safe and alive."

Yely nodded.

"Now let's go."

Another nod from Yely and she walked by John and across the room. As they both stepped into the hall, Yely, said, "Wait.'

John was about to ask her what she was doing, then saw her run into the other bedroom. Yely opened up the top drawer, rummaged quickly a bit and pulled out a large brown, envelope.

"What is that?" John asked.

"I don't know. My mom called and said I needed to know what was in here. I had to show it to someone."

"She didn't say what it was?" John asked.

Yely shook her head. "The call was breaking up."

"Did you wanna open it now, looks awfully thick."

"No. I'll wait. It's waited this long, right?"

"Right." John gently placed his hand on her back. "We can always come back here if there's anything you need. Right now …"

"Prepping."

"Prepping." John nodded. "Let's go."

"Did it land?"

"It did."

"What now? What happens now?" Yely asked.

"I'll be honest, I thought I knew. But it came early, that

changes things. I do know one thing," John said. "We're gonna be alright."

CHAPTER TWENTY-FOUR – FACE REALITY

Yely never really thought much about the rectangular shapes called shutters. She believed they were decorations only, although she could never figure out why they were used as decorations.

In fact, she didn't know much about them, but was surprised that John's were real.

It was like a lesson as they moved through his home.

"Storm shutters and in the day, when they were invented, there weren't blinds," John explained. "Today we close them and open the windows to make sure none of them explode."

"The windows will explode?" Yely asked.

"Oh, yeah, in about …" John looked at his watch. "Six minutes when the pressure winds come. The shutters will keep the air flow and the ejecta stuff from blowing in because we have the windows open. Like with a tornado, the pressure breaks the glass."

It was shortly after that, John handed her ear plugs.

Admittedly, Yely was clueless on what he meant by pressure winds. All she knew was that she opened every window in his house and he pulled the shutters closed.

He placed in his ear plugs and she did the same. She readied to pull them out to ask him a question when it happened.

Explanation of pressure winds came to her in physical form.

While she didn't really hear them, she felt it. Everything vibrated. She could feel the pull and push of the winds. Shutters blew open and she saw outside. The big trees across the street lifted and flew.

It was like a tornado, things just blowing, but it wasn't in a random direction, it was all pushing away.

Her blood felt like it was pushing against her skin, and the pressure behind her eyes was so great, she feared her eyes were going to pop out of the socket.

And Yely realized why he gave her the earplugs, she couldn't imagine if he didn't. She felt the pressure there, like going up a mountain, changing altitude.

When it was done, no amount of opening her mouth, trying to yawn, would make them pop.

She could barely hear, it was as if she still had the plugs in.

"Are you all right?" John asked.

His voice was muffled, but she knew what he said.

"Yes." She nodded. "Is it over?'

"This part yes. Are you sure you're all right?"

"Yes. Scared. My ears are clogged."

"Imagine how those not prepared are feeling right now."

Those not prepared. Yely didn't think about that.

"What might of happened to them?" Yely asked.

"Ear drums ruptured, loss of hearing, you name it," John replied. "Now let's open the shutters, close the windows and get the hose."

"The hose?"

"We have to water down the houses. Get em nice and wet, hopefully it will stop the houses from catching fire."

Yely felt confused, John had a plan and was ready. She wasn't. She wished she asked more questions.

Fire? What else was happening?

He must have seen she was worried or scared because he placed his hand on her shoulder with a firm reassuring grip. "Listen, it's not the whole world. Not yet. Not until the cold sets in. After we feign off the ejecta, I'll fire up the generator and try to pick up some news elsewhere. Okay. Right now, we have about thirty minutes."

Another countdown. It was minutes to the wind, minutes to the ejecta, whatever that was, and then he was going to fire up the generator and find news.

What about his friend Jarvis? And Megan? Was he worried about them? Yely assumed he was, but John was focused on the moment and their survival.

Yely would do what he said, but she couldn't help but think of her mother.

The comet struck and with its impact came the impact to Yely that more than likely, her mother was now gone.

* * *

"Is he going to be okay?" Jarvis asked the doctor, in the crowded emergency area. "I just need to know that he's going to be fine."

"Yes," the doctor replied. "You however, are you okay?"

"Yes, I feel fine."

"I think you're in shock."

"What no. Well, yes, I am in shock, but I'm fine."

"You realize we need to put you on the list for surgery. If you think you're not feeling pain, I think we need to do it soon, because if you can go without anesthesia, we can get you done."

Jarvis was totally confused about what he meant. After all his arms and legs felt fine. He was tired, that was it. "Doctor, I—"

"Jarvis!" Megan called out. "Jarvis!"

"Megan?" Jarvis returned the loud call and looked around.

It was so crowded, he was in the hallway that was lined with cots and it was better than an exam room where they had six people crammed in one.

He spotted her as she walked down the corridor, looking at every cot.

"Megan!" he raised his arm.

She spotted him and made haste his way.

"Jarvis, are you ..." Megan stopped. "Oh my God." She turned to the doctor. "Are you going to help him?"

"Yes. Can you take his son, the baby is fine, but he insists he is as well. He's in shock," the doctor explained. "That's why he's not feeling anything, and I told him let's do this now." He cocked his head to the left and called out. "Nurse, can you move this patient to OR three? We can get him done."

A nurse approached. "He's not a red."

"He will be if we don't do something and right now is the perfect time." The Doctor looked at Jarvis. "Give your son to your friend."

"My son," Jarvis looked down to Denver. "Oh, he's not …"

Megan cut him off. "He's fine, Jarvis, he's fine. I have him. Take care of you." She reached for the baby.

"I'll see you in a few," the doctor said and walked away.

The nurse followed, telling Jarvis, "I'll be right back."

Jarvis shook his head. "This is insane. Why did you cut me off when I was about to say he wasn't my son?"

"Why do you have the baby, Jarvis?" Megan asked.

"Because I was traveling with his mother and she died. I'm hoping to take care of him until I can find out where his family is."

"If you want to do that, you can't say he's not yours," Megan said. "They'll take him. He's an orphan. Just worry about you."

"Nothing is wrong with me."

"You don't think?" Megan said sarcastically. "You really don't feel it?"

"No. Feel what?" Jarvis then lifted his fingers gingerly to his face. He felt something on his cheek, hard and sharp. "What the hell?"

"Glass," Megan replied. "One of about…" Her eyes cased Jarvis. "Twelve, it looks like, twelve shards of glass all in your face."

"For real?"

"For real."

"Oh my God," Jarvis said. "Well it can't be that bad." He noticed the look on her face. "Is it that bad?"

Megan nodded as she balanced the baby on her hip. "It's that bad."

CHAPTER TWENTY-FIVE – DAY TWO

The water pressure wasn't what John wanted, but at least it was there. The power had gone out with the pressure winds and he doubted very much that the line workers would be out to fix it. He went out and began to water down the roof of his home and Yely's. Grateful both were single story homes. He expected to see others out doing the same, but they weren't.

The few who remained on the street, those who didn't abandon their homes for a westward run, were outside assessing the damage, the broken windows, looking at John.

"You might wanna hose down your house, we have a fall out coming," John hollered to the young couple across the street. He used the word 'fallout' because he just didn't have time to explain the word ejecta.

They looked at him like some old guy spewing forth nonsense.

Yely came out several times and John sent her back in.

"Keep trying that radio, I can't have the generator running too long," John told her. "We'll need it."

"I want to help."

"You're helping by trying to lock in on something coming from out west."

John didn't know if the ejecta would cause a fire, but there was a chance. He wished he knew where the comet landed, that would help. All he knew was that it was closer then originally thought.

Actually, he wished Jarvis was around. He had all the information.

Jarvis.

Was he alright? John hadn't heard anything in a while from him or Megan and all he could hope for was that they were okay and made it back to him within the next day because if they had to walk, there was no way they were surviving the heat that John knew was coming their way.

There was an orange tint to everything outside, Yely stood on the porch watching it snow red ash. Most of them turned gray as they landed on the ground, losing their heat. Some, however, did not.

She helped John cover the truck with a tarp, then they wet it down. He needed to protect the engine.

As deadly as it was, there was something pretty about it raining tiny specks of fire from the sky. Like Christmas lights falling.

They were about an inch big. Occasionally, they'd land, igniting a small fire. Nothing major, nothing that couldn't be put out. Yely figured the orange appearance to everything was from fires. According to John, bigger ejecta was falling elsewhere.

They were lucky.

It wouldn't last long and it actually didn't. It was intense, and she held her breath a lot hoping the house was safe. It was.

She didn't think she'd get a chance to see it. Yely had been in the basement and had just located three signals when John came in, shut off the generator and had her go outside … just in case.

But now that it was over, John brought her back in.

He restarted the small generator and joined her in the small room. "Okay, take me where you found the signals," he said.

"Okay."

"You're shaking."

"I'm a little chilly."

"Yeah, well, enjoy, that won't last long, then you'll be cold again. After we hear something, you go get some sleep."

"What about you?" Yely asked.

"I'll rest." John pulled up a chair. "Show me."

Yely turned the knob in the direction she heard voices. There were there, it sounded professional, but blips of words, and nothing made sense.

In fact, even though she was picking up signals, it wasn't the information that they needed.

John snapped his finger. "I have an idea. Come with me."

Yely did.

John had an even smaller generator in the closet of the living room.

"Why is that up here?" Yely asked.

"Because I need one up here and these things are heavy." He set it down near the window and went back into the closet.

When he returned, he had this small boxed item with a screen. It looked like an old computer. He moved his flat screen television over and placed it on the entertainment center.

"What is that?" Yely asked.

"An old TV."

"No, it's not."

John chuckled. "Yes, it is. Trust me."

Yely couldn't believe it. The thing was small yet bulky and silver. She moved closer to see what he was doing. Buried behind the entertainment center, coming in through the wall below the window was a flat cable. It was next to the cable television wire that came in.

"Hopefully this still works." John blew dust from it then proceeded to hook it to the old television.

"What is that to? Cable?"

"No, an antenna on the roof. It came with the house. It's a doozy, big one. You never noticed it?"

"You mean that metal thing?"

"Yep."

"I thought it was a cell phone booster."

"No. It's a booster, but for analog signals. It doesn't work on the newfangled televisions because they don't have the connection thingy's in the back." He finished hooking it up and then extended it to hook metal things from the top of the old TV. "Rabit ears we called them," he explained, then he fired up the generator.

It was louder than the one downstairs, John opened the window.

He clapped his hands together and rubbed them right before he turned on the television.

It was funny, and Yely didn't mean to find something funny under such tragic circumstances, but when John used the word, "Squiggle Vision.' She giggled.

"I'm serious, that's what we called it. See how it's not just white noise and static. It's squiggling." He adjusted the rabbit ears. "Almost …" he slammed his hand on top of the television and suddenly, a slightly distorted picture of a woman came on, but her voice was nearly completely clear.

John froze. "Keep an eye out. I can't move."

"Are you hurt?"

"No, just in case something on my body is helping the signal."

"Is that possible."

"I don't know. She's speaking …"

"The ejecta like particles have fallen," the newscaster woman said, "Will we see it here in Cincinnati?"

Another male voice came on, "Not likely, if anything ask. Remember the impact is greater than three Yellowstone eruptions."

"They confirmed that the impact happened a thousand miles off the coast of Norfolk," she said. "So we're safe?"

"From the wave, yes," the male answered. "I mean, Florida is gone. Half the state of Georgia, Virginia, Carolinas …"

John whistled. "We dodged a bullet."

"Safe from that," the man explained. "What comes

tomorrow is an intense heat wave, we will feel that, not as intensely as say West Virginia and Pennsylvania, however when the cold hits, it hits everywhere. Southwest is now the place to be. Keep in mind, that the farther west the more chance that essential services will keep running."

"Are you saying that it can't be survived from let's say, Kansas to the east coast or even the Northeast?"

"I don't believe …"

Static.

"What?" John hit the television again. "Oh, balls. Sorry."

"We're gonna die," Yely said frightened. "Aren't we?"

"We aren't gonna die. We'll be warm. I promise."

"Do you think we should move the wood inside?" Yely asked. "Or as much as we can. Because when it gets cold, you can't miss that wood out there, people will come."

"You, Missy, are absolutely right. That is good survivor thinking. Let's go get my wheel barrel. I have a lot in the garage, but let's move as much as we can inside."

"We should do it before the heatwave huh?"

"You're catching on," John told her. "Let's do this, then let's cook off some of the food in the fridge and feast before it goes bad."

Yely nodded. She was actually excited to help, it stopped her mind from thinking about her mother. She would rest and sleep later, there wasn't time for it now.

"John?" she asked, sheepishly. "Do you think Megan and Jarvis are okay? Shouldn't they be here by now?"

John paused before answering. "I think they probably are. Not the answer you want, but the best I can give. We deal in reality right now and reality is, we have things to do. It's worse than I planned on, but it's not as bad as it could be."

John wasn't speaking as directly as he usually did. Maybe he was worried now that he would upset Yely, or he just didn't have an answer.

She guessed no one did, although he insisted Jarvis had answers in a brief case or bag.

But Jarvis hadn't arrived, and Megan went out looking for a stranger.

Yely didn't understand why Megan went all in to search for a stranger, she only hoped that one day, soon, she'd get a chance to ask her.

❋ ❋ ❋

The hospital had provided Megan with some formula for the baby, a small child whose name she didn't know until Jarvis not only emerged from surgery but woke fully from anesthesia.

She slipped naturally into a caretaker role, holding back the tears at times thinking about her own son as she comforted the baby in her arms.

Megan worried less about the formula than she did about the water to make it. She knew John had plenty, it was just getting back to John.

When Jarvis woke, he told her the baby's name was Denver and he was six months old.

Six months old. Immediately, the mother in Megan started thinking of feeding the child if the formula ran out. He was old enough to eat some solids.

She changed his diaper, wrapped him tightly in a smaller blanket provided by the hospital and softly sang to him while Jarvis recovered.

The recovery was short, Jarvis wanted to go.

He looked better with stiches in his face compared to the glass that had protruded from it. But suddenly he was feeling the pain that his adrenaline had buried.

The doctor gave him only seven pain pills, which he gave to Megan to hold.

Jarvis said he'd push through the pain, he wanted to get to John's.

It wasn't that far. Fifty miles to Ripley. A two hour trip taking backroads that Megan was sure were open.

They had a mile walk to the car, Megan offered to carry the baby. Jarvis kept talking about how the car wouldn't be there or wouldn't work, despite Megan's reassurance.

His luck had run the gauntlet and it was now one delay after another.

"It works."

"You're sure?" Jarvis asked as they walked. "We had those blast winds and some pretty intense Ejecta."

"How do you know?" Megan asked. "You slept through it."

"They told me."

"Well, we're fine." She adjusted the baby. "The car is fine. I'm optimistic."

She knew that the short walk to the car wasn't a lot for her, but it was for Jarvis. He struggled with each step. There was a sense of awkward normalcy in the early hours of the morning. While Jarvis was in surgery, Megan witnessed the arrival of the winds that blew out most of the hospital windows, the moment she felt the pressure, she held her hands over the baby's ears, while her own felt as if they were going to explode.

Denver cried loud and shrill, like a child with an ear infection and there was nothing she could do. When that ended, not long after came the ash.

More fell than she thought. They walked through it, a slight dusting, each step causing clouds of dust to rise up.

Jarvis moved slowly. Even though it was only a mile, that six month old baby seemed to get heavier for her, especially since she shouldered the bags.

She didn't ask how he ended up with the baby, Megan figured that would be a conversation for when they got in the car. Her new friend was exhausted, but didn't complain.

When they finally arrived in Marmet, the town was different than when Megan had left. It as quiet. No crowds, no riots. The Kroger's looked like an abandoned cemetery. Dark, dismal, and broken down.

In the parking lot across the street, the same one she had

positioned herself while waiting for Jarvis, she had Jarvis sit on a small concrete wall. One that was there to stop people from entering the lot.

She gave him the baby. Megan could tell by his passive attitude that he didn't think there was a car.

She was fine with that. She could see her car in that same position she left it. Her fear wasn't getting the car or even starting it, it was driving it home.

Since the meteors fell she hadn't seen a car moving or running.

As if she were the criminal, Megan made her way to her car, looking over her shoulder and left and right.

In the quiet she knew the engine would ring out loudly, especially her old car.

She slipped into the drivers seat, and cringed as she cranked the engine.

It started

Using the wipers she removed the ash from the windshield, creating a smear. She'd use the washer fluid later, but first she needed to get them out of the town and on to the backroads.

She slowly backed up, making her way to Jarvis.

Leaving her door open, she hurriedly jumped out to help him herself. He kept his bag on the floor and Megan secured the seatbelt over him as he held the baby.

"Thank you," Jarvis said. "I promise I'm fine just groggy from the anesthesia."

"I know. We'll be in Ripley soon." She closed his door and raced around, hopping back in the driver's seat.

"How long?" Jarvis asked.

"An hour and fifteen minutes maybe a bit more. We're taking back roads. Are you hungry?"

"No, but he may be," Jarvis said of Denver.

"He's not crying. Wait until he fusses. We may be at John's by then."

"How do you think John will react to me bringing the baby?"

Megan thought about it. Honestly, she didn't know. John's

youngest was around Denver's age when he died. It would either be hard for John or a blessing.

"I don't know,"

Megan replied. "But it doesn't matter does it." She began to drive from town, keeping her focus on the road and ready for someone to try to ambush them for the vehicle. "Jarvis, why don't you tell me how you ended up with the baby."

"I almost walked away," he said.

As Megan pulled out of the back street into the main one, she listened to Jarvis recant his story.

He seemed relaxed and relieved that he was in the car.

Megan would feel relieved once they made it to John's.

※ ※ ※

At first John wondered what the hell Yely was doing banging around. Wasn't she tired? They spent three hours moving wood all while eating what could go bad in the fridge. From dawn until the morning turned a bright orange like something out of a nuclear war movie.

Bellies full and muscles sore Yely went into the back bedroom and John crashed on the recliner. Then he heard the banging. He was in a pretty deep sleep. Figuring he'd been out for hours, John was surprised when he looked at his watch and saw he hadn't been sleeping that long.

And it wasn't Yely banging. In fact, it wasn't banging at all. His slumbering state confused the knock on the door with a louder sound. After doing his typical struggle to get out of the chair, John made his way to the door.

He didn't peek out like he usually did, maybe he should have.

Standing on his porch in the haze of the aftermath was Giles and Pastor Judy

"Well look what the comet dragged in," said John as he glanced at his watch. "Didn't realize town was so far that it took you six hours to get here."

"We've been busy," Pastor Judy snapped.

"So have we," John retorted.

"Where is she?" Pastor Judy asked.

"She's sleeping."

"I want the girl," Pastor Judy ordered.

"Is that why you brought the law? You have no claims on the child."

"Neither do you."

John looked at Giles. "Giles, really? Are you honestly here to take the girl?"

Giles shook his head. "I come as a peacekeeper. Pastor Judy feels Yely will be better off at the center."

"Do you?" asked John.

"Honestly? No."

Pastor Judy gasped. "It doesn't matter, her mother-"

"Her mother took off on a secret vacation leaving the kid behind," John barked. "It doesn't matter what the mother wants now, she should have thought of that before she packed her bags. Yely stays here. I'm not waking her. She's slumbering off a hefty food coma. You wanna see and speak to her then come back later. Giles. For all I did for the town get this woman off my porch."

"Mr. Hopper she's just concerned." Giles defended.

"I get it, I do. But I can handle the girl. And it ain't like we're a hundred miles away. You can walk here. The girl wants to stay with me. Let her stay. Check her if you want later. She's fine."

Giles turns to Pastor Judy. "Right now, there nothing I can do. With all that's going on, I don't know how we can enforce this."

"John Hopper," Pastor Judy turned to him. "That girl's been through enough. You don't know her or her family."

"And you do?"

"Yes." Judy nodded. "And that's why I don't think it's a good idea for her to be with you. When you find—"

"Good Lord on a cross." John pushed the screen door open and stepped onto the porch stepping beyond Judy and Giles. "They made it." He looked at Judy. "Do you trust Megan with the girl?"

"I do."

"Then you can go now," John said stepped off the porch. "She's here."

He smiled and they didn't see it. John was thrilled and relieved when he saw Megan's car finally pull up.

CHAPTER TWENTY-SIX - PEACE

John wasn't planning on breakfast or rather, lunch company, but he had a houseful. More people were in his small house than he ever had before.

And Yely was still sleeping.

Before Megan came in, looking worn and tired. Before Jarvis, injured plopped in John's favorite chair, before all that. They stepped from the car.

All pettiness, arguments and back and forth about Yely went out the window.

Pastor Judy and Giles weren't far behind.

"Jarvis?" John said in shock when he saw him. "My God, what happened to you?"

"I had a little run in with exploding glass," Jarvis replied, "I'm fine. So is he. His mother didn't make it."

That was when John saw him. The baby.

Something about seeing the little boy just melted John's heart.

"Here, give him here." John held out his hand, they trembled a little, but when John took hold of him, and brought him close to his chest, all those instincts that he thought were gone, came crashing back. "Hey little guy. Let's get you inside and wipe that face, shall we?"

Judy rushed to Megan. "Are you okay?"

"Yeah. It's been a ride."

John turned to her. "Megan, I'm proud of you. You went to get him and stuck to your guns."

Giles asked. "Do you need a doctor? Any of you? Doctor Parch is in town."

Megan shook her head. "We were at the health center in Marmet."

"Let's get inside," John suggested.

Pastor Judy extended her arms. "Do you want me to take the baby for …"

"Nope. Got him. You're not getting your hands on this one either."

"Mr. Hopper," Giles caught up to him. "The child's mother died, technically …"

"Technically my ass." John opened his door. "Rules are different now. Unless you have a plan to find his dad, or grandparent. You got a working phone?" John stepped into his house. "A radio. I do. We have a hell of a heat wave coming in about twenty-four hours, that should be everyone's top priority before the ice age."

Jarvis spoke up as he hobbled in. "I have information. Just from memory. About Denver, the baby. Things Holly, his mom told me while we were traveling. We have a direction when things are clear."

"We have a while," John said. "Things won't be clear for a while."

It was somewhere in that point of conversation, everyone just made themselves at home.

Travis in the chair, Megan, Judy and Giles at the dining room table.

John handed the baby to Megan and made coffee with the percolator on the Coleman stove.

He was pretty sure the half and half was bad by now and put out the powdered creamer, all while asking himself why he was being the host with the most.

Why were they just all sitting at his table, except for Jarvis who was moments away from falling asleep.

Judy and Giles thanked him for the coffee.

"This is the first cup I had all day," Judy said.

"Now that I am your dealer of caffeine," John sat down. "Why are you two still here?"

Pastor Judy exhaled. "John, we just need to make sure Yely is alright and now, this baby …"

Megan jumped in. "The baby is fine. I can't think of a better place to be."

Judy looked at her. "So, you're not coming to the community center?"

Megan peered at John. "Unless, he doesn't want me here, than I am staying."

"Of course, I do," John said. "First you fed me corned beef, really great corned beef, me and the kid finished it off by the way. Second, that baby needs a mother's care until we find his family. That's you."

Megan lowered her head some. "I will do the best I can. I appreciate that John. It's been a long time since I got to mother."

"I feel you on that one. And I didn't know you were a mom, but you put out those instincts with Yely."

Giles finished his coffee and stood. "Pastor Judy, I think we can go. We can come back if need be."

Pastor Judy nodded, sipped her coffee and stood. "John, I didn't mean to cause trouble. I'm just worried and want the best for Yely."

"The best for Yely is here because she wants to be here. You can take that cup with you."

"Are you sure?" she asked.

"Yep. Because you know where to find me and I know where to find you. Enjoy it."

"Thank you." Judy lifted the cup. 'I hope your friend heals well and know that Doctor Parch is in town if needed."

"Thank you," John said.

They began to leave, and Giles stopped. "Mr. Hopper, you're part of this town, if you need anything."

"Same goes on this end, however," John said. "If you're

worried, maybe that couple across the street. They're young, they seem hell bent on staying put and I don't think they have anything ready."

Pastor Judy looked at Giles. "I think they have that newborn."

"All the more reason," John stated. "Put them Christian skills where needed. We're good here."

Before she left, Judy embraced Megan and looked at John with gratitude.

He followed them to the door and Pastor Judy stopped.

"John," she said. "Is it really going to get that bad?"

"That fella there." He pointed to Jarvis. "Has a lot of scientific information. When he wakes and feels better, I'll get him to share. But to answer your question. Is it really going to get that bad?" John paused. "I think worse than you can imagine."

CHAPTER TWENTY-SEVEN – DAY FOUR

The road trip of survival. That was what Giles Matthews called it. Just before the comet hit, half the town's population remained. But after the big comet and Librarian, Joel Monroe announced that he picked up news in Cincinnati, half of those remaining packed up and left.

One hundred and ninety-two people remained in town. A little less than before the comet. It made rationing easier.

According to the Cincinnati news that Joel Monroe monitored, northwest was best for the heat wave, then a two-day transition to get to the south when the cold front, or as John called it, the ice age hit.

John preached to stay put. While Ripley was no longer the safest place on earth as predicted, it still had a lot of nature's protection.

The temperatures would never get as high as some places, and when the cold hit, there were plenty of things to burn to stay warm.

Giles believed John worried about the heatwave more than the cold, then again, John bought out all the firewood in the county.

The day before when the heatwave started, temperatures started to rise and they didn't stop. They reached ninety-eight by evening and barely dropped. Perhaps because there was really no nightfall.

It was dark, but that orange look to the sky remained. During the day it was extremely orange and hazy.

Jarvis, as Giles learned, was pretty brilliant, providing charts and explanations on what all was happening. Pastor Judy and the Mayor had come to John's to hear his explanation.

John wasn't present during the meeting, but he didn't need to be. He was prepping something he called, 'The Cold Room' because he didn't want Baby Denver exposed to the heat for too long.

It had to be in the basement, because that was where they started moving the people at the center. There and the basement of the church.

Three days. Three days that was it.

Jarvis laid out the paperwork and charts. The mayor and Pastor Judy nodded in understanding, but Giles got lost. That was when Jarvis gave him the laymen lowdown.

"All the orange we see to the east, those are fires still raging. It was too close to the coast and a massive fireball just lit everything up," Jarvis explained. "All those fires are shooting smoke up. Right? Debris is in that smoke, it will create one giant massive storm cloud. Because when the comet hit the Atlantic, all that water went up. What goes up, must come down."

"Rain," Giles said.

Jarvis wagged his finger. "But those clouds will block eighty percent of the sun so it is going to be darker and cold."

"Snow," Giles, then said.

Jarvis nodded. "Lots of it. Demographically, we'll see about two feet before it just will get too cold to snow anymore."

Pastor Judy asked. "How cold will it get in the south, southwest."

"They'll get snow, nothing that will stop essential services or break the grid. My concern is those traveling. They don't have two days once the heat stops. They have maybe one day. Because the heat breaks with rain, which will cause massive fog. The rain will get cold and it won't be icy rain that falls, it'll be like slush. It's going to be a mess."

"So we can't go out in it?" the mayor asked.

"After the rain and snow. That's about a week. You don't want to be caught out in the snow. The cold, well, if you have arctic gear you can," Jarvis stated. "John has it."

Gile interjected. "We hit the sporting goods store for some. John gave us the heads up."

"Good." Jarvis nodded continuously. "Like I told John. Get as much as you can ahead of time so you don't have to go out."

The mayor said, "I think we're fixed for food and water. Maybe find more water. Send a couple people out."

"Good idea," Jarvis stated. "Right now it's pushing a hundred. The temperature will peek in a few hours and moving about will be hard."

"There are a few things I can gather," Giles stated.

Megan who hadn't been present must have heard and injected into the conversation as she entered the room. "Are you headed out to get supplies?"

Giles chuckled. "Don't tell me John needs something. I thought he had everything."

"He did. He does," Megan replied. "For adults. We weren't expecting a baby. I'd like to go with you Giles."

"I can get it for you," said Giles.

"I'd like to go."

A semi excited, "Me too" rang out as Yely raced in the room. "Can I help? I want to do something. John said everything is covered here and I don't want to read that mouse and the man book."

"We can use the hands at the center," Pastor Judy said. "Organizing the water so we can ration it. Help unload things when they bring it in."

"The center?" Yely asked. "You're not gonna try to kidnap me again, are you?"

With an 'Oh' and a wave out of her hand, Pastor Judy shook her head. 'You have been hanging out with John too much." She gathered her things. "Let's head out. Where?" She used her folders to fan herself. "Lord, it's hot."

"Yeah," Yely said innocently. "It is hot. I had no idea."

Everyone looked at her curiously.

She placed her hand on Pastor Judy's arm and Pastor Judy jumped.

"Yely, why are your hands so cold."

"John's cold room."

Giles didn't know what that was, but apparently, according to Yely's hands, that cold room was working. The thought of going down to feel it under the guise of just checking it out, crossed Giles' mind, but time was running out and they did need to get more supplies.

❉ ❉ ❉

Megan watched Giles tap the temperature on the squad car's digital read as if he though hitting that '105' would make it change.

"At least the AC works in here," Megan said.

"Barely."

"It's not a hundred and five in here. We could be walking."

"True," Giles replied. "I'm just so grateful we aren't having looter problems here."

"You should have seen it in Marmet. Just after the meteorites hit it was chaos. They went from calmly waiting for Kroger's to open to storming the store and running out with what they wanted."

"We secured our store. I think doing that and distributing it to people instead of letting them in was a big deal. We did the PharGreens, too"

"How much is in the stores?" Megan asked.

"A lot went to the center. PharGreens is still pretty full except for the bottled water," Giles answered. "That's locked up and the gates are closed. It looked untouched yesterday."

"Well, we are remote. People aren't going to find our town so easily if they don't know about it."

"Hey, thanks for telling me how John did his cold room. Jarvis made it sound like a big secret."

Megan laughed a little. "It's just that John went overboard for something for a few days."

"Unless he plans on using it as a hot room, too," Giles said.

"Possibly."

"Well, I think I might be able to make one. Hopefully."

"I have faith in you," Megan replied.

They pulled into the lot of the PharGreens. Once a major chain store, bought out by someone a few years earlier. They kept it pretty much the same, and Megan was relieved to see the gates were still down and though some of the windows were shattered, she attributed that to the comet.

Giles pulled up to the door, took a deep breath then shut off the car.

It didn't take long, almost immediately, once the air conditioning stopped, the car felt hot. Megan opened her door, and waited by the entrance for Giles.

Jingling his keys he searched through his packed keychain, then found the one he was looking for and unlocked the gates. He slid it up enough for them to slip under. He unlocked the main door, closed the gate and fastened that lock again.

Inside the store was dark and it wasn't as hot as it could have been. Megan imagined the store would be darker the farther in the back that they went.

Megan grabbed a buggy and so did Giles.

She had one direction she was going.

The baby aisle.

"Giles, when you checked in with that young couple across the street from John, did they need anything for the baby?"

"They said no, they were fine. They picked up the distribution we did at Kroger's and they said they had stuff. They said they knew where to find us if they needed something. I tried to talk them into coming to the center."

"They really should," Megan said, pushing her buggy.

"I'll pop by again, make sure they have enough water. There

is only one of five families that didn't go to the center. So, I will make my rounds until I can't."

"I'll check on them as well, since they are across the street. I'll grab some stuff. For them just in case."

At the center point of the store, Megan veered right as Giles went left.

Her primary focus was scavenging and taking as much as she could from that baby aisle. She wasn't taking from anyone else's needs in town. According to Doctor Parch, Denver and the baby across from John's, were the only two babies in town. The families that had really young children had left town.

For the time being, she would take what she could for the immediate and beyond. And she did just that. It didn't feel as hot in the store when she first started, but by the time she was done, Megan felt out of breath and tired, but she trudged on. After filling the cart, she put what she could into those larger reusable bags, and she loaded them into the car.

Giles picked up a lot as well, in fact that squad car was packed. It was also hot. It was hard to breathe even with the windows down and the AC blasting to the point it blew her hair.

It was the second day, Jarvis said it would be the worst, Megan didn't want to imagine how bad it would get. She felt bad for people who, unlike her, didn't have access to a basement or a John cold room.

❋ ❋ ❋

It was the one nice thing about getting old in a heatwave. It didn't take much for 'cold' to be too cold and John's fingers to get that prickly feeling. He didn't plan on spending all his time in the cold room, and it really wasn't that cold. But it didn't have the thick humidity that made it worse.

The room was big enough for them all to sleep in. Insulated, ventilated. A portable AC unit vented out through an old dryer vent hook up. It was powered by a small generator. Running four hours on, one hour off, John had enough juice for four days. He didn't need more.

One thing John made certain was that Denver wasn't in the heat too much. John knew babies didn't process heat well and that was what crossed his mind as he looked at the house across the street.

He was peering out his window like a nosey old neighbor but he did it with concern.

The drapes were drawn over their broken windows and John was worried.

In the silence of the world now, sound traveled.

He didn't hear that newborn, who, four days earlier when everything was loud, wailed like there was no tomorrow.

The young couple really wanted nothing to do with anyone. Even when Giles popped by, they were dismissive, and adamant that they were fine.

Were they?

They said they didn't need anything, but after seeing the canisters of baby formula the hospital gave Jarvis and Megan, John kept thinking back to his wife when his middle child, his son was born.

There was a heat wave and she just wasn't getting enough fluids, she couldn't breast feed.

Maybe the young mother across the street was already using formula, but just to be safe, John decided he was going to take her a can.

He had a bad feeling, and it was something John hadn't felt in a long time.

Worry.

He stopped caring, never bothered with neighbors, now all of the sudden he was worrying about people.

He blamed that on Yely.

In fact, formula in hand, he opened the door as she walked in.

"Damn you," John spat.

"What did I do?" Yely asked innocently.

"Making me like people again, you and your emo state. I thought you were helping at the center."

"I was. Pastor Judy said to take a break." Yely nodded at the can of formula. "Is that for across the street.?'

"Yeah, it is."

"That's nice. I'm going to the cold room. It's hot," she said

"It is."

She giggled.

The girl never giggled. John watched her with a 'hmm', wondering what she found funny as she walked away. Maybe she met a boy or something.

John stepped out, it was even hotter out there. The air was thick, damp and hot.

There were two things that happened as John crossed the street. He noticed they didn't have a basement. It was the first time, probably because he had never bothered to look before. Never thought about it.

Then came the scream.

The all too familiar mother's scream. It took him back immediately to that day with his wife.

He knew that scream and even with his legs not wanting to move like he wished, John picked up the pace and hustled to the house.

The screams continued, then adding to that was the father's voice.

"No, no, no!"

John froze as he reached for the door to knock. Frozen solid in a state of being triggered. It didn't matter how long before it was, he was instantly transported back to that day at the campsite.

Suddenly he wasn't on the neighbor's porch, but outside that cabin, wanting so badly to rush in.

He didn't then on that day, he listened to the sheriff instead. Perhaps if he had listened to Fred Price and stormed the house, things would have been different.

With that thought, John didn't know, he stormed in.

The father didn't turn around, his back was to John as he raced to the wall. The mother was on the floor.

"What happened?" John asked. "Do you need help?"

She cried, unable to answer and John looked around.

He could barely breathe and he didn't know if it was the heat or that he ran and charged into the house. Turning left and right, he saw the cradle and with his heart beating out of control, John walked over.

The baby was in there on his back, wearing only a diaper. His color was off, pale, but not gray. Lips blue, belly slightly distended. With a trembling hand John reached down to him, he had barely touched him when he saw the baby blink. Then his hand, on the baby's chest, he felt it move and John jumped back.

"He needs cooled down," John said. "He needs cooled down." John reached for him.

"What are you doing?" the mother screamed. "What are you doing?"

"It's the heat, we have to cool him down." John lifted the baby gently, it was near lifeless, but he was alive.

"No, don't take my baby!" the mother screamed.

Was she insane? Had the heat caused her not to think reasonably, John wasn't stealing the child he was trying to help him.

"I'm gonna help your son," John told her, he shrugged from her grip and charged out of the house, straight across the street to his.

When he entered his home, he called out, not that he thought anyone could hear him.

"Yely!" he yelled as he headed to the basement. "Yely!"

When he reached the bottom of the stairs, he squeezed through the hallway still calling out for her.

John made it quickly, spry for a man his age.

The cold room door opened and Yely ran out. "Are you calling?"

"Go. Go to town, get help. Doctor Parch, a fireman, someone."

Yely nodded and looked at the baby. "Is he ..."

"No. But we have to cool him down."

Jarvis jumped up from the small couch. "There's cool water down here. I'll get that and a towel," he said. "Place him on the futon, it's leather and cool."

"Hurry, Jarvis, I don't know what to do."

"You're doing fine."

John nodded, he noticed Denver sleeping on the small couch with a blanket.

A blanket. That baby was cool and now John was faced with a child that was dying from the heat and John had the means to prevent that from even happening.

He hadn't even considered it or thought about it.

How horrible was that?

John had the means to help the child before, but saving him was out of his hands now.

CHAPTER TWENTY-EIGHT – REALITY CHECK

The temperature in the squad car read that it was 108 outside. Too hot to be moving, working, or even running.

Yet, when Giles spotted Yely running toward the community center, he knew something was wrong. He pulled over and jumped out.

"Yely, why are you running?"

Yely, red faced, caught her breath. "To get help. The baby across the street. Something is wrong. John's trying to cool him down."

"Get in the center, get the doctor ready. Stay put," Giles said. "I'll be back with the baby." On that, he jumped back in the car, and sped off.

"The baby?" Megan asked. "Heat stroke."

"Sounds like it.'

"Oh my God."

Giles sped the several blocks to John's house, came to a screeching halt outside, and without missing a beat, popped the trunk, jumped from the car, grabbed the medical bag, and raced to the house.

The young father, Ben, from across the street was sitting in a chair, head buried in his hands. A wailing woman's cry carried to him and Giles followed that sound to the basement. All while his hands worked frantically to unzip the bag.

He knew what he wanted to grab, the small oxygen canister. They could rig it to work with the baby.

He made his way down the narrow stairs, though a hallway lined with water honing in on the cries. They were muffled.

At the end, oxygen freed from the bag and in his hand, Giles looked to his right.

Jarvis stood outside a closed door, holding Denver. He said nothing, but only shook his head when he saw Giles.

Giles opened the door and stepped inside, the mother Anna, her cries along with instantly cooler air blasted him. Anna had crumbled to the floor, curled up and John was at the end of the small room, kneeling before a futon.

"Come on, baby, come on. Come on, baby, come on," John beckoned.

Giles rushed over, he could help, he knew it, at least until they moved the baby to the car.

Get him in the car, get him to Doctor Parch.

"John, let me take him. The car's out front ready to go. We'll get him to Doctor Parch."

"Okay," John said, rushed. "Okay, thank you. Help him, please." Using the futon as support, John stood and Giles took his place.

Giles lifted the infant into his arms, cradling him deeply against his chest, feeling a heartbroken loss and uselessness overcome him. As he walked quickly from the room, the mother looked up.

She knew.

Ben upstairs knew, so did Jarvis.

Giles knew. They all did. Except for John.

The baby was gone.

Saying nothing, Giles took the baby and held him as Megan drove them to town.

Maybe, just maybe he was wrong. Perhaps something could be done.

He would fast learn, that wasn't the case.

John sat at his breezeless, open living room window that night, staring out at the sky. He watched the lightning flash continuously. Heat lighting, loud and scary, lighting up the dark sky.

It looked like a storm, but that wasn't coming. Not yet.

It also ominously lit up the house across the street. John stared at that, too.

It was dark over there, but he knew the young couple was home. He offered them to stay with him, but they declined. Pastor Judy offered as well.

He knew what they were feeling, he knew, they wanted nothing but the darkness because at this moment, that was what was in their heart. Dark pain that would never go away.

In a sense, John was trapped in their tragedy.

Reliving his own.

The only difference was, his whole reason for living was to keep his family alive in a way and to see justice delivered to Reed.

It didn't much for John to imagine where they were mentally.

Yely's soft voice didn't startle him. "Here," she said. "Hurry before it gets warm."

John turned from the window, she held a small pan with water and a rag. "What's this for?'

"Cool down. I filled it downstairs."

"I'm good." He returned to looking out the window. "Thank you."

He heard the sound of water, slight splashing, then he felt it. A cool wetness gently on the back of his neck, water slowly tricking down his back under his shirt.

Yely wouldn't take no and placed the rag on him.

Her kindness was an overload. John closed his eyes tight, to fight off emotions. He reached for her hand, bringing it down. He squeezed it, looking at her. "You're a good kid." He then took the rag. "Thank you again. I needed that more than I thought," he said, meaning it wasn't just the rag, but Yely didn't know that.

CHAPTER TWENTY-NINE – SOLEMN DARK

John took the rag wiping off his forehead and back. He didn't realize how badly he was sweating.

"Is this heat really supposed to break tomorrow "Yely asked

"That's what they say. That's what Jarvis said."

"I know he keeps saying it. It doesn't make sense to me though."

"What doesn't?"

"Why it's so hot and won't be for long."

"The fires will burn out," John explained. "The rain will come."

Yely jumped when the lightning brightened the sky. "Tonight?"

"No, tomorrow. Ever have a summer day that just got hotter and hotter until it rained?" John asked

Yely nodded.

"Sort of like that. Only it won't get muggier. That rain will cool it down and keep cooling."

"We can stay warm right?"

"We're good. We may all have to stay in the living room, but we'll be warm."

"I saw you gave Giles gasoline."

John nodded. "He needed it for the bulldozer. So they can bury the baby while the ground is soft. And a couple others in town that died from the heat." John sighed and looked out again, setting down the rag.

"Did you know Ben, Anna and the baby very well?"

"No. No I didn't. Until you moved in, I never spoke to a neighbor."

"At all?"

"Except to tell them to get their ball out of my yard," John said almost stagnant.

"I thought you knew them. I'm sorry you're so upset."

John glanced at Yely with a closed mouth smile. "It's just um, I feel their pain. You know. It's not only a painful reminder, but it's a …" John brought his fist to his heart. "Shared knowledgeable pain. It don't matter how many years go by the pain is there, and things like this just bubble it to the surface. I spent all this time getting ready to survive this comet, all my money. And I couldn't save a baby."

"Nobody could. You tried."

John huffed out a breath. "Guess I suck, as you kids say, at helping people."

"That's not true. You're helping me."

"You don't count."

"John? Does what happen to the baby remind you of your family in the picture?" Yely asked.

"Yep."

"You don't talk about them."

"Nope."

"I won't ask."

John looked at her, then down to the pan of water and back out. He took a deep breath. "Forty years ago, a sick man, he took my family from me. My wife, my three kids. One was a baby. Denver's age."

Yely gasped.

"You're acting shocked," John said.

"I am."

"You saw the old pictures."

"I thought they left you. I mean in a van or something. I'm sorry. That's horrible. He must have been a horrible person."

"He wasn't. I knew him. He had a great wife. A baby that was on the way. He was just … he lost his mind and in doing so, killed my family and in a sense, killed his."

"Thank you for telling me."

"Don't go blabbing it. We all have stories. All of us. In this house we all carry tragedy."

"Megan and Jarvis, too?"

"Megan more than him. He just got left by his famous wife," John said. "Welp." He slowly stood. "Gonna go cool off. Are you coming?"

"I'm gonna stay and watch the lightning."

"Not too long. Don't make me come up and get you. It's still over a hundred degrees."

"I won't be long."

John started to walk and stopped. "Did you eat today?"

"Pastor Judy fed me."

"Okay. I know my head wasn't in it." He stopped again. "Do you have any more of that marijuana? Seems like a weeding kind of night."

Yely giggled. "I don't smoke marijuana."

"Yeah right." John started walking toward the basement and paused when the entire room lit up from the lightning.

Yely was engrossed.

"That lightning you think is so nifty? John said. "Ask Jarvis. That's nothing compared to what's coming."

※ ※ ※

Denver's little lips puckered as he slept and Megan could stop watching him. She could have gone to the center or even home, but she stayed to be with the baby and not just for the cool air.

It wasn't a bad thing john had the cold room.

If it was under normal circumstances, it wouldn't have been cold, but the temperature at seventy-eight degrees was a freezer compared to how it was outside.

It hit one fifteen and stayed there most of the day.

Which was nothing compared to what the radio was saying those down south were experiencing. Temperatures that were not survivable.

The exodus was like a mouse in a maze, Head one place, stop and go to another.

North for the heat, south for the cold and the window to travel between wasn't wide.

The cold room was only eight feet wide by ten feet long. John had two futons facing each other and a single reclining chair.

Like Yely, Jarvis opted to sleep on the floor, it was cooler.

Denver slept on a futon and Megan just watched him.

The night before John opted for the chair, but he was in and out of the cold room.

Yeley was finally asleep like Jarvis and Denver. Megan wasn't tired. She worried too much about the baby, Yely, was Jarvis healing all right and John. He just wasn't himself.

He was in and out of the room. Now he was at that radio again.

Megan could hear it. People were transmitting information. How hot it was in Arkansas, which routes were open, and how to register for a refugee shelter in Nevada.

One thing she did hear, and that perked her interest was about red cross ships. Some had made it to the US. Some hadn't, they were lost when the comet hit.

She supposed John was gathering all the information, because when he returned to the cold room, he had a spiral bound, flip top note pad.

"Anything good?" Megan asked, "I mean I heard some."

"Same old, same old, but that will change when the weather does. They're saying tomorrow around noon."

"How do they know?"

"Well they can still reach the satellites," John said.

"I heard something about red cross ships."

John nodded as he sat in his chair. "They didn't say much, just some ships arrived."

"Yely's mom …"

"I know. She was supposed to be on one of them. Maybe she made it."

Immediately, Yely sat up. "Do you think?"

John groaned. "How'd I know you'd hear that."

"Yely," Megan said. "We don't know. All the radio said was that some of the red cross boats arrived. We don't know which one or where."

"She was supposed to go to Savannah," Yely said.

John replied. "We'll find out. If she made it Yely, she won't be able to make it home yet. The weather will be too bad. It'll be a while."

"How long?" Yely asked. "I know you said three hundred days …"

Jarvis groaned out. "The weather will calm down in a few months. It'll start stabilizing around Christmas. The three hundred days is until we see warmer weather. If she's going to make it home, she'll start heading home in a few months."

"If she doesn't show up?" Yely asked. "Does that mean …"

"No," John cut her off. "It doesn't mean that. If she doesn't show up, well, then we go looking."

"Do you mean that?" Yely asked.

"I do. I'll take you myself, we'll steal that big truck Giles bought after his divorce," John replied.

Megan asked. "What about gas?"

"I have my stash. Don't you worry about that." John winked. "Right now, worry about what's ahead."

CHAPTER THIRTY – DAY SIX

There were one hundred and ninety-two Ripley residents remaining after the comet hit. Pastor Judy did a head count on the day of the burial, one hundred and forty-five remained.

Eight died from heat related illness and the other thirty-eight had left town, and that included the Mayor, Jim Rollins.

Pastor Judy was feisty and expressed her dismay about it to John just before the funeral for the eight lost residents and the baby.

John's attitude was different. The mayor did what he had to do to try to keep his town safe, then made the decision on what he thought was best for his family. According to Judy they were riding out the heat wave in Ohio, then heading to Nevada.

The weather had cooled, dropping to ninety for the early morning service. Nearly everyone attended.

John kept thinking about how hard Giles had worked in the heat digging the graves, and how once the cold weather set in, the burying of the dead would have to wait.

Ben and Anna attended the service not saying much to anyone.

John wanted to talk to them, share his wisdom, but didn't know them well enough. They didn't speak to him and he didn't know if it was because he failed to save their child or they were just lost souls drowning in their grief.

Nearly everyone that remained in town gathered for the service. Jarvis stayed back at the house, his face was healing really well, but it was still too warm to bring Denver outside.

And then, it started to rain, a light drizzle that fell steadily.

All those at the church cemetery held out their arms, lifting their face to the sky, laughing and rejoicing as if it was a form of relief. It was physically, for the moment, the cold rain felt refreshing, but John knew it was short lived.

"Right on time," said John to Yely and Megan. "Let's head home."

"I want to run to my place," Megan said. "Some things I want to get. Memorabilia. I don't' want it to freeze and get ruined, some things can't be replaced."

John nodded. "That makes sense. Are you ready Yely, we have a walk to go in this."

"Can I go with Megan?" she turned to Megan. "Unless you don't want me to go."

"No, I could use the help. Can she John?"

"Just make sure she's covered and doesn't get too wet. The girl's gonna spend a lot of time shivering, I don't need her catching a cold."

"That's nice of you to worry about her," said Megan.

"Not her. Me. She gets sick. I get sick, we all get sick. See you at home."

He watched the two of them head off to Megan's place, not far from the church and John walked home.

Smart enough to bring an umbrella, he wasn't embracing the rain like everyone else. He shielded himself, as he walked home.

Ben and Anna were a good half block ahead of him, widening the distance with each step because they moved faster. John decided as he watched them, he would go over to make sure they had the means to stay warm. Even at the risk of being chastised about not extending the 'do you have a means to stay cool' invitation.

That worry was probably more in his head.

They were no longer in sight when he reached his home.

Jarvis was on the porch with the baby.

"Everything okay?" John asked.

"Yeah, wanted him to get fresh air before we're stuck inside again."

"Good idea," John said. "Jarvis, you're doing really well with him."

"Thanks. I just hold on, you know, thinking about my family, and knowing they're probably gone, and I have something left."

"I'm sorry."

"We all are." Jarvis sighed. "Who thought I'd be a father at the end of the world."

"I think you're going to be fighting Megan over that one. But it takes a village, isn't that what they say?"

Jarvis nodded. "They do. Speaking of Megan, where are her and Yely?"

"They went to get some things from Megan's home. Anything new on the radio?"

"Um, uh … how was the funeral?"

"You didn't listen, did you?"

Jarvis cringed.

"It's fine. How's the face? It looks good."

"Feels good."

"Excellent. Before this evening I'll need you up on the roof to hit the antennas with Frost Guard."

"I thought you bought the artic shield?" Jarvis asked.

"I did. I want to double down. It'll be a few days before it's safe enough to go out. Even with Arctic gear."

"Tell me what I need to do and I'll …" Jarvis' eyes strayed.

Noticing that Jarvis was looking elsewhere, John turned around. He saw Ben and Anna loading the car.

"They're leaving," Jarvis said. "I mean they can't leave, right, it's a little late in the game."

"Yeah, if they don't get somewhere safe by dawn they'll get nowhere. Excuse me." John stepped off the porch and walked across the street.

Ben saw him and waved.

John returned the wave and kept walking to them. "Are you leaving?" he asked.

Ben closed the back door after putting in a suitcase. "Yeah, we are. We're gonna try to head south."

"Do you have a route?" John asked.

"We do, back roads," Ben replied.

"Good. Good. The weather is going to change pretty quickly. Do you need supplies?"

"We're good."

At that moment, Anna came out.

"Is there anything I can say that will get you to stay?" John asked. "It's dangerous and you're welcome to stay at my place. I'm ready for the freeze, I have food."

Anna approached him. "You've done enough."

At that point John really felt that she was going to go off about not inviting them to cool down.

Anna continued, "You have. Thank you so much for trying so hard to save Steven. We will always remember that and your kindness."

"I've been there," John said. "I have been in your shoes."

"We've heard," Anna said.

"Damn Yely." John mumbled.

"What?" Anna asked.

John shook his head. "Just be safe, please."

"Thank you." Anna walked to him and kissed him on the cheek. "We're gonna chance it. We have nothing to lose."

John tightly closed his mouth and opened the car door for her. "I hope you get to where you're going."

"It doesn't matter, just know, we appreciate you trying to help us." Anna slid in the car.

"You stay safe, Mr. Hopper," said Ben. "Take care of that teenager and yourself."

"Will do."

"Who knows. Maybe when this is all done, we'll see you again."

"Let's hope. Now get going, the weather isn't kind." John stepped back.

Ben got in the car, and John moved fully out of the way.

He knew the young couple had quite the journey ahead, time was not on their side.

If they didn't make it far enough south, they would stand a chance of being stuck and freezing to death.

John knew that it probably didn't matter either way to them.

* * *

Jarvis had the knowledge, but even then, a part of him was doubtful of what he knew. Maybe he was wrong.

He wasn't.

He wished he could talk to his ex-wife. She knew it all, and perhaps she was who the news got their information from.

After Megan returned, Jarvis gladly turned baby duty over to her. Yely offered but said she drew the line on diaper changing.

They no longer needed to stay in the cold room, the temperature had dropped enough to be tolerable. Not enough to start heating the place.

The switch had been flipped. It went from short term survival in extreme heat to long term survival in the almost barely survivable cold.

But survival was going to be more than firing up the fireplace.

John, of course, had a plan. Behind the garage, covered in a tarp, was a small, very small, geodesic dome green house. It was no bigger than a small tent. The smallest one Jarvis had seen. He remembered a year earlier when he told John about them, how they had them in the arctic.

John said he got one. It was built, but not finished and he informed John they didn't have much time to do so.

For the tens of thousands of dollars John paid for it, Jarvis didn't understand why he just didn't pay to have someone get the plant beds ready.

John simply explained that he didn't think that a mini ice age was going to happen. Then he just wanted to spend his money because he was old and had no one to leave it to.

"Look at it this way," John said. "Now we have something to do."

"If we don't freeze to death walking from the dome to the house."

And even though it sounded as if Jarvi was being sarcastic, he was serious.

There would be a time when the storm settled, that even moments outside would be deadly.

While Yely did the non-stop diaper changing Denver duty, Megan worked in the kitchen. It was a mess from making meals there and taking them down below. Everything would be different once John got the fireplace going, they would cook food on it. But until then, it was the propane stove.

Jarvis and John listened to the radio.

The signal wasn't as strong, and it would only get worse until the weather calmed down.

During the storms they'd lose a lot of information, but Jarvis didn't need it. He knew what was coming.

The information he didn't have was about those red cross ships, which John seemed to be focused on.

Jarvis knew why.

Yely.

Her mother was on one. They said something about the Savanah ship, and John was leery about telling Yely. Simply because the news announced they were hunkering down in Savanah.

With the comet landing so close to the shore, even if Yely's mother made it, hunkering down in Savanah with a tidal wave a thousand feet high, moving five hundred miles an hour, wasn't promising.

After listening to the news, Jarvis, along with John braved the weather and headed into town to deliver updates and figure out a way to communicate with Giles and Pastor Judy, because they weren't replying to John's radio call, and there were things they needed to know.

John conveyed his gut instinct that they weren't prepared enough.

The 'new' John, as Jarvis mentally called him. Six months earlier, John couldn't care less if the entire town froze, at least that was how John put it.

Now he worried. Was there a change? Or was John just putting on a tough front?

Jarvis met him because by chance he caught the podcast. Some guy was just ranting and raving. Sometimes it was funny, like the time he went on a rant about the woman whose cat pissed in the frozen food section of Kroger's. Other times it was serious.

Jarvis was hooked, him and fifteen thousand other listeners. But they struck up a friendship.

He believed in John and he wasn't wrong. Jarvis crossed an ocean to survive and if John wanted the town to live, Jarvis was going to help him.

Though it was now raining steadily, it was still drivable and because it was out front, Jarvis borrowed Megan's car for the short drive to the center.

The leadership was down to Giles and Pastor Judy with a couple men as the helping hands.

John pulled Judy and Giles aside.

"I know I told you things," John said. "But it's important that you listen to him."

"Your face looks much better," Judy told him.

"Yeah," Giles added. "I don't think you'll scar."

"Can we stop. Thank you," John said. "Now, Jarvis is smart. This is what he does. He's not as smart as the wife that left him, who is tucked away in a government shelter, but he's smart. Tell them what you told me."

"Tonight it starts. This is the last of the full sunlight we will have for months. The brightest it will get will be like just before dawn on a rainy day. So it'll be cold, but I must tell you, do not go out in the rain after it gets dark. It will be so cold, it'll feel like acid on your skin and it will burn it, too."

"But it's not hot," John added. "It's cold."

"Nothing is on the radio about it," replied Pastor Judy.

"Yeah maybe they don't know," John stated. "He does. Speaking of radio. You aren't communicating with me, I'm calling out and calling out. No reply."

"What channel?" asked Giles and looked down at his radio. "I'm on fourteen."

"I don't have channels, I have frequencies," John snapped.

"I can get you a radio," Giles said. "But they'll die if we don't charge them."

"Get me them all. I'll keep them charged." John waved about his hand. "It won't take much generator juice."

"And on that," Jarvis added. "Do you have enough to stay warm, I mean, fighting warm."

John snapped a quick look at him. "What the hell is fighting warm? And why is this the first I am hearing about this."

"It's the deep freeze," Jarvis said nervously. "I told you deep freeze, it'll start tomorrow sometime and hit hard and fast. It will take a few days to level out. No one can go out, they won't live. Fighting warm means keeping the means of heat going. Constantly. A week from now it will level out cold enough to venture out if dressed properly."

"Fighting warm." John grumbled. "Is that a real term."

Pastor Judy waved out her hands. "It doesn't matter. What I am hearing is we keep it hot and as steady as we can for what? Seven days."

"Five will be good."

Giles asked. "How will we know when it's over?"

"The radios," John replied. "Turn yours off to conserve power, we can determine what times you turn it on to check in."

"To be honest Mr. Hopper," said Giles. "I don't think even turning it off will conserve the battery life for five to seven days."

"We picked up generators. Use that," John barked.

Pastor Judy looked at Giles then back to John. "People took them. We have one. And barely enough gas to run that. We have things to burn to stay warm."

"Keep as many people as you can in one room." John said. "Body heat will generate heat."

Jarvis glanced at John. "What about the two-forty. You have three of them."

John grimaced.

Giles huffed a little in disbelief. "How many generators do you have?"

"Small ones," John replied. 'Enough. But none of them power too much. They won't run heat. Don't ask for too much gasoline, I don't have that to spare. But get in that squad car before the death rain hits and I'll give you one."

"Thank you, Mr. Hopper," said Giles, "And I promise to check in."

"And you have the means to burn without killing yourselves with carbon monoxide?" John asked. "Maybe move everyone over to the historical society. They have a fireplace."

"We're good at the center," Pastor Judy replied. 'We can't fit everyone at the historical society. Al, the firefighter, has us rigged. I think we're good."

"Each log burns about an hour and a half," John explained. "You need more than one log. I'll go through a dozen a day. What are you burning."

Pastor Judy. "Of everything, we're good on wood. We may have to rethink and revisit after the fighting warm."

"Okay, well stay in touch. I mean it," John wagged a finger. "Let's go Giles. Let's get you a generator."

Did they get all the information they should have? Just to make sure, Jarvis figured he'd stay behind, check everything out for himself, then head back.

They weren't like John, and Jarvis knew that their perception of 'good enough' may not have been.

He hoped it was, because at this stage in the game it was too late to do anything about it.

CHAPTER THIRTY-ONE – ON THE ROAD

A slight hiss of wind made its way somehow into the car. Anna wondered if there was a crack in the window somewhere.

It didn't matter. She held tighter to Steven's baby blanket, smelling it every so often.

She and Ben had made it nearly to Louisville Kentucky. A drive that typically would have taken just a little over four hours, took longer utilizing backroads.

What they didn't count on was nowhere to stop for gas.

They weren't the only ones that had that problem. All along the route they saw abandoned cars, people walking.

Anna didn't want to deal with anyone but her husband. She was swimming in pain, but when she saw the man and woman walking and carrying a toddler in the icy rain, they stopped and offered them a ride.

"There's a town three miles ahead," the woman said. "If you could drop us off there."

"Absolutely," Anna told them, and they got in the car.

They were shivering, the child was the only one that looked warm, they had shielded her from the weather.

It had gotten dangerously cold outside, Anna felt that when they opened the door and got inside.

The couple said very little, except expressing their gratitude for the ride.

Just as they said, three miles later, was a small town. It was mostly dark, a few glows of light.

Where would they go?

They didn't know, they were hoping for the best and were confident someone would take them in and shelter them. Anna and Ben dropped them off at bar and grill that had a light on, probably candles, they didn't know.

The couple begged Anna and Ben to join them, but they declined. They waited until they saw the couple make their way into the building, and they drove off.

In silence, that was the way the trip had gone.

Neither of them had much to say nor wanted to.

For the most part, in Anna's mind, they were just going. They could have stayed in that small town, been safe, maybe for a little while, but it wasn't time to stop.

The rain went from steady to slushy, to icy.

The roads were treacherous, the car slid a lot despite moving slowly.

So many cars were abandoned, off the road, it was desolate and it got to a point where they saw no one.

Everything was happening so fast. The sky lit up with violent lightning and the thunder was so loud, not even the closed windows of the car deafened it.

Finally, an hour after dropping off the family in that town, sixteen miles from Louisville, the car puttered and jolted on its last ounce of gas and drifted to a stop. Before the car completely died, Anna looked at the temperature reading on the rearview mirror.

Ben tried his hardest to maneuver the car to the side of the road.

It didn't matter.

No one was out there. They tried to hear something on the radio the whole ride, but there was nothing.

Alone, quiet, they sat in the car.

The rain sounded like steady, tiny pebbles hitting against the car windshield and with each passing minute, the car grew colder.

The windshield didn't take long to ice up.

"And here we are," Ben said, reaching over to grab Anna's hand.

"I'm not surprised," she replied. "I honestly didn't think we'd make it this far."

"Me either, but we tried."

"To do what?" Anna asked.

Ben paused. "To say we wanted to live. To try to live."

"We could have lived back home."

"Did you want to?"

Anna shook her head. "No."

"I saw the sign. Louisville isn't that far."

Anna smiled slightly. "It's fourteen miles. It might as well be a hundred. I saw the temperature before the car died."

"Minus fifteen."

Anna nodded. "And probably dropping fast."

"Yep. We could stay here, wait."

"For?"

Ben shrugged. "I don't know. Just wait. Or …" He exhaled. "We walk."

"We won't make it."

"We won't make it here either." Ben paused. "I heard freezing to death is the way to go."

"Says who?" Anna chuckled. "Anyone that did isn't around to say."

"Did we do the right thing, Anna?"

Anna knew what the question meant. They both knew, at least she did, they were on a one way ticket.

If it was a year from then, maybe she'd care, but she was in so much pain and torment from losing Steven, that she wanted to die. It didn't matter. Even though there was very little they could do, she blamed herself.

Clutching the baby blanket, she squeezed her husband's hand. "Let's go."

"Let's go."

He opened his door first and then Anna did.

She wasn't expecting the cold blast to hit her as hard as it

179

did. She had never felt anything so cold, she could barely take a breath.

The rain that hit her hurt.

It was like rocks of burning ice, and it took all of ten seconds for her hair to become frozen.

Barely had she gripped Ben's hand and she felt the pain, the pain of the cold.

Little did they know they were in the middle of the freeze that Jarvis had warned the town about. They had no clue.

Not that they cared.

Twenty feet from the car, both of them slowed down. Anna couldn't walk.

She was drenched and her clothes immediately froze. Rigid, hard, cold.

She could feel her fingers crackling and her lips instantly cracked when she moved them.

Anna tried to bring the blanket to her face but couldn't move her arm. Her heart pounded, and it was slow.

She was freezing to death.

It took everything she had to look at Ben, one last time, his face was white and frosted over. She tried to speak, but no words emerged. Even if they did, would he hear her over the storm noise.

Finally, she stopped. Maybe they made it ten minutes of walking, it seemed like forever with the pain and cold.

But the moment she stopped, she started to not feel the pain, a warm sensation took over her chest. She couldn't let go of her husband's hand, they frozen together and that was perfectly fine with her.

At the same time, both of them dropped to the ground.

Still holding hands.

Still holding that blanket.

Anna was able to lock eyes with her husband, trying desperately to tell him she loved him and everything was all right.

She saw it in his eyes and felt a sense of peace.

Theirs wasn't a journey to live, to survive.

It was a means to end their pain.

At that second, there was none. Just tiredness for Anna.

In reality their life was over when their son took his last breath, and now they took theirs.

CHAPTER THIRTY-TWO – DAY TEN

It wasn't the end of the entire world, it was the end of civilization as people knew it for seventy-five percent of the world.

That was what made it so difficult and frustrating for John. He planned on being part of that seventy-five percent and now he wasn't.

His world was definitely different and he knew once the worst weather had passed, and enough time had passed, he'd have to venture out. And if he and the others weren't self-reliant by then, could they reach out to the rest of the world?

Would they help?

Evacuation and rescue crews were promised, That was before their radios went silent and periodic newscasts went off the air, and it wasn't because something was wrong, they went off the air to conserve power because with the horrible weather, there was no way to get a signal through.

At least one that bounced off of towers and satellites.

His radio communication with town worked. Albeit a tad glitchy during the rain and wind. But enough to have check ins.

John knew it was a vast country that was affected, any rescue, if it came would be months if not years. But the rescue wasn't something John wanted to know. He wanted to hear about the Red cross ships that left the Bahamas and other islands in the Caribbean. He heard it was a successful evacuation even with the short time table,

Just where those survivors went was left out.

Two of the three red cross ships headed to Savannah made it.

Savana was a casualty of the comet and surely they knew that and moved those people out.

But where?

He needed the information because if there was a chance Yely's mother made it, he wanted to know.

That information was now in limbo.

Much like life.

They were in the 'Fighting Warm' stage. Right smack in the middle of it.

It wasn't that it was snowing, it was, but the wind was brutal, John had the foresight to close his shutters. Still, he could hear the wind howling and often a frigid breeze made it in.

It was the peak of it, Jarvis claimed. It would get better.

John would check in with Giles and it was always the same. "How's it going?" John would ask.

"You know, fighting to stay warm."

"I hear you."

But John's battles, he guessed weren't as bad as everyone else. He had a small home, a large working fireplace and even if the house wasn't toasty warm, they were nowhere near suffering from hyperthermia.

"Stay warm," John told him. "You know the drill. Hopefully by tomorrow the weather won't kill you in five minutes. I'll check in this evening."

They mainly stayed in the living room. John brought up his radio gear to the dining room, it was too cold below to stay there. He could have turned the cold room into a hot room but chose the fireplace. It worked. It did what it was designed to do.

He'd be lying to himself if he said he didn't worry about the roof. The way the wind whipped, he wasn't just worried about his antennae, he worried about the amount of snow and the roof caving in.

It was reinforced, that still didn't stop him from worrying.

Megan was making supper, using the last of the fresh meat that survived.

Ground chuck.

A pot of chili and it smelled wonderful. He was going to give Denver some whether his adopted parents liked it or not.

John often thought of Denver's mom, a young girl, traveling somewhere, trying to find an aunt to take her in around Cincinnati.

That was the only relative she mentioned to Jarvis. He had a picture of her. Her driver's license. He got that with a few other items in her purse. He wanted to have a photo to show Denver.

Poor girl.

Megan hollered that supper was done. And John walked from his radio. He paused by the dining room window and looked out. The snow had reached the window and still falling.

He estimated three feet. Thick snow, too. He couldn't see anything outside.

When he returned to the living room, he tossed another log on the fire.

"We don't need that yet," said Jarvis. "It's warm."

"Well, I think after a good meal, we may all pass out, better safe than sorry." John sat in his chair, looked down at Yely. "What do you have there?"

"It's a missing poster of Megan's son," Yely replied.

John immediately glanced up to Megan who was serving up the dinner. "You okay with that?"

"Yes. It's part of my life. It's part of my story." Megan handed John a bowl of chili.

"Wow, this smells wonderful." John sniffed it, pausing before taking a bite of the steaming substance. "Whatever is left …"

"I know." Megan handed a bowl to Yely. "Pack it and put it by the back bedroom window. It'll keep."

"Good girl." John then noticed something else. The brown envelope Yely had taken from her home. "Did you open it yet?"

"What?" Yely asked.

"The envelope."

Yely shook her head.

Jarvis asked. "What is it?"

"The last I spoke to my mother. She said to get it from her drawer," Yely explained. "She said I needed to know what was in it. That after someone sees it they'll know."

"Who?" asked Jarvis.

Yely shrugged. "I don't know. The connection was bad. I'm scared to open it."

Megan sat next to her. "It's only scary because you don't know. You'll open it when you're ready."

"The longer you wait," said Jarvis. "The more the suspense is going to make you afraid. It's probably nothing. And John what are you doing?" He asked as John creeped over.

Busted.

John winced. "I just blew on it to make it cool. Was giving some chili sauce to Denver."

Megan gasped. "Do not give the baby chili. Not while he still has baby food."

"Just think we need to break him in now, that's all. Get him ready for food that's not baby ready." John put the spoon in his own mouth and returned to his chair. "But I'll do as you say. For now."

"As I was saying," Jarvis continued. "Your mother wanted you to know what was in that envelope. Important enough to make it one of the last things she said to you."

"Maybe it's not that big of a deal," Megan added. "Maybe it's about some property your mother has."

Yely chuckled. "No. My mother didn't have anything."

Jarvis said, "Maybe it's about your father. Where to find him."

Megan asked. "Why would she keep it so secret? I mean putting an envelope in her drawer. That tells me it's something she was going to wait to tell Yely."

"It's not about my father," Yely said. "I don't know him."

"There you have it." Jarvis held out his hand.

The hard 'clank' of John's spoon drew everyone's attention. "Why does it matter? Leave the girl alone. She will open it when she's ready and who cares what's in there. It's a secret, obviously, that her mother kept. When she's ready, she'll share that story. Speaking of which, share your painful story, Jarvis."

"What?" Jarvis quipped, switching Denver to his other side so he could eat. "I don't have a story."

"You're all about uncovering secrets."

"I don't have a story."

"Bull," John barked. "Your big shot, smart wife left you and here you are."

"John!" Megan scolded. "That's his business."

"And that envelope is hers."

"No, no." Jarvis waved out his hand. "I'll share. It's entertainment. Right? I mean, I know everyone's story. Here's mine. I thought we were happy. She wasn't. She left me. I mean, we're still friends, but she left me."

"I feel that," John stated.

"Mine's not as tragic as yours," replied Jarvis.

"No one's is," said Megan.

"Not true." John looked at her. "Yours is tragic."

"Mines not," Jarvis said. "She left me."

"Why?" asked John. "Were you mean? Did she leave you for someone nicer? Smarter? Younger?'

"Dumber." Jarvis replied. "She left me because I was too smart and she wanted someone not on her level."

"Maybe he's not that dumb," said John.

"He's dumb."

"How dumb?" asked John.

"He thinks the earth is flat."

John shrugged. "That don't make him dumb, it just means he believed something different."

"He asked what Hitler's last name was," said Jarvis.

John paused then said, "Okay you have a point. How's that working out for her?"

"She's happy and they're in the shelter."

John was about to comment, when he heard it, he wasn't sure anyone else did, but John heard it loud and clear.

A crackle and hiss.

The radio.

Setting down his bowl of chili, John got up from his chair.

"John?" Megan questioned.

John kept walking to where he set up the radio. A crackle and hiss meant someone was trying to reach him.

When he got to the radio, it repeated, it wasn't coming from his main radio, it was coming from the walkie talkies he had to reach town. He heard Giles, "John."

Why was Giles calling out to him? He had just spoken to him two hours before, during the check in. It wasn't time for the last call of the night.

Maybe it was and John didn't realize it. He swept up the radio and depressed the button. "Hey Giles," he replied. "This is John. I read you. Over."

"John," Giles said and the radio glitched. "Help."

CHAPTER THIRTY-THREE – THE FALL

It happened as a sequence of events from what Giles witnessed.

Did they not keep it warm enough?

He believed they did. Blocking off as much as they could of the community center. People were cramped in one small area, but it helped with the heat that was provided by an old pot belly stove McGrugle Antiques had and Al, the fire chief fitted for safety

There were times during the Fighting Warm stage when Giles didn't wear a coat or blanket.

He was told by Jarvis and the last radio transmission they picked up that when it stopped snowing, things would settle. Temperatures would stabilize and the snow would firm up enough to move on.

The temperatures wouldn't kill instantly.

So when it happened, Giles tried not to panic, but he did. In his mind, he was counting down minutes.

Ten days in, how would they survive? They probably wouldn't.

It started as a whistling sound, then someone mentioned they could feel cold air coming from somewhere.

Then just over in the far corner a dusting of snow started to seep through.

"Kill the potbelly," Al ordered. "We have to move. Everyone has to move."

"Why?" Pastor Judy asked.

"Listen." Al pointed up. "Everyone shut up!" he shouted then lowered his voice. "Listen."

The creak and cracking. Giles finally heard it.

Al walked across to the other side of the center then returned, speaking calmly, in a raised voice, "Everyone, grab your stuff. We have to move to the other side. Quickly now."

Gile heard it and felt that warning, he rushed over with Pastor Judy to the potbelly stove. Should they put it out? How would they move it?

They were there. Right there, both of them. So close to the potbelly, the heat was intense.

Giles wanted to yell out for Al, asking him how to move the potbelly or kill it as he said.

But people were grabbing their things, they were listening.

Now the crackling was louder and more snow filtered through.

Just about the point where people started to move, and Giles wondered if the chaos and rush to go could have been a slower thing ... it happened,

It happened fast.

In a snap of a finger, it came down hard and fast

Save for a tiny section, the roof of the entire corner of that community center came down. The portion where they stayed, they portion they had kept warm.

The screams were brief because when the roof came down so did the three or four feet of snow that was there on top, weighing it down.

Snow they couldn't remove because the temperatures would kill them.

Now the temperatures were in.

Was it luck? No. Torture.

Giles was standing on one side of the potbelly, pastor Judy on the other side. They watched it just drop, like a rock and a billowing cloud of cold billowed out as if it were a snow explosion. The force of which knocked Giles back against the wall near where the rigged Potbelly was positioned, his arm hit it and instantly it sizzled and burned. He felt it, but not for long.

He tried to get up but something was on his leg. He wasn't in pain, but he couldn't move.

He couldn't see anything, hear anything. A wet sharpness hit his face for a few seconds. Snow against his face.

It came from above, blowing his way.

Eventually, he could see the flickering emergency light above his head, he gave enough light in the darkness for him to see with every flicker of the light, just the white of the snow.

It wasn't debris that had him pinned it was snow, from his thighs down.

Giles tried to move, he couldn't. It was heavy.

He closed his eyes, thought about his situation, and tried again to move his legs.

Nothing.

Then he heard Al's voice, slightly in the distance, muffled.

"Grab what you can," Al said. "Quickly now. We're headed to the historical society. I have wood there. Go. Go. Go."

Wait, Giles thought, *Wait.*

He could hear them moving, they sounded so far away. Was the snow that much of a sound proofing?

"No," Giles weakly called out. "Help. Help!"

He believed he was shouting, he knew he was shouting, yet it sounded deadening, as if he were in some room jammed packed with foam, blocking all noise.

"Help! Don't leave!" he called out.

It was the scariest thing.

Voices there, muffled, then getting softer, fading, fading …. silence.

Giles closed his eyes. He tried to move again. He reached down to grab whatever pinned him and he felt the snow, like a block on top of him,

A few deep breaths and he called out. "Can anyone hear me? Anyone?"

No one responded.

"Is anyone here?"

After a second, he heard Pastor Judy's voice. "I am. Giles. I am."

She was close.

"Are you okay?" he asked.

"I'm not hurt. Just stuck. The snow is heavy."

"I know. They left."

"I heard."

"Anyone else?" Giles shouted. "Anyone else alive?"

No response.

It was strange, his legs felt heavy and yet, trapped beneath the snow, he wasn't cold. That was when he realized the potbelly was still going.

How long would it last?

Enough warmth to keep them alive, but for how long? Would Al realize there were others alive or did he assume they were all dead.

Pastor Judy whimpered not in pain, but in defeat. "I guess this is it. I don't hear anyone."

"Some got out," Giles said. "Al and some of the others got out."

"It's still in that time frame where we can freeze."

"It's supposed to be a peaceful death," Giles said.

"I doubt that."

"Me, too."

"Once the stove stops," Pastor Judy said, "We're done."

"Maybe they'll come back before then."

The potbelly was not only a saving grace it was also a curse. It would keep them alive long enough to agonize over what was happening.

It wouldn't stay warm long enough.

Maybe it would melt the snow enough for him to move.

To get help. But what help was out there?

Then it dawned on him ... John.

"Can you move?" asked Giles.

"No. It's like a thousand pounds on my legs."

"Me, too. Hold on." He maneuvered his hands down to his waist.

"What are you doing?"

"Please work, please work." His fingers felt the radio on his hip, only a little snow was covering that. Giles was able to grab it.

"Giles?"

"The radio." Giles grunted. "I got it. I got it."

Another whimper came from Judy, this one sounded different, not in pain or sorrow, but relieved. "John."

"John."

"Giles wait."

"What?" he asked.

"The weather is too deadly."

"We have to try." He brought the radio up to his face and turned it on. It hissed. "John." He winced. "John come in." He paused, then pressed the button again. "John please, are you there. John."

Static, hiss, cracking.

"Hey Giles. This--John. I read you. Over."

Giles joyfully exhaled with almost a laugh. "John. We need help."

"Repeat. You need help?" John spoke.

"When you can get here, if you can. The roof collapsed."

"Repeat that, Giles, you're breaking up."

"If you can help. Please."

Static.

"John."

Nothing but a rush of static came over the speaker, then silence.

"He heard the call," said Judy. "He heard it."

"Yeah." Giles replied. "But can he do anything?"

She said something, Giles wasn't sure what it was. He was too preoccupied with thoughts of what could happen.

The potbelly stove would keep going for a little bit more, a few hours at tops, but after that, if John didn't come, then it was over.

The snow fell steadily, the frigid winds cut through the warmth of the close potbelly stove.

Every minute that passed it got colder, wetter.

Giles knew that in a few hours when the last of the wood burned out of the stove, not only would it get too cold to survive, but he would be buried beneath the snow that fell steadily on him.

CHAPTER THIRTY-FOUR – DAY ELEVEN

"John, stop," Jarvis told him, physically blocking John from putting on his artic gear. "Please."

John had pulled everything out, placed it by the front door. It was so new he was ripping off tags.

"They need help. I'm going to help," John said.

Jarvis shook his head with a huff of breath. "Six months you didn't care who else survived, now you're all about saving everyone."

"That's because six months ago, I thought it was a joke. This buying all this survival stuff was a game, a way to spend the money I had no one to leave to. I didn't think it was happening Jarvis. It is. They need help."

"I get that. I know. I heard. We put the call out to the help channel."

"They aren't coming, we're it," John was adamant.

"I know. But it's also twenty below. Not counting the windshear and it's snowing."

"I spent a lot of money on arctic gear. You have gear, too, put it on."

"We don't know if it will work," Jarvis said. "These elements are untested."

"No they aren't. These are arctic conditions. Besides, Dannis Quaid did it."

This caused Jarvis to pause and stammer. "What?"

"Dennis Quaid. Ice age, walked from Washington Dc to New

York City to save his son."

"Are we talking about a movie?" Jarvis asked.

"Yeah, an old one, but he did it."

"It was a movie!"

"I'm sure they researched. Now gear up or I'll make Megan gear up."

"Can we wait? Just until morning. It's eight hours from now," Jarvis pleaded.

"They'll be dead."

"So will we."

John peeked out the small open window space next to the front door. One of the few windows without shutters.

He saw nothing.

Blackness.

Occasionally he'd hear the snow hit the window, but it was so dark, he couldn't see.

As much as he hated to admit it, they had to wait. They couldn't see to walk there and how could they see to rescue anyone.

He didn't know if Giles could hear him, but he called out on the walkie talkie.

"Giles, I'm coming, but I have to wait until I can see."

Static.

"We're holding on," Giles said. "Still have some shelter. The pot—still going. When you can. Help."

"I will."

"Maybe Al will be back."

His words were smothered with static, but John heard it.

Al was the fire chief of the volunteer fire force. If Giles was hoping he would come back then Al had left.

Why? Was it to help people, get them to safety?

With the glitches and static it was hard for John to piece together exactly what happened. All he knew was that Giles wouldn't call for help if he didn't need it, and Giles wouldn't have radioed if he really believed Al would come back.

There was nothing John could do and he felt helpless.

His gear was ready and John was, too, he just had to wait.

Jarvis rested up and John stayed by the door. It was cold, but he didn't want to waste a second of time once it got light out. Even though daylight was still dark, he could see enough to move, to know what he was up against.

John used those hours to pack an emergency kit. Supplies, mylar blankets, food and water. He ventured into the basement to find that old World War One canvass stretcher he bought off an auction site long before he heard about the comet.

It was six dollars and John happened across it. It was worn, didn't look sturdy, was over a hundred years old, but a 'neat' thing to have. He put it somewhere, and it passed the time looking for it.

When he uncovered it, his fingers were cold. The stretcher was heavier than he remembered and he carried it up the stairs, placing it by the front door next to his gear and backpack.

Then John waited. He waited for a hint of light. When it arrived, be it still dark, he summoned Jarvis and they geared up.

John knew it was light enough when he saw how much snow was on his porch. The reason he couldn't see anything was because the snow had to be at least four feet high.

It partially covered every window on the first floor.

He knew one thing, they wouldn't be able to open the front door.

That's when he realized the kitchen door could be open. If the awning was still standing, they could get out that way.

What were the chances?

Of course, that awning was erected long before John moved in and was made of a product long since forgotten about. It was from the sixties. Hard aluminum. And sure enough, when John looked out only a portion of the awning had fallen.

The kitchen door would open to about two feet of snow that blew in.

Once fully in gear they went out that way, pushing the screen enough to move the snow and slip out.

John didn't know what to expect nor did he know how well

his gear would keep them warm. He was covered from head to toe, including his face and protective glasses.

He didn't feel the cold, not drastically and that was a good sign.

John carried the backpack and Jarvis carried the stretcher. He felt like that movie actor when they got to the wall of snow. Jarvis clawed his way out, climbing to the top of the four foot mound. He lifted John's backpack then held his hand out to John.

John knew the second that he saw the backpack resting on the snow that it was firm and they wouldn't sink in.

Climbing up that mound with Jarvis' assistance reminded John he wasn't a young man. He got winded, but when he reached the top and caught his breath, he felt rejuvenated.

He didn't feel the cold in his body, just a bit on his face. He figured that would change during the half mile walk to town. The wind was fierce, pushing them back. The weight of what he carried helped his footing, but they had to be careful. Every once and a while, they would sink some, where the snow wasn't quite hard. They didn't talk much on the walk, it was better that way. He had seen deeper snow in his lifetime. This snow was three or four feet. At the moment it was blowing and causing drifts.

Three or feet of snow before the comet was plowable, people shoveled. This was heavy and hard and no sun or heat was going to appear to warm it up and melt it.

The houses on his street looked barren, dark and empty. They were. No glow of lights or smoke from fires burning.

In fact, the only smoke he could make out was from his house.

John hoped as they neared town, he could see something, anything to indicate they were keeping warm.

All John could pick up from the broken radio call was that they needed help. He didn't know the measure of or what kind of help they needed, but it had to be bad if Giles was calling and asking John to take the chance.

They moved slowly, but made good time, and that was when John saw just a hint of thin smoke lifting to the gray sky. He sighed out in relief but it wasn't a lot of smoke, as they turned the bend, he knew it wasn't coming from the community center, because John saw the community center.

He saw the reason for the call for help.

From where he stopped cold in his tracks, he saw the community center had collapsed.

The heavy snow on the roof seemed to bury the one side and it appeared that fresh snow had blown and caused a drift, and everything was frosted over.

Any source of heat they had was long since extinguished and any hope John had of finding people alive, collapsed within John, just like that roof.

Still, both he and Jarvis walked to the center.

CHAPTER THIRTY-FIVE – WHEN HOPE FAILS

Jarvis could have gone anywhere.

When he booked his flight long before the world knew of the comet, he could have gone anywhere, he had thought about Arizona.

Temperature wise it would never really see the snow, not like he was seeing in West Virginia. It would be cold, but not as cold, and snowy, but certainly not for as long.

However, his ex-wife cautioned against it.

"You aren't meant to live in a Mad Max world," she told him. "And Arizona, Nevada, Mexico, that is what it will be like. The strongest survive. Not the smartest."

She told him to find a place that was habitable. Though the severity of the mini ice age would last three hundred days, they were hopeful the federal government would start to distribute aid long before that.

So, Jarvis decided to go to John.

A man he befriended after listening to his radio show. It was a man bitching about everything, saying what most people really wanted to say.

He had been listening to John, AKA Reed before the comet was confirmed.

John was a trusted friend even before he started speaking to him. He was funny, wise, and when Jarvis told him about the impending apocalypse, John sunk all his money into surviving.

Jarvis felt somewhat responsible for John's financial losses. What if Jarvis was wrong? What if his ex-wife was wrong about Ripley.

She was.

But Jarvis wasn't about what was needed to survive.

John had it all and more. However, in spite of all that, Jarvis kind of wished he picked Arizona and rolled the dice on a Mad Maxx life.

Ripley looked like something out of a time forgotten picture.

The weather was not kind. Jarvis didn't know what it looked like before, but it certainly was desolate.

And the arctic wear. Sure, he wasn't freezing, but it was cold. He didn't feel like the actor Dennis Quad, Quid, whatever his name was, trudging through a movie apocalypse.

Jarvis felt defeated and cold. Especially when he saw the center.

"Why are we trying?" Jarvis asked. "John, why are we going there?"

Maybe John didn't hear him through the sound of the wind. He followed John to the community center, wanting to stop him. There was no way anyone was alive. Maybe they got out. After all, there was some smoke coming from somewhere.

Jarvis didn't want to go closer, he knew what he'd see.

In fact, he did.

Bodies.

Protruding from the snow were hands, feet, and faces. The faces were white with frost, frozen over with eyes wide open, some bloody. The color of blood bright like a color replacement in photoshop.

Why had they gone in there.

It was heart wrenching.

John walked slowly and carefully looking down and around.

"John, please," Jarvis called. "John."

Then John picked up the pace, heading somewhere, deeper into the fallen center.

Or rather through the front door. What was he thinking?

John was careful where he stepped. He knew roughly ninety people were in that center and they were all walled in a section in the back third of the community gymnasium. Walled in with old bleachers to keep in the warmth.

John saw the bleachers, some crushed and toppled over. Most of all, he saw the bodies.

It wasn't so much the ones buried in the snow from the collapse, it was those at the edge of it that tried to crawl out.

They didn't last at all.

Those were the faces he checked carefully.

The others it was obvious they died nearly instantly from the collapse, but he knew Giles didn't. He lived and was alive enough to make the call for help. John swore he also used the word, 'We'.

Meaning he wasn't alone in survival.

Where? Where would he call from. Giles wasn't one of the ones outside. That was when John got the idea to go into the center, maybe he was in there.

"John!" Jarvis called out.

Thinking, *Damn it, doesn't he know to conserve his breath*? John spun around and waited until Jarvis was close. "What?"

"What are you doing?"

"Finding Giles. He radioed, he survived this initially."

"Maybe he's over there." Jarvis pointed. "There's smoke. Not a lot. His radio probably died and he's there. Let's go check there."

"Here first."

They walked inside the double doors, the linoleum floors were like an ice rink, the walls were iced over, luckily the doors to where everyone was staying weren't far down the hall.

It took a bit of nudging, but John got the doors open.

It took his breath away seeing it from the inside.

It didn't take long for the snow to blow in through the open roof leaving a layer on the floor of the gymnasium giving him some traction.

John stepped further inside, looking at the destruction. His eyes shifted left to right as he walked slowly. Everything was still there. The roof collapsed, giving no one time to get what they needed. He could see the cases of water, the food. Snow covered and iced, but their rations remained.

"John, he's not here."

John stopped as he said that, almost believing Jarvis was right until he saw. There was a small pocket to John's left, on the interior wall of the gym, the roof collapsed, but it formed a triangle. Not big, but it was an opening and John hurried there.

The tipped bleacher, white with snow, balanced a part of that wall.

When John arrived at that triangle opening, it was black, even darker than outside.

He pulled out his flashlight lifting a foot to step through.

"Careful John, it's not stable."

"It collapsed eight hours ago." He shone the light on the bleacher. "I doubt it's going to come down this minute."

Realizing he wasn't fitting through with that emergency backpack on his back, he lifted it off to set it to the side, when he did, the beam of his light entered that opening and John saw him.

Giles.

CHAPTER THIRTY-султанSIX – FREEZE

There were three of them, all shielded from the snow but not the cold. At least for several hours. They were near the potbelly stove when everything went down. John didn't understand why they were so close, but it saved their lives … at least for a little while.

Pastor Judy, Giles Matthews, and a man John knew from church as Roger the Usher.

All three of them were pinned under a section of roof. Roger had the worst, the roof wasn't just on his legs, it was on his chest, probably making it hard to breathe. Like Giles, he was on his back. Roger was farthest away from the stove, his face had ice on it across his eyelids, nose and mouth. His skin white with a hint of blue. The flashlight beam reflected the crystallization.

Pastor Judy was on her side, twisted some. Her hand was distorted as she reached up to try to touch Giles. She wasn't as iced over, but her skin was darker and her eyes wide and black.

Giles looked like he survived the longest. He still had some color, although he was turning blue from the cold and his lips were blue.

His eyes were closed, and just to be sure, John removed his fastened glove and reached down for a pulse.

His skin was cool to touch and he couldn't feel anything. He retracted his hand and stood upright.

Nearly scaring him to death, John stumbled back in shock when Giles' eyes opened and he gasped out the word, "John."

* * *

"He can't stay here!" Al, the firefighter, blasted.

John ignored him. He didn't have time for it. It took almost an hour to move that piece of ceiling, pull out Giles and drag him to the stretcher.

His legs didn't look broken, but it was hard to tell, they had to worry about injuries later, they needed to get him warm.

They rolled him on top of the stretcher, wrapping him in a mylar blanket as they did so, tucked several of those 'Shake them' warming packs around his body, and secured him across his chest and legs with rope from the backpack.

All the while Jarvis kept repeating that he couldn't believe Giles was alive.

John honestly didn't know for how long.

It was such a rush of energy and adrenaline, John didn't feel cold. The hardest part of carrying Giles was getting him out of that gym, once they hit outside, they trudged through the snow right to the historical society building.

That was where the smoke came from.

It was a small log cabin building that people used to make fun of, joking that it was small so Ripley probably didn't have a lot of history.

They didn't listen to John, had they done so, they would have prepped the historical building as a just in case. Instead, the survivors broke in, the door jam was busted. After making it up the couple steps of the porch with Giles, it took only a push to get in and move the small barricade holding that door closed.

When they did, John was immediately met with the barrel of a rifle. Al held it on him.

"Put it down. It's John Hopper, I have Sergeant Matthews." John led the way to the right side of the room where the fireplace was located.

The fire didn't roar, it was minimal, but there were a dozen people in that room including Al.

John could feel the warmth. It wasn't toasty but it was noticeably warmer.

The furniture was broken and piled in a corner, that was their firewood.

"Let's bring him close to the fire," John told Jarvis.

"John!" Al screamed. "He can't be here. I don't have the resources."

"He doesn't need your resources, he needs the heat," John barked back as they set the stretcher down by the fire.

"He can't stay."

"Shut your damn mouth, Al. You obviously left him to die."

"No." Al shook his head. "I led these people to live."

"Well good on you for being the Moses of the apocalypse." John took off his gloves, then face covering. "Now be the Jesus of the apocalypse and help me save him."

Someone, a woman, gasped out, "Blasphemy. Pastor Judy would …"

"Pastor Judy is dead," John told the woman. "They were alive when the roof collapsed. She's dead now. Maybe someone should have gone back."

Al defended. "It was the middle of the night."

John waved him off and looked at Jarvis. "What do you think?"

"I'm not a doctor," Jarvis said.

John looked around. Maybe Doctor Parch was there. He wasn't and John sat on the floor next to Giles. "Giles, come on. I need you to stay awake."

Giles opened his eyes.

"We're trying to warm you. As soon as we do and get some color back, we'll lug you back to my house."

"I'm not cold," Giles weakly replied.

"Of course you're not," John said. "You're pretty close to death."

Jarvis added. "But we're gonna try to stop that."

John gazed up at Al. "You have some medical training. Help."

"You broke in."

"Oh, stop. Help this man. What can we do."

Al huffed and set down the rifle, crouching by Giles. "He's hypothermic."

"No shit."

"John, he's not gonna make it. I can barely find a pulse. The only choice we have is to try to warm him up, get his heart rate up, breathing steady."

"And then?" John asked.

"If we can get him warm, get his heartrate up, then ... we can address whatever else there is wrong with him," said Al. "I'm not a doctor."

"Can I move him to my place?" John questioned.

"Yes. But not yet," Al replied. "You move him too soon it can reverse any good you do. You have to warm him and wait." He sounded irritated, and acted it, walking away as if that room was huge.

John nodded and looked at Jarvis. "One of us needs to go back to my house to let the ladies know what's going on. I know Yely, if she doesn't hear from us soon, she'll come."

"I'll go," said Jarvis. He grabbed his own face mask and gloves to place back on. "I'll be back."

"I'll wait here."

Jarvis stood, looked around then headed to the door.

John focused on Giles. The packs still felt warm and he moved them around. "Come on. Hang in there." He could feel everyone looking at him, staring, watching.

No one said anything.

Feeling strangely uncomfortable, John not only wanted Giles to warm up, he wanted Jarvis to not be gone that long.

Al walked back over. "John. We'll need water."

"There's three feet of snow."

"Are you serious?" Al snapped. "You want us to drink that?"

"If you get desperate enough you will. There's three feet. You can walk in that. We did. The mega pharmacy is down the road. Supplies are still there. You realize the majority of the town's rations are still at the center, right?" John stated. "You have supplies there. Send people over. They may be frozen, but they'll thaw. If there's something you need that you can't find, I'll try to help you out."

"Can you take in twelve people?"

John just stared at him. He didn't answer.

"That's what I thought," Al replied. "You wanna help You'll see what you can do. That's what you say, empty words."

"Now, hold on there," John waved out his hand. "That's a tall ask. Twelve people. I don't have the supplies for twelve people. I'm stretching it with what I have."

"And we're not?"

"There were enough supplies, albeit meager for ninety people. There's a dozen of you," John argued. "You'll be fine."

"You think we look fine?" Al waved out his arm, pointing to the people.

"About as fine as we do at my place."

Al huffed a laugh. "This was not set up for survival. We all know you are."

"You don't know that."

"Please," Al scoffed. "We need help."

"Why didn't you go back to see if anyone back there needed help?"

"I saw it go down. I thought they were dead. I saw the roof ready to go. I didn't know how much time we had, I just started gathering people to get out, we were all that got out. It was too dark to go back." He threw out his hand. "Why am I defending my actions to you."

"You don't have to."

"You really won't take us in?'

"I can't."

"You won't."

John said nothing.

"You know what, John, you really are what everyone says."

"And what might that be?" John focused on Giles.

"A bitter old man, who cares about no one because no one

cares about him."

"Maybe so."

John thought that was the end of it, until he heard the sound of the pump action of the rifle. Slowly he looked up to see it pointing at him. "Put that down."

"Get out."

"Al …"

"Get out," Al said stronger. "Take your friend and go now. You won't help us, we won't help you."

"You have got to be shitting me."

Al lowered the rifle to Giles. "You gonna let us in now?"

"No."

"Then you leave. I won't hesitate to shoot. He's dead anyhow. He's already on the stretcher …"

"When Jarvis gets back, I'll go."

"No, you'll go now. I mean it, John, I'll shoot. Get out."

At that minute, John knew Al wasn't joking. His finger rested on that trigger and John worried that anything could cause him to accidentally shoot.

"Okay. All right." John lifted his hat and mask, placing them on. He double checked the blanket and the ropes they had on Giles, and then he stood. Reaching down for his backpack, Al poked John with the rifle, then used it to push his arm away.

"That stays with us."

Murmuring, "Asshole," John bent down grabbing the handles of the stretch and lifted.

It was heavy and John could barely get a good grip, let alone walk backwards, dragging Giles' that small distance to the door. At least Giles didn't slide off.

Even though it was difficult, John didn't want Al to see how hard it was nor was he going to beg for his life or Giles.

He made it to the door and once he pulled Giles over the threshold, the door slammed.

John took a breath and set Giles' down near the two steps to the porch.

He had to take a moment, he had to think about how he

was going to do it. He looked outward to the horrific winter wonderland. It was snowing again. He could stand there and wait for Jarvis, but he stood a chance of being shot. Going anywhere else wouldn't be wise. Jarvis wouldn't find them. The snow would cover their tracks.

"Think, John, think," he said out loud. It wouldn't have been so bad if Jarvis was there to help carry the half of mile back to the house.

When he thought of Jarvis helping to carry Giles, he remembered Jarvis carrying the stretcher.

The stretch was old, it folded in half for storage and the sides snapped in place when opened. There was a strap for carrying. Jarvis used to toss it on his shoulder.

Stepping off that porch, John didn't have to bend down to look under the stretcher beneath Giles' head. John saw it.

He had an idea. Hopefully it would work.

After unzipping his snow suit, he undid his belt and pulled it out.

He looped it through the strap, then through the buckle and pulled it tight.

"Yeah, that might do it." John zipped up again, then looked down to Giles. "I'm covering your face. You're not dead. Just keeping you covered."

Giles blinked, looking up to John.

He covered his face with a blanket. "Good boy." Then lifting his shoulder as he took a deep breath, John grabbed his belt. "Hang on, it'll be bumpy."

Holding that belt and pulling, John slowly stepped forward, inching until he felt the stretcher go down the first step, then the second. He glanced back to make sure Giles was still attached and hadn't fallen off. Then John, pulling the stretcher, started walking.

It moved easier on the snow, but it was just the beginning of a long walk.

It wouldn't be easy for long.

CHAPTER THIRTY-SEVEN – GOOD FRIENDS

Yely tried to focus on baby Denver. He sat in a baby seat while she dangled items to keep his attention. "An hour and twenty-seven minutes," she said.

"I know," replied Megan, as she crocheted a blue blanket.

"It doesn't take that long to walk into town."

"They're helping people."

"Maybe they need help."

"They don't," said Megan.

"If they do. We need to set a time."

"For?" Megan asked.

"When I go after them."

Megan set down her work. "You are not going after them."

"One of us has to."

"Yely, it's negative ten out there, snowing and who knows what the windshear is."

"Well, the people of Yakutsk, Russia, deal with an average temperature in the winter of almost negative thirty," Yely said. "Daily. Daily. And there are three hundred thousand people that live there and deal with it. I'm pretty sure if I put on my sled riding stuff I'll be fine for a half hour. I can be Yakutskian for today."

"If that is even a term." Megan tilted her head. "You're a vat of knowledge. How did you know?"

"John. He told me a bunch of places, I remembered that one because it had a lot of people. Please let me go. I can do this."

"Do you have your snow suit?" Megan asked.

Yely laughed.

"What is so funny?"

"It's not a snow suit. It's a sled riding suit."

"Is it one piece? Then it's a snow suit. And you layer, okay?"

"Okay." Yely jumped up.

"Where are you going?"

"To get my layers and sled suit. Good thing John made me bring that over."

"Good thing. Yely?"

Yely stopped. "Yeah."

Megan nodded. "Your envelope is on the floor, you might not want to leave it there."

"Oh, yeah, sorry. I was thinking about opening it." she hurried back in, grabbed the brown envelope, put it on the bookshelf and darted back out. Her sled suit was in a box in the dining room closet. John made her put all the pieces together so she wasn't looking for a glove. He gave her sun goggles, too.

Her extra clothes were in a bag on the floor.

She figured a couple of shirts, a pair of sweatpants and the suit would be good enough. It would be hard to move and she'd feel like that kid in the old Christmas movie, but she'd be warm enough.

Yely didn't want to put the sled suit, hat and gloves on until she was ready to walk out. She knew if she was too over heated before leaving, it would defeat the purpose.

After about fifteen minutes of pacing, Megan finally told her to go. Then Megan thought of something not even John and Jarvis did.

Take a radio.

John had four of the ones from the police station and they were still there.

She tested it to make sure Megan heard her, then Yely went

into the kitchen to get ready.

At the point, she was nearly done, in between loud talking back and forth with Megan, making promises to be careful, she heard it.

A shuffling outside.

She was relieved, yet a part of her was disappointed she couldn't go out.

All she had left to do was to pull down the face covering, and put on her goggles and gloves.

Boots on, Yely was ready to unzip when she saw Jarvis. He wasn't coming in, it was then, Yely worried.

Hurriedly, she pulled down her facemask and opened the door only wide enough to come out.

"I'm not coming in," Jarvis said. "Why are you dressed for going out?"

"I was coming to find you."

"I came back so you wouldn't. John is with Giles, he's in bad shape, we're trying to warm him up. Long story. We'll fill you in when we get back, I have to run back now."

"I'm coming with you." Yely pulled the door closed.

"John specifically wanted me to come back here and stop you, because he knows you."

"Then he knows I won't listen. Let me come, please. Megan gave me permission. You guys might need help."

Jarvis looked at her for a moment. "An extra set of hands will be good. You look ready. All right. Let's go."

"Yes." Yely opened the door, just a creak, popped her head in and yelled. "I'm leaving. Be back soon."

Then she closed the door.

Of course, she was worried about Giles, but he was with John and there was no one better, in her mind, that he could be with.

* * *

"Taking a break," John said weakly. He stopped moving, but

didn't let go of the stretcher. "How about that? Lloyd Peterson's house. Eight blocks from my place. We should count down."

He breathed heavily, he was just glad that pulling Giles took his mind off of the cold.

"Bet you're wondering, how I know it's eight blocks. Well, Lloyd died shortly after I moved to town. You probably don't remember Lloyd. You had to be twelve or thirteen when I moved here twenty years ago. Time to get going." After a deep breath, John started walking again. "Anyhow … his widow, Patsy, if you can believe it, had the hots for me. Yeah."

John trudged on.

"I probably shouldn't be talking. It's making me winded."

"Then …. don't."

John paused and looked down. "Look at you, still hanging on."

"Sixteen."

"What?" John walked again.

"I was … sixteen. Twenty … years ago."

"You look good for thirty-six. Me? I was a mess. Look almost as old as I do now. Which makes no sense for Patsy having the hots for me," John said. "She used to say we," he gave his voice a higher tone. "We only live eight blocks from each other." He returned to talking normally. "That's how I knew it was eight blocks."

It was another block and Giles spoke up. "Am I blind? I can't see."

"The blanket is over your face. Eleven blocks. Eleven blocks."

What John didn't verbalize was how tired he was. Pulling Giles was harder by the second. Moving in the snow made him feel like he was trying to run in a dream.

Trudging. Trudging. He lost count of how far he walked, all the houses looked the same. Snow covered, partially buried.

"Getting close," John announced, his words and legs slowing down.

"Thank you."

"I don't know how you're alive. But you are." John paused,

then continued. "You're one tough son of a bitch." He drew in a breath and it didn't sink in his lungs. John's legs felt like rubber, barely able to move. "Sorry, Giles. I'm not," his words slowed down. "As tough as you."

On his last words, the belt he used to pull Giles slipped from his hands. The stretcher dropped into the snow and John fell to his knees to take a break. When he did, he sunk into the snow, arms and all, he couldn't move. He didn't teeter forward or back, just legs dug deep into the snow, arms to the elbows, he then lowered his head.

"It's not that cold," Yely said as they struggled through the deep snow. Some steps easy across the hardened white surface and sometimes, they just sank "The snow makes it hard to see."

"I can see you," Jarvis said. "The world can see you."

"What do you mean?"

"That's an awfully bright pink snow suit."

"It's a sled suit," Yely defended. "My mom got it for me a couple years ago."

"Bet your friends had a lot to say about it when you went sledding."

"I didn't have any friends."

That made Jarvis pause. "Yely, I'm sorry. No friends?"

She shook her head. "Not really. John."

"John can't be considered a friend, he's old."

"No, Jarvis ..." she pointed outward. "John."

With a quick jolt of his head, Jarvis looked outward, the snow made him hard to see, not like he was wearing something like Yely. But he did see him along with the stretcher.

He tried his best to run, it was difficult.

"Please don't be dead, please don't be dead," he pleaded out loud.

If John wasn't, surely Giles was.

How long were they out there? Why did they leave the

historical building.

"John," Jarvis called out as he was close.

"Don't," John replied, his head still down. "This is a deep soft spot. You don't want to get stuck like me."

"Okay. Okay." Jarvis held up his hands. "Are you seeing something, John? Are you hurt? Your head is down."

"I was trying to figure out where I was and what I fell into for so long, my head stuck. I think. I also think I stepped into that obnoxious pond of the Whitners. Just walk carefully."

"You're trapped in ice?" Jarvis asked.

"No."

"You said the pond."

John grunted. "The hole for their pond. They didn't fill it yet."

Jarvis turned to Yely. "Yely, you barely weigh a hundred pounds. See if you can get his head up. If you sink, I'll get you."

"Yely!" John said her name hard. "I sent you back to make sure she didn't come."

"Well, good thing she did."

"I can do it," Yely said, but she didn't move straight. She moved to the right. "I don't know the Whitners, but I know the pond." She stopped. "Is Giles dead? He's covered."

Muffled and weak, Giles responded. "No."

"Oh, good."

"Can you get his arms out Yely?" Jarvis asked. "If we can get his arms out we can pull him."

Six feet from John, Yely did a belly crawl to him, sliding across the snow.

"Hey, John."

"Hey, Yely can you lift my head."

Yely snickered.

"What's funny?"

"Nothing. You look like a bug with your face covered and those black goggles on." She reached under his chin and lifted his head. It was stiff and heavy for her, that and John, groaned out, 'ow-ow-ow' the whole time. "There."

"What in God's name are you wearing? You say I look like a

bug? You look like Barney the Dinosaur."

"He's purple, I'm pink." She started moving snow from around his arm. "Can you wiggle while I do this."

"My arm?"

"Yes."

She removed handfuls of snow, one after another until John's right arm was free, then she went to the other side and he was able to help a little until the other one was free.

John let out an audible sigh of relief. "Thank you."

Face to face, Yely asked him quietly. "How are you?"

"Tired, sore, I feel beat up," John replied just as quiet.

"We'll get you out. Extend your arms as best as you can." Yely inched back until she reached his hands. She looked over her shoulder. "Come on Jarvis, on your stomach. We'll get him out. It shouldn't cave."

"It caved on John, how about I pull your legs and you hold on."

"That's silly, because you'll have to pull us both." Jarvis nodded, got down and crawled close. "Okay, I'll take one arm, you take the other, and John ... you try as we pull. Got it."

"Got it." Then John turned his head to Yely. "Thank you."

"I wish I could see you smiling.," Yely said. "I know you are."

"Have to keep my face safe. Unlike cowboy cop back there with freezer burn."

"I heard that," said Giles.

"How the hell is he still alive?" John shook his head.

"Okay, ready," said Jarvis. "Pull."

It took a lot of tries, more than likely the weight and heat from their bodies softened the snow enough for John to get leverage while they pulled.

But he was freed after spending an hour stuck in a snow pit with temperatures and windshield dipping far below zero.

Jarvis took over the stretch, using the John method of tugging him with the belt.

But he was heavy. Yely could see Jarvis struggled and she wondered how John did it.

She knew he didn't do it without it having an effect on him. John staggered, moved slowly, lost his footing several times, but kept going.

Yely stayed by his side. She just wanted to make sure he got home and was all right.

CHAPTER THIRTY-EIGHT – DAY FOURTEEN

"They say the beginning is the hardest," Jarvis said.

John didn't need to open his eyes to know that was Jarvis. In fact, hearing Jarvis say that was what woke him up. They were in the middle of a conversation he supposed or maybe Jarvis was talking to him. He could hear the baby laughing about something. That was a good sound.

He remembered getting home and being exhausted. Every bone and muscle in his body ached. His head, too.

Megan was a mad woman, barking out orders, left and right.

"Yely, take the baby," she had said. "Jarvis get that fire hot, I mean hot, lots of wood, we'll worry about it later. I'll get them out of those damp clothes. Hurry now, hurry."

John was weak, he appreciated her help but wished she fussed more over Giles. He was in worse shape.

But it didn't take long and John was in just his long underwear, on that couch, covered in a blanket and out like a light.

Now he was awake. He appreciated that nap.

"I would think like near the end," said Megan. "Waiting for the better weather."

"Nope, they say the beginning is the hardest," repeated Jarvis.

'Who says it's hardest?' John thought.

Megan said, "Certainly is the coldest."

"It takes three weeks to break a habit."

"Is surviving a habit?" asked Yely.

"No," Jarvis replied. "Giving up the comforts of every day life."

"We have comforts," Megan said. "Maybe not the everyday life we're used to, but better than others. Better than those at the historical building. Wouldn't you think?"

"They can be fine if they dig out the center and get the supplies," Jarvis said. "Just have to work for it."

John grumbled out, "Assholes." Then lifted himself, surprisingly he wasn't as sore as he was when he laid down.

"Oh!" Yely said excited. "John's finally awake."

"Is Giles dead?" John asked. "I don't hear his voice."

"I'm doing better than you, old man," Giles replied.

John looked over at him sitting by the fire, a blanket, over his shoulder. His face looked like he had a horrible case of severe sunburn, beet red and blistered. "Are you superman? How did you get better so fast. I'd bet dollars to donuts you'd be dead."

Jarvis explained. "It's crazy when people freeze. The organs protect themselves, you need less oxygen. There was a woman in the 1980's that was in temperatures like this for six hours. Frozen like a popsicle. They found her in the morning, put some heating pads on her and good as new by evening. And it helps that he's been healing for two days."

"Two days?" John sat up all the way. "I've been sleeping for two days. No wonder I have to piss like a racehorse on crack. You people let me sleep for two days!"

"In our defense," Megan said. "We tried to wake you. You got up a few times, sipped some water and went right back out."

Giles said. "You suffered a trauma carrying me. I'm grateful John."

"Well, like I said. I need to use the head." He stood and teetered, but caught his balance.

"I'll fix you soup," Megan told him.

"Thank you." John walked across the living room and paused

before he left. "Any sign of the historical bunch? They're bad news. They're gonna come after us. We need to get armed, have watch duty and protect out mini greenhouse out there."

Giles lowered his head for a moment, "John, I know what Al did was wrong. It was. There was no excuse, but they're scared and Al's a good guy. I really think they aren't going to attack us like some post apocalypse movie trope. Good people make bad choices. Good people realize it and don't make them again."

Jarvis then added, "But desperate people do desperate things."

John snapped his finger and pointed at Giles. "Exactly. They're desperate. Mark my words," he said. "They're coming."

CHAPTER THIRTY-NINE – DAY NINETY-ONE

"They're not coming," John said softly, bundled up and looking out the window next to the door. "I thought they would. Maybe a little longer."

"John," Megan said with concern. "Quit looking for them."

"I'm not."

"Every day you stand at this window for a good fifteen minutes."

"Same time every day.'

"Yes."

"I'm not looking for them," John replied. "I may say in shock every day that they aren't coming, but that's not what I'm looking for."

"Then what is it?'

"The shadow."

"I'm sorry."

"See this." He pointed to a scratch in the wood. There were several above it. "I'm marking the shadow. Every day, little by little it gets brighter. Still not sunny, still dark, but we have been getting a shadow from the porch post for the last week. It's getting brighter faster. Jarvis and his three hundred days."

"Jarvis didn't say it was going to be dark for three hundred days, he said it will be three hundred days until the weather starts to return to normal."

"That's March twenty-third. Maybe it will be spring," John said.

"That's the week before Easter."

John looked at her. "How do you know that?"

"I work at the church. We get all the calendars ahead of time."

"I'm sorry about Pastor Judy."

"Yeah," Megan responded sadly. "Me, too."

John lifted his head when he heard the sound of the kitchen door opening and stomping of feet. "I don't understand why they can't sweep off the back porch and stomp their feet out there."

"It gives us something to do."

"We have enough to do," John replied. "We don't need to mop up water." He walked away from his window, through the living room and to the kitchen.

Jarvis, Yely and Giles stood there.

"John," Jarvis said. "It feels like a heatwave out there. Who would have thought one degree was a heatwave."

"Heatwave, please. You will mop up that water." John pointed.

"Sorry," said Jarvis. "It's done."

Giles added. "We cleared a path or rather cavern to your greenhouse plus we dug out a path, so no more climbing to get out of the house. Next is the antennae."

"The geodesic just needs set up," Yely said.

"Why didn't you set it up before?" asked Giles. "I mean it's pretty cool."

"I didn't think we'd need it," John answered.

"Do we know how to set it up?" Giles questioned.

"No." John lifted a finger. "But, it came with a two inch instruction booklet. Breaking it down will give us something to do until the radio works again. I'll go get it. Stay here." He held out his hand. "I don't need water in the living room where Denver can roll on it."

Leaving the tree of them in the kitchen, John made his way to the living room and to the book shelf. When he reached for the booklet he saw Yely's envelope. Grabbing them both, he walked back to the kitchen. "Yely?"

She glanced up.

"Did you forget about this?" he asked of the brown envelope. "Or did you hide it on purpose?"

"Oh, I decided not to open it yet. My mother had that put away for me and I think she wanted to give it to me."

"Yely," Jarvis said her name with a soft compassionate tone. "You're mother …"

John cut him off. "Was headed to a red cross ship, Number four, is that right?"

Yely nodded. "John you only saw the bad side of her. She's a good person who just made bad choices."

John heard those words, words told to him before. "Well, if the girl wants to wait to see her mother, then we wait until we can find out what happened to that ship." He handed the book to Jarvis. "You and Giles warm up and head back out there. Yely, get dry. I have something I have to do."

"What is that?" Giles asked.

"Being that it's a heatwave, I think I need to see if good people that made bad choices are still out there."

"Al?" Giles asked.

"He never came. You said because he knows he made a mistake. I think it's because he's dead. I wait and look for them every day. It's time I stop."

"Wait," Yely said. "Can I go."

"No. You're babysitting Denver," John replied. "Megan is going."

It didn't take long. Megan must have heard him from the other room and instantly, she raced in with the baby on her hip, "What?" she asked.

"Suit up," John told her. "You have boots, coat and gloves. You'll be fine. It's a heatwave, I'll even not wear the arctic stuff."

"John, I am not going out there."

"Yes, yes, you are. You're the only one that hasn't left. In months. It'll do you good. Blow the stink off of you."

Megan gasped. "I wash every day."

"You know what I mean. Let Yely take off the snow suit, quit hiding behind Denver, give her the baby, and get ready. Then you two." John pointed at Jarvis and Giles. "Get that greenhouse ready. Or the antennae.'

"John," Giles said. "I'm glad you're going to forgive Al."

"Oh, I don't forgive him. Bastard sent me with a dying man out into the cold. I'm just going to check the threat."

And John meant that.

It really was time to stop looking out the window guessing when they would come and find out what was going on out there.

❈ ❈ ❈

The only pleasure Megan derived in the frigid cold walk to town was the fact that John didn't wear his arctic gear out of fairness to Megan. He was cold, she could tell, but he wasn't giving her the pleasure of knowing for sure.

Megan, on the other hand, made no bones about it.

She didn't mean to audibly groan her discontent so loudly, but she did. It started not long after they left the house and grew worse when John said, "Watch the pond."

It was almost to the point she didn't feel her feet, they were so cold, even though she had four pairs of socks on.

"This weather is not conducive to my bad shoulder."

"I thought you got that replaced," John said.

"That was the other one. And these boots were not made for walking in this cold and snow."

"Oh, hang in there Nancy Sinatra, it's just up around the bend."

"Nancy Sinatra?"

"Yeah," John replied. "Let me put that song in your head." He then proceeded to sing but didn't make it too far into the tune.

"Please don't."

John laughed.

"Then what, John?"

"What do you mean?"

"What happens once we get there?"

"See that the threat is eliminated and see them dead, then go home."

"I don't think they're dead."

"What makes you say that?"

Megan pointed to the sky. Two distinctive thin streams of smoke rose up.

"Damn it."

"John!" Megan gasped.

"What? I thought they were dead. Well, some of them aren't. They have enough food, they won't come after us for that. They can't be doing that well."

When they turned the bend, Megan realized that wasn't the case.

They went from trudging through deep snow to shoveled out paths everywhere. It reminded her of a hedge maze. Passages that had walls of snow, almost like she used to do when the snow was deep and she was a kid.

One led straight down the main street and every twenty or so feet, another path branched off to a business in town.

Megan slowed down in her pace when she saw the community center and how the roof had collapsed. There were, of course, paths that led there.

"Looks like they're doing well," said Megan.

"Yeah, let's go, they don't need us. That's all I needed to see."

"You don't want to check to see how they're doing?"

John looked at the historical building. "Nope." He turned.

Al called out in the distance. "John!"

John gave a scolding look to Megan. "You and your dallying."

"What did I do?"

"Megan?" Al called with question.

Placing on a pleasant look, Megan turned around. "Al."

"Hey, um, glad to see you're okay," Al said.

"Are you?" John quipped.

"John!" Megan scolded.

"Do you guys need anything? Is that why you came?"

"Nope," John replied. "I came to see if you were dead. That didn't happen. I'm on my way."

"John," Megan repeated her scolding. "Looks like you're adjusting."

"We are, we are." Al nodded. "The weather stopped being so bitter a week ago and we decided to make it easier to get around and get things that we need. We got both fireplaces going in the historical building, and have been using the supplies from the center. We intend to bury the dead once the weather breaks. We'll let you know so you can attend the funeral."

"Please, do."

John huffed. "Gonna be a while."

"Maybe when help rolls through, but I think most of the people left will go with them," Al said.

John scoffed. "Help isn't coming."

"Yeah, it is, John," Al stated. "Walt got the station radio up and picked up the FEMA recording two days ago. It was a recent recording, they gave the date. Some part of the government is still running."

This caught John's attention. "Radios are up."

"Transmitting from the south, I guess."

Immediately John turned again and started to walk. "Come on, Megan."

"John stop." Al caught up to him. "They're sending emergency transport to areas that reach out. Get people to habitable areas. It might not be for another three months, but still. We ... we ... we can't send a message, we can't transmit. Maybe you can try ... maybe at least let them know our location. If you can get through."

Megan answered before John did, "Of course, we'll try. You know John and his radios."

"I do," Al said. "Reed Warner."

"I'm sorry, who?" Megan asked.

"Don't you worry," John said.

Al replied. "Reed Warner was John's radio pseudonym. The guys at the fire house listened to his podcast all the time. We knew it was John."

John huffed. "If you listened, you knew about the comet before the public."

"We didn't believe it, John."

With a grunting, 'eh' and wave of his hand, John tried to leave again.

"John, please," Al said. "I was going to come and ask you tomorrow."

"Damn it," John looked at Megan. "He was coming, see."

"Can you try, please," Al said. "We need them here. Anna Johnston is five months pregnant."

"I'm going to try my radio, it isn't because you asked."

"John," Megan scolded his name again.

"I get it." Al held up his hand. "I do. The way I acted, what I did, what we all did, was wrong. I know it. I knew it when I did it. But we were desperate, scared, everyone around us died. We lost family. We weren't thinking correctly. I'm sorry, I really am."

John nodded.

"How's Giles?" Al asked.

"Dead."

"John!" Megan gasped.

"Oh, stop with saying my name like everything I say offends you."

"It does," Megan replied. "Giles is not dead, Al. He's alive and well."

"I would have said the same thing," Al said. "Thanks for trying the radio, John, even if it's not for us."

John nodded again and turned, he started walking away and wasn't stopping.

Megan reached out, touching Al's arm. "Thank you for apologizing. He isn't showing it, but it means something."

"I'll be in touch."

Megan passed on a gentle smile, then hurried to catch up to

John. 'You're not waiting for me?"

"I figured you'd catch up. Right now, I want to get home."

"He gave you an apology."

"Nope. He gave me more than that. Information I didn't have." John shook his head. "Why didn't I think of that. I was waiting to try again. Of course, the government is up and running. Of course, they had a plan. Jarvis' wife is there. That should have told me about their contingency."

"You seem energized."

"I am. I am getting home, making sure that arctic shield is uncovered and put the Frost Guard on the antenna. I'm reaching out."

"You want to get on the transport?"

John grimaced. "Oh, heck no. I got everything I need here. It will be habitable soon enough."

"You seem so excited, I just thought…"

"You know why I'm happy? I got a teenage girl and a baby boy living at my house. They have a whole life ahead of them. The radio, the transport, the government … the world is not over. Not yet," John said. "And not by a long shot."

John walked a lot faster on the way home. A man with a purpose. He shed his coat and boots outside the kitchen door, then went inside with them in his arms. He set them on the plastic he had laid on the floor and marched right into the living room.

Giles and Jarvis sat by the fire. Denver was asleep on the floor and Yely was reading the green house dome manual.

"Slackers," John said. "All of us are slackers."

Jarvis laughed and looked up. "We're taking a break and warming up."

"You think the historical building maniacs take breaks?" John said. "We were there. Sadly, they're alive and motivated. They got paths dug out all over town, we got one. One. And the damn porch isn't swept."

"John," Giles said. "There's a dozen adults there."

"And there's four here. If they dug twelve tunnels, we should have dug four. We are behind the eight ball. Jarvis, did you go to the roof and hit the antennae."

"Not yet."

"Now's the time, you and Giles need to clear it," John said. "Al told us they heard a radio transmission from FEMA. They're taking reservations for transport to safe places."

Shocked, Jarvis looked up. "You wanna get on a transport."

John huffed. "No. I'm not running away. I want to reach out so they can get those who want to go, I mean, Al has a pregnant lady for goodness sakes, she can't have her baby here. Bottom line is the radios are back. We need to tap in."

Giles stood. "On it. Jarvis?"

"I'm with you."

"Good," John said, "I'll be out to join you in a minute."

"You mean to micromanage?" Giles asked.

"That, too."

Once they had left, Yely stood up. "John, do you think the safe places may know about my mom?"

"I don't know, but the radio is a good start, and a good sign, that this does have a light at the end of the tunnel. There's hope out there," John said. "We're gonna find it for you."

CHAPTER FORTY – THE CONDUCTOR

Ever since Jarvis and Giles cleared the roof and antenna, John didn't leave the radio. It was getting dark, and Megan could still hear him trying. He'd call out, turn the controls and listen to static, curse and continue.

She brought him broth for lunch, which was barely touched when she brough him his supper. There were things and routines they had gotten into to make being stuck in the house less boring.

Sundays and Tuesdays were reading nights. A quiet reflection time.

Monday was Mystery Meal Night, where blindfolded, each person reached to the shelf. A protein, vegetable, and starch, then whoever's turn it was to cook had to make a creative meal.

Wednesday was 'Tell your movie', where each of them took turns telling about a movie from beginning to end. John's was always brief and always a movie that had a tough guy actor and generally didn't leave room for questions or comments because John always interjected his own..

Megan's favorite was when he talked about a movie, saying, *"He was cop in the future, food was scarce. Like now. Over crowded, not like now. Rich people got lettuce, poor people ate people who volunteered to be turned into crackers. Then he got shot because he told everyone the people were crackers. Never understood why, let well enough alone."*

For the last couple of weeks, especially since he rigged a

battery for the radio, John hooked up the generator once a week to the projector and DVD player and they'd watch a movie on the wall.

It was that night and Megan tried to get John away from the radio, even offering to delay movie night, but he said he wasn't in the mood to watch Scooby Doo.

They ate, watched the movie and all without John.

Finally after everyone settled and it was pushing midnight, Megan had to tell him enough was enough. She walked into the dining room where he had his set up.

It was cold in there and again his dinner was barely touch.

"John, you're going to get sick. Take a break."

"I thought at night it would work better. Still too many clouds, I gather."

"John …"

"How the heck is Al getting a signal? He's got to be lying," John said.

"He's not lying. Maybe you should ask him, see what he's doing."

"No. I don't need to ask him. He's lying. There's no way he's hearing it and I'm not."

Megan sighed out. "Maybe Jarvis needs to adjust the antennae for you."

"Maybe." John groaned. "Or my radio is a piece of crap. Didn't think it was, it worked before all this."

"Not as good as the police station?"

"I swore it was better. Piece of crap." He smacked a dial. "Still nothing."

Speaking soothingly, Megan placed her hand on top of the radio. "John, there is nothing …"

Static.

A voice.

"Hot damn."

In her excitement, Megan clapped.

Silence. No sound.

"What the hell? Did you break it?"

"No," she snapped. "All I did was touch it like this."

The moment she put her hand on the radio, the voice came back on.

"See, I didn't break it." she removed her hand.

John looked at her when the voice stopped again. "Put your hand back on there." He chuckled giddily when the voice returned. "Leave it there. Don't move."

"Why?"

"Because I think the metal from the shoulder replacement is the conductor boost we need."

"Glad I can be of help."

"Yep, you now have a shelter purpose."

Megan gasped, offended.

John laughed and adjusted the volume down, he had it up when he was trying to listen for a signal. It was clearly a recording that they caught the end of. A few minutes later it repeated.

'This message was recording August 25 ...' the male recorded voice spoke.

"Yesterday, it is new."

"Al was right."

John grumbled.

"Emergency services and national defense is now back in operation. Work has commenced in clearing pathways into the impacted cold zones. If you are in an effected area and need assistance traveling to the southern safe zones, transport will be available once roadways are clear enough. Do not respond to this channel. If you are able, transmit on 47.42 MHz Information can be obtained on 146.520 MHz both frequencies are manned between six am and six pm daily. This message will repeat in seven minutes."

"Do you know what those numbers mean?" Megan asked,

"I do," John replied. "It means Al wasn't lying and I can reach out." He looked at his watch. "We have six hours. What do you want to talk about?"

"You want me to stand here for six hours?"

"Yes."

"No." Megan removed her hand.

"Hey, that's coming back on."

"I don't care and I'm not standing here with you for six hours listening to a recording, you got the information, go to sleep. I am."

"I suppose you have a point." John pushed his chair back and tried to stand. "While I'm stiff."

"Is it any wonder."

"Might as well eat my dinner now." John lifted his plate and sat back down.

"You're not coming."

"Nah, I'll be in after a few. I need to relax, that was stressful." John took a bite of his rice concoction, then reached down to the floor, lifting a bottle of gin. He poured some in a glass next to his radio. "Want some?"

"No, I'm good. Good night, John."

John held up his glass to her, took a healthy drink and sighed out. "Night."

CHAPTER FORTY-ONE – DAY ONE SIXTY-SEVEN

The man's laughter carried across the radio speaker. "John," he said. "You are funnier than you want to admit. Are you doing a show tonight?"

"I'll do a broadcast."

"The guys and I like to listen. The Christmas Special was really good. Jarvis has a great voice," the man said.

"Don't he though? And it was a holiday special, Carl, I want everyone to feel included."

"I stand corrected and will listen tonight," Carl said. "You're clear on the transport."

"I am. It'll be here in four days. Sometime around eight am. Why the heck did it take so long?"

"John, it's taking a lot of resources to clear paths."

"Oh, I get it."

"And John, when you go tell people, make sure you let them know that this might be the last for a while."

"Why is that?" John asked.

"Not only do we have to deal with the mini ice age, we have winter setting in for those of you up north. We don't know what that will be like."

"I can almost guarantee it won't be as bad. Where is the transport taking people?"

"Yours is slated for Atlanta Processing."

"Atlanta!" John said in a fake shock. "They aren't going to live there are they?"

"For a little while, just until they process and they find them a permanent place to live. There's a lot of the United States operational now. It's almost six months. People have jobs, they work, pay bills, and go to Starbucks."

"How about that. I take it there's electricity."

"The grid is back up."

"How long do you think it will take the grid to get back up here?" John questioned.

"Honestly, years if ever. That's why you should consider getting on that transport."

"Nah, I got a home here. Eventually this will all break and warm up."

"John," Carl said. "You can always catch a transport back if it's not for you."

"Again, no, I'm good. I have supplies. I'll wait it out and then we'll see." John paused. "Carl, you've been avoiding it and I've been avoiding asking. Did you find out anything about the ships?"

After a moment, Carl answered. "I did and it's not much. There were four red cross ships and two naval ships coming from the islands, plus one carnival cruise. All slated to arrive in Savannah. Only four of the seven ships arrived. I couldn't find out which ones, but I know a good bit of them were moved out with the evacuation."

"Well, that's a lot of information Carl, that is. Is there any way to find out if Yely's mother was on one of those."

"They took names of everyone. I don't have that information. Processing does, wherever they were processed."

"Atlanta?"

"Could be Dallas. But they're all online so Atlanta could look for the name."

"Okay, well, I'll go talk to those getting on the transport and have them ask," John replied.

"That's a good idea, they can get word to you either way.

Maybe … maybe even Yely can get on that transport. Up there is no place for a kid."

"Being in a strange place alone isn't a place for a kid either, but I'll talk to her. Right now I'm going to walk into town."

"John, it's still cold out there. Send one of the others."

"Nah," John replied. "I'll go. Exercise is good and … we all can't be 'a Megan', sit around and never leave the house.

At that moment, Megan gasped.

Carl chuckled. "She's right there, isn't she."

"Of course, the radio doesn't work without that titanium arm."

"Talk to you later, John,"

"Talk soon." John set down the microphone.

Megan moved her arm from the radio with a groan. "Oh, God, I thought you'd never stop talking. I can't wait until it clears up enough for me to stop doing this."

"Seventy percent cloud coverage." John stood. "A couple months ago we were at ninety. We're getting there. My guess is fifty percent. Until then." He tapped her cheek. "Keep up the good work."

"Are you going to town?"

"I will. But first," John said. "Yely."

Yely was tucked away in the place she had been going steadily for two weeks. The geo dome, which reminded John of a little igloo.

He only wore a jacket, the fifteen degree weather felt balmy and when he stepped inside the Geodesic Dome. He didn't know how they worked. Just it was something to buy. He did plan on using it eventually even if the comet hadn't come. He had a contractor come and put in the foundation and the geodesic dome place did the rest. They told him it was ready to go.

It was the only thing that didn't have an abundance of snow on it.

He stepped inside the small archway door then into the

actual dome. He could feel the temperature difference. Yely was sitting next to a counter. Rectangular green planters by her while she read the instructions book.

"Hey," John said as he entered. He gently touched the soil. "You are getting ready."

"Yeah. I didn't do the seeds yet. We need a bit more sun."

"Good job. I'm proud of you taking on our farmer role."

"Thanks." She looked up at him. "It beats babysitting."

"Yeah, Denver is tough. He's walking now."

"I worry about the fireplace."

"Me, too," John said. "So…" he cleared his throat. "Carl, got some info."

Yely's attention was caught. "What did he say?"

"Four Red Cross ships, two navy and one Carnival Cruise hit the islands to evacuate. Only four made it to Savannah. He wasn't able to find out which four."

"Seven ships for all those people."

"I know. But your mother said she was waiting to get on one, right?"

Yely nodded.

"Maybe she did."

"We'll never know."

"That's not true." John wagged a finger. "All the processing centers are online, meaning they can share information. Carl said the processing centers take names and would be able to tell us where she is. She may be in Texas."

"Or not at all."

"Yely, there's a sixty percent chance she made it."

"But I have to go to a processing center to find out."

"At this time yes." John nodded. "And lucky for you, a bus goes there in four days."

"What happens if I go there and she didn't get on a ship or her ship didn't make it?" Yely asked.

"Well, you come back when a transport comes or you stay. You can also go there and find out your mom is in Tulsa."

Yely gently smiled. "You told me that when you thought she

wasn't in the Bahamas."

"Who knows. Maybe it's a premonition." John put his hand on her shoulder. "Think about it. Okay? I'm gonna head to town to let Al know about the transport."

Yely nodded.

"Keep up the good work in here." John walked to the door.

"Good luck with Al."

"Yeah, I know." John shook his head. "Maybe I should tell him the transport isn't coming."

"John."

"Kidding." He pointed a finger before walking out. "Think about it."

* * *

Even though John wanted to sport that canvas jacket, he opted for a winter coat. It was nice to walk without the wind hurting his cheeks every time it blew. He wished the sun would shine, it was still heavily overcast, but at least it started looking more like daylight. Now instead of it looking like it was just before dawn, it looked like seven in the morning on a rainy day.

It was a lot easier walking to town, Al and his crew had cleared a path, not that John walked there much, but Jarvis and Giles did to check on things.

Plus, more diapers were needed for Denver.

Al spotted John before he spotted Al, calling out and jogging up to John as if they were old friends.

John noticed his people moving things, boxes and so forth toward the library.

"Hey, John was coming to see you."

"Is that so," John said. "I was coming to see you."

"Is that so."

"Just got off the radio. Transport will be here in four days."

"We heard different dates," Al replied. "But nothing specific."

"Well, I got specific. Four days. Picking up on Fourth and

Main just before the junction to the highway. He said between seven and eight am."

"Thank you. Are you or anyone from the house getting on the transport?"

"I'm not."

"John," Al said. "What's here for you? Come start a new life somewhere warm."

"There's about as much out there for me as here. I have my home. I'm staying put. As for the others. I don't know. I'll ask. What were you coming to see me for?"

"We're moving all the supplies to the library," Al explained. "We've cleaned out most of the town, empty houses, loads of nonperishable food and water. It's there for you if you stay."

"Thank you. That's nice of you to move it to one place."

"It passes time."

"Time is a killer."

"But your weekly radio show helps."

Blushingly, John lowered his head. "I appreciate that. Good luck to you all and thanks again for the supplies."

"No problem. Good luck to you," Al said. "And John, I do hope you and your people change your minds."

"Appreciate that." John turned, he said all he needed to say and decided to leave. He probably didn't express it well, but he was happy for the supplies they were leaving for him.

As far as Jarvis, Megan, Giles or even Yely catching the transport, John really didn't know what they were thinking or what they wanted to do.

While he made his way home, he realized it was time to find out.

❈ ❈ ❈

When John arrived home, he didn't expect everyone to be in the living room, by the fire having soup. He didn't realize it was lunch time. Actually, John took a bit longer to get home. He kept thinking about all the supplies they moved in town and every house, John passed, he finally noticed they had markings on them.

He supposed that was Al's way of saying the house was clear.

"Oh, John, just in time for soup," Megan said. "Sit down. Warm up."

"Thanks." John took off his coat and looked around.

Denver was getting so big. He sat on the floor between Jarvis' legs eating something. Giles face had sustained so much damage from the freeze he looked like he had an uneven suntan.

"John?" Giles called his attention. "Are you alright?"

"Yes. I ... people ..." he took the mug of soup Megan offered. "Thank you." He then sat down. "We need to talk. The transport comes in four days. It goes to Atlanta and there they process you, maybe send you somewhere else. They have power, they have things running, they have Starbucks. I want you all to know, in case you're worried about me, I want what's best for you. For the baby, and Yely. I just need to know who is going on that transport."

Everyone looked at him.

"Giles?" John asked.

"No. Not yet. Maybe later. But not yet."

"Megan?"

Megan shook her head. "This is home. Ripley is my home. I'm seeing it through."

"Jarvis, you have Denver."

Jarvis nodded. "I know. But we sent that message out like three times to my wife."

"Ex-wife," John corrected.

"Still." Jarvis waved his hand. "She'll get it. Carl said he would make sure she got that I was here. She's with all the important people. The president."

"Okay," John said. "What does that mean for you?"

"Maybe instead of sending people to take us, she'll send help to make the town what it was always labeled, the safest place on earth."

"Jarvis, you have a good heart, but I doubt right now that your ex-wife gives two scraps about Ripley."

"I am not giving up on that."

John then turned to Yely, she sat on the floor by the couch. It was at that second he saw she had the envelope. "What are you doing? I thought you were waiting on that?"

"My mother … my mother wasn't on those ships," Yely replied. "I feel it. I'm not going. I'm staying here and it's time I opened this for my mother."

"Yely, I think you should wait." John looked at everyone else. "Tell her."

Megan replied. "We tried. Let her open it."

Giles added. "She's been ready for days, John."

"Okay, before you do," John said. "It's obviously something about you or your mother. Just know whatever is in there, will never change who you are. It won't change you."

Yely took a deep breath and undid the clasp. "Anyone wanna guess?"

Jarvis guessed. "I think it tells about your father."

"Me, too," said Megan. "Or maybe there's money somewhere for you."

Giles shook his head. "Not that money matters. Whatever is in there, her mother said she had to show it to someone, so someone has to explain it. Hopefully, one of us can. Whatever it is, she was waiting for Yely to see."

Cautiously and slowly, Yely opened the envelope. It was thick. A folded old newspaper with something folded inside. A note was clipped to the newspaper. "A note. It says," Yely read. "This is why your grandmother wanted us to live in Ripley so bad. I think it was to make up for it somehow."

Yely unfolded the newspaper, more clippings fell, along with papers and photos. She looked confused. "I don't understand."

Megan looked over her shoulder then peered up. "Oh my."

"What?" Yely asked.

Megan locked eyes on John.

'What?" John asked, then walked over and sat on the couch

behind Yely. He glanced down to what she held.

"What is it?" Yely asked. "What does this mean."

"John," Megan said. "That's you, right?"

John nodded. He looked down to the newspaper that Yely had unfolded. On the front page, were two pictures. John was in the picture on the right with a woman.

"Do you know this woman in the picture?" he asked Yely. "The one holding the baby."

"Yeah," Yely nodded. "It's my grandmother. She is young."

"Peggy," John said. "That man is me. That baby, Ruby." He closed his eyes. "Ruby Warren."

"My mother. You knew my grandmother?"

John nodded. "I did. That man." He pointed to the picture on the left. "If Peggy is your grandmother, then this is your grandfather."

'But the headlines say Murder Suicide ..." Yely gasped. "John. John. My grandfather was the bad man that killed your family."

"Sick man. And I am afraid so," John said. "Your mother was probably waiting until you were old enough to understand. Maybe she knew you were going to meet me."

Giles was shocked. "John, her grandfather is the one ..."

"Yep. Ruby. I remember the day Ruby was born. Yely, your grandmother ..." Before John could finished, Yely dropped everything, jumped up and ran.

"What the hell," Jarvis said. "What the hell was wrong with her mother? That was too big of news to put in an envelope for a kid to read."

"I think she had it as a just in case," John said. "Just in case something happened to her and Ruby didn't get a chance to tell her."

Giles asked. "Her grandfather was really the one who killed your family."

"Yep."

Megan stood. "I'll go talk to her."

"No." John stood, handing his soup to Megan. "I have to be the one."

He left them in the living room knowing well, where Yely had gone. He heard the kitchen door and that meant she ran to her special place. The dome.

He didn't have on a coat and he walked to her. After stepping inside, he found Yely crouched on the ground, her head buried in her arms, knees brought up.

"Yely."

"I'm sorry John." She sobbed. "I didn't know."

"Of course, you didn't." John lowered to the cold ground to sit by her. "How could you."

"I feel bad. She knew, she knew when we moved next to you. She knew when she came over and fought with you."

"Yeah, well, she's a pistol."

"She knew. You have been so nice to me and my grandfather took everything from you."

"Yely, yeah, he did. That has nothing to do with you," John said.

"He was my grandfather."

"And you didn't know him. He was a good man that made a bad choice. A phrase we repeat around here."

"He killed your family, that's more than a bad choice. And my grandmother …"

"Was a wonderful woman and a victim, too. Your mother as well," John said. "That's why I think you should get on that transport and look for her. Find out. Because if you don't, you'll never know and you'll never have resolution."

"I'm scared, John. Scared to go alone."

"You won't be alone. I'll go with you. I can always come back. But you need to know. Yely," John said. "Lift that head."

"I can't." Yely said muffled through tears. "I can't look at you. You must hate me."

"Hate you? Yely lift that head."

Yely slowly lifted her head and wiped her eyes.

"Hate you" John leaned closer. "I had nothing. Nothing. An old miserable man. I lost everything. I didn't care. I care now. Why? You. You, Yely are the best thing to come into my life. Hate you? Far from it. I love you."

Yely's lips quivered. "I know you said not hugs ever."

"Yeah, that was before I realized how great you are." John reached out and with both his arms, pulled Yely into his embrace, and he held her.

"I love you, too, John," Yely cried from within his embrace.

That was it for John. He couldn't speak, he wanted to keep his emotional strength, but it was hard. He just held on to Yely and would do so for as long as she needed.

She may have found out the story of her grandparents and their connection to John, but her story wasn't over. She still needed to find out what happened to her mother and John was going to make sure she did.

CHAPTER FORTY-TWO - DAY ONE SEVENTY-ONE

They were lining up not far from the Korger's like a school field trip.

Al and his people, John and his.

He had one bag, as did Yely. Not much. John didn't plan on staying in Atlanta long, but he couldn't let Yely go alone. He also wanted to go, not just to find out if her mother made it, but if Ruby did, John wanted to get to know her.

She was Peggy's daughter and John adored Peggy.

"I hear the bus," Megan said. "Do you have everything you need?"

"Yes," John answered annoyed. "I don't understand why you three had to come and see us off, dragging that baby into the cold. Like we're going off to war or never coming back."

"We have been inseparable for six months," said Giles. "Give us this."

"Well, I better not come home to a messy house. The minute it warms up, start getting the house ready for summer."

Megan nodded. "We will."

John looked as the bus was pulling up. It was a school bus only green.

"And watch her greenhouse," John said.

"I'm on it," Giles replied.

"Jarvis?" John called his name. "Watch that baby."

"I will. I'll keep in touch with the radio and keep trying Amy," Jarvis said.

"Who?" asked John.

"My ex-wife. She's going to send people here to rebuild Ripley."

John waved out his hand. "Keep dreaming. I'll try to keep in touch. But know I'll be back."

The bus pulled up and the airbrakes squealed.

"Yely, you ready?" John asked.

Yely nodded. She hugged Megan, then Jarvis and Giles and kissed Denver.

"See you soon," John said, lifting his bag over his shoulder. When he did, Giles lept forward embracing him tightly. "Good Lord, Giles I'm not dying."

"Just wanted to thank you."

"Yeah. Yeah." John patted him on the cheek. He walked with Yely to the bus, the last ones in line. Before boarding he looked back. Even though the temperatures had warmed slightly, the town was still white, frozen and looked barren.

He stepped on the bus. Yely picked the seats near the back, and John took the window seat. As much as he didn't want to show it, he was going to miss his friends and he pressed his hand against the window, watching them as the bus pulled forward.

He didn't know what the road ahead had in store for him, but John knew where his road would end.

That was Ripley. No matter what. He was coming back.

* * *

The bus ride was long, made longer by the frequent stops they made for people to get out and walk around. They called them rest stops. Six in all and only three had porta johns. No real restrooms.

John slept a lot on the ride, not that he was tired, he

was bored. Yely held that envelope and didn't say much. John supposed she was thinking about what she would say or ask her mother, or maybe what she would do.

No one really said or told them much. The chatter was minimum on the bus, John honestly didn't know what to say to Yely.

He couldn't believe he left Ripley. Without a second thought or even doubt, he went with her.

He felt lost, like a traveler in a far off land. The bus window gave him a view of piled up cars, moved to the side of the road all part of the heavy snow that had fallen.

However, the farther they traveled, the less snow they saw.

At six in the evening, eleven hours after thy left, the bus driver informed them they were arriving in Atlanta.

John had been in Atlanta and that was nearly twenty years earlier.

It still looked the same.

The bus stopped on the freeway, a quarter mile from the processing center. They were told they had to walk the rest of the way.

Glad he packed lightly, he disembarked the bus, grabbed their things and he and Yely followed the line of people.

The skyline of the city was in the distance. It was dismal, gray, and frozen.

It was a lot lighter than it was in Ripley, more daylight, the temperature was warmer. So much so, John took off his coat. It wasn't hot and humid, but it was near forty or fifty degrees. A far cry hotter than Ripley.

They walked for a while, aimlessly, like refugees going to some camp. John couldn't see the front of the line so he didn't know if someone was leading the busload or they were going on their own.

An hour later they arrived. The line extended outside the convention center and it moved slow.

Atlanta may have been a processing hub, but it was in bad shape.

Abandoned cars everywhere, some looked burned. It seemed as if a riot had broken out and no one controlled the chaos. Burned buildings, busted windows.

There was a certain amount of regret that set in as they waited in line for the processing center, but he didn't want to tell that to Yely.

He listened to the conversation around them, people chatting as if they were waiting in a black Friday sales line.

They arrived in Atlanta at six and it was ten pm when they crossed the doorway into the processing center and nearly midnight when they made it to the table.

What surprised John the most was the attitude of those who were working there. He expected people to be miserable, stale in personality. But Trisha, who proudly wore a big name tag was neither of those.

"Can I get you anything?" she asked with a bright smile.

She was a young woman, not much older than Yely.

"Coffee? Water?"

"Water," Yely replied.

"I'll have a coffee, thank you." John said.

She brought the beverages back along with a sandwich wrapped in paper. "I'm sorry, it's taking so long. I promise once you get registered, we'll have a bed for you."

She was that way, that nice to everyone.

Standing on his feet was taking a toll on John, he really wanted to sit down.

Finally, they reached the registration table. There were four people working it. Two men and two women.

John and Yely approached a man, middle aged, glasses, dressed in a shirt and tie.

He had a laptop computer before him and john nearly forgot that half the country had fallen apart ... "Thanks for your patience," he said. "Once we get you in, I promise it will be no more than an hour before we assign you a tent, get you a cot and you can rest. Tomorrow, at some point they'll find you and tell you where you are going."

Yely asked. "What do you mean, where we are going?"

"Housing varies. We're a lot quicker since the upgrade." He placed his hands on the keyboard. "Did they give you a bus number?"

John replied. "Northeast Seven."

The man moved his fingers on the keyboard. "Name."

"This is all well and fine, and I'll give you our names," John said. "But I was told you guys can give us information on red cross ships."

The man paused. "What do you mean?"

"Her mother," John pointed to Yely. "My daughter in law was in the Bahamas. She called, said she was getting on a ship. My radio contact said this is the place to get information on where she is."

"I see." He looked up to John. "I can't do that but … but I can find someone to help you. But right now, I need to get this line moving. Can we do that and I will forward your request."

John didn't believe him, but when he looked at Yely, she looked not only exhausted but defeated.

Reluctantly, he agreed.

After providing his information and Yely's, they moved down the line. After being assigned a tent number and cot number, they were given a box of toiletries and ushered into a food tent.

Neither him nor Yely was in the mood or hungry enough to eat the beef stew.

By the time they were brought to their tent it was pushing three in the morning. Nearly twenty-four hours of traveling.

The entire area around the convention center was one big tent city. The woman led them to tent Three Four Three, she told John that usually, housing was done within three days and assured them the tent situation was temporary.

By the time they got to their cots, both him and Yely weren't thinking much about anything but sleep.

The tent was quiet, warm and big. They were in the corner. It was comfortable.

Yely lay on the cot, holding on to her bag. "I'm sorry, John."

"For what?'

"For all this."

"Eh, it's fine. It's a nice tent. Warm, look." He wiggled his fingers. "My fingers aren't numb and white. Get some sleep."

He watched her close her eyes, and when John was certain she was asleep, he covered her.

It was quiet and late, and figuring he wasn't getting any answers soon, he too lay down for some sleep.

The man at the check in line kept his word.

John was out not even an hour when a woman came into the tent.

"Mr. Hopper," she said softly. "Sorry to wake you. I was told you're looking for someone."

John immediately sat up. "Yely, wake up there's someone here to help us."

Yely slowly sat up.

The woman pulled up a chair and placed her laptop on her legs. "They said you are looking for someone that came in on a red cross ship."

"Yes," John said.

"Red Cross Bahamas Four," Yely added. "That's what she told us."

Her fingers clicked on the keyboard. "We have a Red Cross Hamas One and Three that docked in Savanah."

"She said she was getting on four," Yely stated.

"Unfortunately, not all the ships that left the island arrived. Some were caught in the wave, The ones that did arrive made the evacuation. We got their names. Maybe she was on another ship."

"And Four didn't arrive?" John asked.

Sympathetically, she shook her head. "We have that listed as lost."

John saw the look on Yely's face and he held out his hand to her while speaking to the woman. "Can you search names?"

"Certainly. What name?" she asked.

"Ruby. Ruby Warren," John answered.

"Age?"

Yely spoke up. "Twenty-nine."

"What?" John snapped. "Your mother isn't twenty-nine. You think she had you at fourteen."

"Maybe. That's what she told me."

"No." John looked at the woman. "She would have turned forty this past October."

The woman typed. "Ruby Warren."

"Yes," John replied.

"She's not coming up."

"Try Jeremy Bernstein." John suggested.

Again, the woman typed. "No. I'm sorry. Is there some other name I can try."

John glanced at Yely. "Anything."

Yely shook her head.

"Can you try again," John asked the woman. "Just one more time."

The woman did. "I'm sorry. But this doesn't mean anything. She may have gotten on another ship, never left with the evacuation. I've seen that."

John nodded. "Thank you."

"I'm sorry I couldn't give better news."

"You tried."

"Good luck to you."

"Thanks again."

The woman closed her laptop and walked from the tent. John swung his legs over the side of the cot. "Yely."

"I knew. I knew she wasn't here. I should have stayed in Ripley."

"You had to know. I had to know. And you know what? We still don't."

Yely looked up at him through the tops of her eyes. "We know better. What now?"

"Get some sleep."

"I mean about going back to Ripley."

"We both know that's not happening any time soon. So, we go with the flow. We go where they want us to go and we will get back home. I promise."

"I'm sorry." Yely began to cry. "I'm sorry I made you leave home for nothing."

"Yely, stop. Just stop. I made the choice to come here. I wanted to come with you. We're together. I like that. It's an adventure. Again, we will get back home. Yely, I need you to know this is the first good purpose I had in my life since my family died. I'm glad to be here with you."

"Thank you, John."

"You're welcome Yely. I for one am excited about where they send us. Now get some sleep, stop worrying. I'm sorry we didn't get information about Ruby. I really am."

"Me, too."

"Get some sleep. We'll talk tomorrow."

"Are you sure you're okay?" Yely asked.

"Yep." John lifted his legs to the cot and stretched out. "I'm good as long as I don't have to deal with Al anymore."

Just then the flap to the ten opened and John heard the voice.

"John, Yely, this is great," Al said. "We're bunk mates."

John silently groaned, closed his eyes, and pretended he was asleep. The situation wasn't all that bad, it could have been worse.

Even though he would have rather been home, he knew he'd get there eventually.

For the time being, and forever how long it took to get back to Ripley, John would make the best of it.

It was a different avenue to his life. The world was a dim, dismal, frozen, chaotic place full of death. However, for the first time since that dark tragedy forty years earlier, the world, John's world, seemed brighter and he owed that all to Yely.

CHAPTER FORTY-THREE – DAY THREE HUNDRED

Yely never thought the day would come. They had been moved to Birmingham Alabama shortly after arriving in Atlanta. Continuously told that they could go back north as soon as transports started again.

But that didn't happen.

She and John moved to an apartment complex. Once abandoned, the government quickly redid them for refugees like Yely and John. They weren't special, they were small and old looking. But they were warm with power.

Yely started school, actually made friends, and John worked at a processing center as an communications expert

Yeky figured he did that to get information and try to reach out.

A few weeks after they arrived in Birmingham, John was able to get a relay message from Jarvis. Jarvis knew they were safe and they were holding down the fort.

But months went by, over four, and just when Yely was resigned to staying in that small two-bedroom apartment, John told her.

"Get your things. We're going home."

She was excited.

Her friends thought she was insane.

Why would she give up electricity, running water, a hot

shower, food and internet to go to the dead zone. And that was what the north was labeled. Dead.

But it wasn't dead. Jarvis, Megan, Giles and Denver were there. And Yely would give up all the comforts of Alabama to be with them and John.

They were family.

They were home.

And she just wanted to get there.

John didn't convey his thoughts to Yely on the journey north to Ripley. They weren't on a bus, they were in a military convoy headed to New York to survey the area and damage.

John was able to catch a ride. But he asked the soldiers to stop back for them if things in Ripley were bad.

While the weather had warmed into the sixties in Alabama, virtually breaking the mini ice age streak, it was still cold up north. Sunny but cold. He hadn't talked to Jarvis in months and John didn't know what he and Yely were headed into.

For all he knew they were dead.

It wasn't a nine-hour journey, it was three days, stopping at different Military posts for the night.

When they finally started driving through West Virginia, John could see it wasn't healed completely like the south.

There was still plenty enough snow on the ground, the only saving grace was the highways were passible. But that was only because the cars that jammed the roadways had been moved aside.

Ripley was a small town so the signs leading up to it were few and far between.

When they arrived, other than being defrosted and the sun shining, Ripley hadn't changed.

They dropped John and Yely off at the Kroger's.

"We'll pass back through here in three weeks," said the one soldier. "We'll look for you and if you need to come back. You can."

"Thank you," John told them.

When they left, he felt alone. Ripley felt barren, silent and dead.

It seemed as if it were just him and Yely.

Hopefully he wouldn't have to go back in three weeks. Not that the apartment wasn't nice, he just didn't like living refurbished tenements from the eighties like they were characters in Call the Midwife.

He knew Jarvis, Megan and Giles couldn't have gone through all the supplies and if God forbid something happened to them, John would find the supplies. They'd be fine until the military returned.

Ripley was quiet and walking back to John's house was different. There wasn't an abundance of snow on the street. The pond that tripped up John was visible.

"What do you think?" Yely asked as they walked.

"I think we need to get to my house and see. Yely, you just need to be prepared."

"I am."

"Are you? I mean we haven't heard from them in a while."

"Yes, I've been with you, John, I'm realistic now."

"Bet you wish you had that marijuana."

Yely just chuckled, a nervous chuckle that spoke her fear more than words.

As they turned the bend to his street, John wanted to dismiss the gloomy feeling he had swirling in his gut. A feeling that Jarvis, Megan and Giles froze to death, or marauders got them.

His house wasn't safe, not by a long shot. The shutters only kept out the elements not the bad people. When he left, they were all basically living in one room.

What if they ran out of wood? Water?

They were barely around the bend, four houses from his own, when he heard the shriek.

A shrill surprise, happy shriek and all John's fears and worries went by the wayside when he saw Jarvis running their way.

Jarvis was screaming in surprise and delight like a teenage girl at a boy band concert, which caused Yely to drop her bag and scream as well.

"Good lord." John closed off one ear. But he picked up the pace, too.

Jarvis hugged Yely, lifting her from her feet and then without warning, hugged John.

"I thought when I didn't hear from you that you weren't coming back!" Jarvis said with glee. "Oh my God, you're back."

"So things are good?" John asked.

"Oh, they're great. Come on."

John wasn't expecting much when they got to his house. Maybe for it to be a bit more in order, but it was more than that.

It reminded him of his house before the world went to pot.

All the survival supplies that lined the hallway and dining room were cleared.

John felt a sense of relief when he stepped inside. He was home.

Denver ran by him, nearly double in size. He didn't recognize John or Yely, he screamed and then ran in another direction.

"Megan," Jarvis called out. "Look who's back."

Megan came from the kitchen and her legs buckled some before she cried out in joy, racing to John and Yely. She hugged them both at the same time.

"You're home. We kept things going for you," Megan said. "Yely your greenhouse is flourishing thanks to Giles."

"Where is he?" John looked around. "Is he dead?"

"John," Megan scolded. "No. He's with the Revitalize Crew. In six months, we're going to be a town again, survivors will be moved here."

"Hopefully Al won't return."

Yely stepped forward. "Wait. The lights are on."

"They are," John said with surprise. "How did you manage that?"

Jarvis boasted proudly. "My ex-wife. I told you she'd come through."

"Just like that?" John asked.

"Yep."

"What's the catch?"

Megan laughed and hugged John again. "Get settled. I'm making dinner. They brought fresh meat to us a couple days ago."

"Oh, yeah?" John asked. "Anyone else in town?"

"A few," Jarvis replied. "A few people returned."

"Ripley people?" John questioned.

Jarvis nodded.

"Good. Who?" John asked.

Megan hesitated and then answered, "Al."

❋ ❋ ❋

"How about that?" John set down a mug of stew for Yely in the dome green house. "Al came back weeks ago. Son of a bitch. He beat us here. How did that happen? And he's working on the revival whatever committee. Eat. You missed dinner."

"I just wanted to come in here. Look at it, John."

"I know. I see."

"I still think Giles is dead and they're hiding it from us," John said.

Yely laughed "He's not dead."

"How are you with everything? Coming back."

"I'm glad to be back and I'm okay."

"Your house is still standing. Are you going to go over there."

Yely nodded. "I think I will. Maybe look for things of my mothers. Things that may have survived."

"I haven't given up hope on her," said John. "Have you?"

"Maybe."

"Can you not yet? Just give it a little bit of time. A parent, you know, they fight to be with their kids. Just give her time."

Yely sucked in her bottom lip, bit it, and nodded. "John." Yely faced him. "You didn't need to do all that you did for me."

"I know. But I wanted to. And I am damn proud of you. You have matured and grown. I'm proud."

"Thank you. I'm proud of you, too."

John tilted his head. "Proud of me. Why?'

"You've come a long way since the day I met you."

"You, too. No more marijuana, bad music ..."

"John."

"In all seriousness," John said. "I'm glad you kicked that green ball in my yard."

"That wasn't my ball."

John smiled. "I know."

"You're funny."

"No I'm not," John said. "But I like that you think that." He glanced around and touched a plant. "Look at all this. Life. We've done well so far, and we'll keep doing well."

"Yeah," Yely replied. "We will."

John took in all around him. A small place filled with life.

Life that he thought would never return,

The plant holders once containing just dirt were now flourishing. Plants that contained tomatoes and lettuce and other vegetation blossomed. From nothing to something in such a short period of time. The air in the dome was warm and moist, a contrast to what was outside and a symbol of rejuvenation, much like John was feeling about Ripley and his own life. Both once dead, barren, would grow into something beautiful like what happened in the dome.

It was happening to Ripley.

It was happening to John.

And the world, it would flourish again as well, it would just take time.

BOOKS BY THIS AUTHOR

Stone Virus

When the outbreak comes to a head, Laney is away from home. Chasing her dream of being the winner of a baking reality show, she is sequestered like a juror. No phone, no internet, no knowledge of what is happening.

When the show evacuates all of the contestants, somehow Laney is left behind. Shut off from communication when the city loses power, Laney is clueless about what is happening and lacks the knowledge of the virus she is facing. Those infected experience a violent fever rage before the virus ultimately consumes them and takes their lives.

She's far from brave and searches for someone to help her. Carrying a backpack with some supplies and very little survival know-how, Laney has a choice. She can wait it out until all infected die or try to make it home to her family. However, meeting the young girl Nika, changes how Laney must view and navigate her journey. Her weaknesses need to become strength.

The journey becomes more than just getting home.

What We Become

Like many, Mackenzie Garret complains about the weather. It is the hottest summer anyone can remember. The high temperatures are out of control with no end in sight. Until it all changes.

Overnight, blue skies become gray, and the hot, humid weather turns to rain, then snow, then ice as the temperature plummets.

The entire northern half of the country is thrown into chaos as blow by blow, storm after storm, nature rips into the world, tearing it apart. Towns and cities are evacuated, and Mac and her family are forced to leave their world behind and face a treacherous journey south to safety.